## *Lady Grace Mabry was up to something.*

Lovingdon wasn't certain what, but he'd bet his last farthing that she had some scheme in mind. Very deliberately, very slowly, her eyes never leaving his, she tugged on each fingertip of her glove and leisurely peeled off the kidskin, exposing her wrist, her palm, her fingers. So slender, so pale. It had been years since the sun had kissed her skin. He wondered if any gentlemen had this evening.

She moved her bared hand over to the other glove, and he cursed her actions and his fascination with the gathering of material, the revealing of skin. Bloody Christ. It was only an arm. Her pale blue ball gown with blue piping and embroidered roses left her shoulders and neck enticingly bare, but the upper swells of her breasts were demurely covered, and yet he found the unrevealed more alluring than everything revealed by any courtesan he'd visited of late.

His world tilted off its axis.

## *Romances by* Lorraine Heath

**ATTENTION: ORGANIZATIONS AND CORPORATIONS**
HarperCollins books may be purchased for educational, business, or sales promotional use. For information, please e-mail the Special Markets Department at SPsales@harpercollins.com.

# Lorraine Heath

# When the Duke Was Wicked

**A V O N**
*An Imprint of HarperCollinsPublishers*

This is a work of fiction. Names, characters, places, and incidents are products of the author's imagination or are used fictitiously and are not to be construed as real. Any resemblance to actual events, locales, organizations, or persons, living or dead, is entirely coincidental.

AVON BOOKS
*An Imprint of* HarperCollins*Publishers*
10 East 53rd Street
New York, New York 10022-5299

Copyright © 2014 by Jan Nowasky
ISBN 978-0-373-60137-0
**www.avonromance.com**

All rights reserved. No part of this book may be used or reproduced in any manner whatsoever without written permission, except in the case of brief quotations embodied in critical articles and reviews. For information address Avon Books, an Imprint of HarperCollins Publishers.

First Avon Books mass market printing: March 2014

Avon Trademark Reg. U.S. Pat. Off. and in Other Countries, Marca Registrada, Hecho en U.S.A.

HarperCollins® is a registered trademark of HarperCollins Publishers.

Printed in the U.S.A.

If you purchased this book without a cover you should be aware that this book is stolen property. It was reported as "unsold and destroyed" to the publisher, and neither the author nor the publisher has received any payment for this "stripped book."

*In loving memory of our sweet Duchess,
who became a member of our family after
surviving Katrina. She never met a stranger,
never had a harsh bark for anyone, and
taught us that dogs do indeed smile.*

WHEN THE
DUKE
WAS WICKED

# Prologue

*From the Journal of the Duke of Lovingdon*

*On the morning of February 2, 1872, I, Henry Sidney Stanford, the seventh Duke of Lovingdon, Marquess of Ashleigh, and Earl of Wyndmere, died.*

*Not that my death was apparent to anyone other than myself.*

*I continued to breathe. I still walked about. On occasion, I spoke. I seldom smiled. I never laughed.*

*Because on that morning, that dreadful morning, my heart and soul were ripped from me when my wife and precious daughter suc-*

cumbed to typhus within hours of each other—
and with their passing, I died.

But in time I was reborn into someone my
mother barely recognized.

All my life I had sought to do the right and
proper thing. I did not frequent gaming hells.
I did not imbibe until I became a stumbling
drunk. I fell in love at nineteen, married at
twenty-one. I did the honorable thing: I did
not bed my wife until I wed her. On our wedding night she was not the only virgin between
our sheets.

I was above reproach. I had done all that I
could to be a good and honorable man.

I was brought up to believe that we were
rewarded according to our behavior. Yet the
Fates had conspired to punish me, to take away
that which I treasured above all else, and I
could find no cause for their unkind regard.

And so I said to hell with it all. I would sow
the wild oats I had not in my youth. I would
gamble, I would drink, I would know many
women.

Yet I knew, with my blackened heart, that
I would never again love. That no one would
ever stir me back to giving a damn about anything beyond pleasure.

# Chapter 1

*London*
*1874*

The Duke of Lovingdon relished nothing more than being nestled between a woman's sweet thighs.

Unless it was gliding his hands over her warm and supple body while she caressed his shoulders, his chest, his back. Or hearing the hitch of her breath, a murmured sigh, a—

Rap.

He paused, she stilled.

"What was that?" she whispered.

He shook his head, gazing into her brown eyes and fingering back from her blushing cheek the stray strands of her ebony hair. "The residence settling, no doubt. Pay it no mind."

He lowered his mouth to her silky throat, relishing her heated skin—

Rap. Rap.

Dammit all!

He winked. "Excuse me but a moment."

Rolling out of the massive bed that had been specially built to accommodate his large frame, he marched across the thick Aubusson carpet, his temper barely leashed. His butler—all his servants—knew better than to disturb him when he was enjoying the offerings of a woman.

He closed his hand around the handle, released the latch—

"There damned well better be blood or fire involved—"

He swung open the door. "—in whatever—"

He stared into wide, rounded sapphire eyes that dipped down before quickly jerking up and clashing with his of amber.

"Sweet Christ, Grace, what the devil?"

Before she could respond, he slammed the door shut, snatched up his trousers from the floor, hastily drew them on, and proceeded to button them.

"Another one of your paramours?" the luscious vixen in his bed asked.

He grabbed his linen shirt from where it was draped over a chair. "Good God, no. She's but a child." Or at least she'd been the last time he'd seen her. What the deuce was she doing out and about this time of night? Had she no sense whatsoever?

After pulling on his shirt, he dropped into the chair and tugged on his boots. He didn't know why he was concerned with Grace's sensibilities. It was truly a bit late to worry about them, considering the view he'd given her when he opened the door. Trust her to take the sight with unfettered aplomb. She'd always been a bold little she-devil, but she'd taken things too far tonight.

He shoved himself to his feet and crossed over to the bed. Leaning down, he kissed the lovely's forehead. "I won't be but a moment in dispatching her." After giving her a reassuring wink, he strode across the room, opened the door with a bit more calm, and stepped into the hallway, closing the door behind him.

Grace stood where he'd left her, blushing deeply from her neck to the roots of her coppery hair. Had her freckles not faded, they would have been obliterated. "I'm sorry to have awakened you."

Is that all she thought she was doing? But then she was an innocent miss at nineteen, and while the lads she'd grown up with were more scoundrel than gent, they had all done what they could to preserve her innocence. For her, their wicked ways were little more than rumor.

"It's after midnight. You're in a bachelor's residence. What are you thinking?" he asked.

"I'm in trouble, Lovingdon, a situation most dire. I need your help."

He was on the cusp of telling her to seek assistance elsewhere, but she gazed at him with large blue innocent eyes that left him with little choice except to suggest they adjourn to his library. She'd always had that irritating effect on him, ever since she was a young girl and looked at him as though he were some errant knight capable of slaying dragons.

Perhaps in his youth when the dragon was little more than her foul-tempered cat in need of rescue from its perch on the tree limb—

But he had learned through harsh experience that he was not a dragon slayer.

After they reached the musty scented room, he crossed over to a table that housed an assortment of decanters. In silence, he poured a scotch and a brandy. He hoped beyond hope that when he was done pouring, she would be gone. But when he turned, she was still there, studying him as though she were searching for something, and he found himself wishing that he'd taken a bit more time in dressing. Her attire was far more formal: a white ball gown trimmed in pink velvet.

He'd known Grace all his life. She was not generally one to need help. Certainly she was not one to ask for it. She'd once spent an entire afternoon stranded in a tree because she was too stubborn to alert anyone to her predicament. Wanted to get down on her own. Eventually, as darkness fell, he'd climbed the tree and helped her to the ground, even though he'd been twenty to her eleven, and much too old to be scampering up trees. Then he'd had to reclimb the blasted elm to rescue her mean-spirited cat. He bore the scars from the encounter on his left wrist.

For her to come to him now, she had to be in very bad trouble indeed.

As he held the snifter toward her, he could not mistake the gratitude in her expression as she wrapped slender white-gloved hands around his offering. While it was entirely inappropriate for a lady to be alone in a bachelor's residence, theirs was no ordinary relationship. Their families were close, and she had practically grown up within his shadow, as he had spent much of his youth watching out for her. If she were indeed in trouble, her parents—the Duke and Duchess of Greystone—were more likely to kill him in a most unpleasant manner if he didn't help her than to harm him in any fashion for allowing her to remain in his residence at this ungodly and scandalous hour.

He indicated the seating area near the fireplace where glowing embers were all that remained of an earlier fire.

Her skirts rustling, her fragrance of roses and lavender drifting toward him, she wandered to a burgundy chair and perched herself on the edge of its cushion. She'd always been a complex creature, never content with the ordinary, not easily defined.

One scent was not enough for her. And neither was one gentleman, based upon the conversations he barely gave any notice to at the gaming hells.

He took the wingback chair opposite hers, slowly sipped his scotch and studied her for a moment. Although he knew her age to be nineteen, he couldn't help but wonder when the bloody hell she had grown up. He knew her as a spindly legged and freckled-armed girl who preferred climbing trees to visiting ballrooms, who preferred galloping her horse over the gently rolling hills to attending dance lessons.

She was nine years his junior. He'd known, of course, that she was growing up, but his realization had been more of a vague sort of thing, on the periphery of his life, like knowing the seasons were changing but not being fully aware of each falling leaf or budding blossom. She had certainly blossomed. She was slender with only the barest hint of curves. Her gown, while revealing her neck and upper chest, stopped just short of displaying any swells of her breasts. He would not have expected her to be so modest, yet with her modesty she became more mysterious.

It seemed she was also fearless. He'd heard that she had no qualms traveling about at night to the foundling homes that her parents had opened. While she generally had a chaperone in tow, she was rumored to be skilled at escaping her notice.

Tonight's little visit a prime example.

He tapped his glass, striving to get his thoughts back on track, to her problem, her reason for being here. "So what's this trouble you're in?"

"You weren't at the Ainsley ball," she responded, no censure in her voice, but still it was laced with something that very much resembled disappointment. He tried to remember when she'd had her coming out, if he'd even been aware of it. Respectable activities no longer held any allure, and he managed to successfully avoid them.

"Did some gent take advantage? Do I need to fetch my pistols?"

She smiled, a warm, amused tilt to her plump, soft-looking lips. "No, but it warms the cockles of my heart to know you would champion me."

Yes, he'd champion her. When she was a child. He didn't have the desire to champion anyone these days. What he did desire was waiting for him upstairs in his bed.

"You've never been one to stall," he pointed out impatiently. "Explain what brings you here and be quick about it."

She held up her hand. Dangling from her wrist was a card, her dance card. "I danced every dance tonight. If previous balls are any indication, in the morning dozens of bouquets of flowers will be delivered to the residence."

"You are most popular."

"No," she stated succinctly. "As you are no doubt

well aware, I come with an immense dowry that includes land and coin. It is my dowry that is popular."

"Don't be ridiculous. You offer a good deal to a man. You're lovely and charming and poised. I'd wager all my estates that you'll be betrothed before the Season is out."

She rose from the chair with the grace to which he'd alluded and stepped over to the fireplace. She was tall. He was well over six feet, and her head could bump against his chin without her rising up on her toes. The long slope of her throat would draw a gentleman's eye. Small understated pearls circled her neck, adorned her ears. She had no reason to be flashy. Her hair sufficed. It was presently piled on her head, a few tendrils deliberately left to toy with the delicate nape of her neck. He suspected the haphazard ones circling her oval face were not planned but had escaped their bounds during the ball, no doubt when she had waltzed.

"But will I be loved, Lovingdon? You know love, you've experienced it. However can I identify it?"

He gulped down scotch that was meant to be savored. He would not travel that path, not with her, not with anyone. "You'll know it because it'll be someone without whom you cannot live."

Turning slightly, she met his gaze. "I do not doubt that I will know if I love him. But how will I know if he loves me? My dear friend, Lady Bertram, was madly in love with her husband. He has since taken a mistress. It's broken her heart. He was infatuated with her dowry, not her. And Lady Sybil Fitzsimmons? Her husband has taken to scolding and berating her. How can he love her if he berates her, in public no less? With so many men vying for my affections, how can I know if their hearts are true? I shall marry only once, and fortune hunters abound. I want to ensure that I choose well."

"Trust your heart."

"Do you not see? It is obvious to me that in the matter of love, a woman cannot trust her heart. It can be most easily influenced with poetry, and chocolates, and flowers. A lady requires an objective person, one who is familiar enough with love to assist her in identifying and weeding out the insincere, separating the wheat from the chaff, so to speak. Someone like you."

"I am no longer an expert in love, and I have no desire to become embroiled in it again, not even from the outskirts."

"Is that why you've turned to this life of debauchery?"

He eyed her over the rim of his glass. "What do you know of debauchery?"

"I've heard rumors." She stroked her fingers along the edge of the mantel as though searching for dust. "And I know you weren't alone this evening when I disturbed you. Is she your mistress?"

"A mistress implies a certain amount of permanence. I have no interest in permanence."

She peered over at him. "A courtesan, then."

"Is that sharpness on your tongue disapproval?"

"I'm not judging you."

"Aren't you?"

She shook her head, a sadness in her eyes that irritated him. "No. You have every right to be angry with fate for what it stole—"

"I won't discuss it, Grace. Not fate, not Juliette, not love. I don't need you or anyone else to justify my actions. I live as I wish to live. I find satisfaction in it, and make no excuses for it. If you want someone who is an expert on love, I suggest you talk with your parents. They seem to have weathered enough storms."

She scoffed. "Do you truly believe I'm going to discuss my interest in gentlemen with my mother or father? They are each likely to inflict bodily harm on any gentleman I am unsure of, simply by virtue of my being unsure of him. Besides, they will tell me to marry whomever will make me happy."

"Sound advice."

"Have you not been listening? Just because he makes me happy before the vows are exchanged does not mean he will make me happy afterward. If you will not bring your knowledge of love to my quest, you can at least bring your recent experiences to bear. Who better to identify a blackguard than another blackguard? I need you, Lovingdon."

*I need you.* Juliette had needed him and he'd failed her.

"Please, Lovingdon."

He almost believed there was more to her plea than met the ears. Where was the harm? He held out his hand. She stared at it as though she didn't recognize what it was.

He snapped his fingers. "I'll take a quick look at your list, assist you in eliminating the cads, so you can be on your way."

"How can you discern a man's feelings for me simply by reading his name?"

"I can identify those with whom you do not wish to invest your heart, those of bad habits and vices."

"If that's what I wanted, I'd go to Drake. He knows men's vices better than anyone."

Drake Darling—a former street urchin and thief who'd grown up within the bosom of Grace's family—managed Dodger's Drawing Room, a gaming hell for respectable gentlemen. Yes, he was certainly familiar with various gentlemen's vices, but he was also very good at holding secrets.

"I need more," she said. "I need you to observe them, to then offer your opinion on them." She knelt before him, and while the glowing embers provided little light, it was enough for him to see the desperation in her blue eyes. "Attend Claybourne's ball. It's the next one of any importance. Be a wallflower, stand behind fronds. Then provide a report on what you've noticed, who you believe truly cares for me."

The thought of being at a place filled with such joviality caused him to grow clammy. It would only serve to remind him of happier times, and how quickly and painfully they'd been snatched from him. "Trust your heart, girl. It won't lead you astray. You'll be able to tell if a man cares for you."

Defeat swept over her features. "I can't trust my heart, Lovingdon. It's betrayed me before."

He felt as though he'd taken a hard punch to the gut. He despised the thought of her hurting. Had some man taken advantage? Why else would she not trust her instincts?

Standing, she returned to the fireplace, presenting him with her back. "When I was younger, I once fell deeply, passionately in love—or as passionately as one can at such a tender age. I thought he returned my affections. But eventually he married another."

"Who? No." He held up a hand. "That is not my concern."

With a sad smile, she glanced over her shoulder at him. "Don't worry. I won't reveal his name. You would think me an utter fool if you knew who he was."

"Just because he took another to wife doesn't mean he didn't love you. Men marry for all sorts of reasons."

"As I'm well aware. Which is the reason that I'm here. Do you not see that you are making my arguments for me? How do I determine that they are marrying me for the right reason, for love, and that their affections are not held elsewhere? I fear that if I were to give my heart to another, and discover that he truly had little regard for it—the devastation could very well be my undoing."

"Little Rose, perhaps it's better not to love."

She glided back to the chair and sat. "Do you truly believe that? Is it not better to hold someone for a short span of time rather than not to have held them at all?"

For the briefest of moments he heard laughter—Juliette's laughter. He saw her smile, felt the warmth of her touch, tasted her lips, felt the heat of her body welcoming his. It had been so long, so very long since he had given himself leave to think of her at all. The agony of it nearly doubled him over.

"I want what you had," Grace said softly. "It was perfection, was it not?"

"I shall never love another as I loved her. That is the honest truth."

She studied him for a long thoughtful moment before asking, "What is it like to have such a grand love?"

It was all-encompassing, permeated everything. How could he put into words an emotion that defied them? "You laugh, you smile. You have secrets to which no one else is privy. You can communicate without words. You know what each other is thinking. There is a sense of euphoria. But it all comes with a price, Grace. Losing it can destroy you, turn you into little more than a hollow shell."

"You cannot dissuade me from wanting it, even if it is only for the blink of an eye. To love someone and to know beyond doubt that he loved me would be the most wondrous experience I can imagine. And therein rests my dilemma—it is not enough to love. I must be loved in return, or what is the point? Will you assist me in my quest for true love? I can think of no better way to honor your Juliette than to help someone acquire what the two of you once held."

Once held and lost. He would not wish his sorrow on his worst enemy.

"I can't help you, Grace. It would serve neither of us well for me to even try. You should be off now, before your father discovers where you are and forces me to marry you. That would be the quickest way to ensure that you do not acquire that which you seek."

"My father trusts you. He knows you would not take advantage."

"Be that as it may, if anyone were to see you leave here, you would be ruined."

"I will not marry a man who does not love me, even in the face of ruination." Her words came with such conviction, but he knew from experience that conviction did not always render the words true.

"Be that as it may, I fear you would have no choice."

"We all have choices." Slowly she rose. "The Claybourne ball."

He did not watch her leave, but instead turned his gaze back to the fireplace, where the embers no longer glowed. She asked the impossible of him— just as Juliette had.

Don't let us die.
I won't.
But he had.

# Chapter 2

As the carriage rattled along the cobblestones, Lady Grace Mabry's thoughts traveled to where they ought not: Lovingdon opening his bedchamber door and standing there proudly in the altogether. She'd caught a glimpse of the woman in his bed, knew she'd not awakened him, yet it seemed prudent to act the innocent.

But doing so left her with questions that a lady shouldn't entertain, but they were there nonetheless, and she wasn't certain to whom she could turn for the answers.

The Duke of Lovingdon did not resemble any statuary she had ever gazed upon. She'd seen Michelangelo's David, among others. Lovingdon put them all to shame. She could have stood there staring at him forever, but she'd forced herself to lift her gaze to his because it wouldn't do for him to know that she'd wanted to touch.

All of him. His broad shoulders, his flat stomach, his...maleness. No, he was not at all like David in that regard. He'd been quite breathtaking. As the memory caused heat to suffuse her, she pressed her cheek to the cool glass.

She'd been fortunate to find his residence not locked up for the night. She supposed that meant the woman wouldn't be staying. She didn't know why relief accompanied the thought. What did it matter one way or the other when the woman was there now?

Grace had been all of seven when she first came to love Lovingdon. Although in retrospect she knew it was little more than a young girl's fancy, but at the time it had seemed so much more to her young heart.

Spring had only just arrived, and her mother had invited the other families—connected by hearts, not blood—to join them at Mabry Manor, her father's ancestral estate. Some of the young boys had taken to teasing her about her red hair, saying she looked like a carrot. She had been curled in a corner of the stable weeping when Lovingdon found her and crouched beside her. He was sixteen, on the cusp of manhood. With his thumbs, he gently wiped away her tears. No boy had ever touched her so tenderly. Her childish heart had done a little somersault. He could have asked anything of her at that moment and she would have granted it. He could have called her anything—Freckles, Coppery, Hideous—and she would have thought it poetry. Instead he had stolen her heart with his words.

"You're only a bud right now," he'd said. "No one appreciates the bud, but before long you will blossom into a beauty as lovely as a red rose that will put all other ladies to shame. Now come on, Little Rose. No more moping about. Someday you shall have your revenge, and it will be incredibly sweet."

Over the years, he had called her Little Rose. Until he married. Then he had no time for her at all, had given her no attention. While her yearning heart had known that was the way it should be, that her feelings were little more than childish affection, it also felt the sharp sting of rejection.

Tonight had been the first time in years since he referred to her using the endearment. And her heart did that silly little somersault thing in her chest, which had irritated her beyond measure. She didn't want it dancing about for him. He had proven to be a disappointment. She loved him as a friend, a brother. Her woman's heart would never love him as more than that.

But he possessed the knowledge she required to achieve happiness. He knew love, and he knew the wicked ways of men. Who better to assist her? Yet he did not care about her enough to take a holiday from all his sinning. She supposed that said it all. His was not a character to be admired.

What a fool she'd been all those years ago to hold

him in such high regard. She could not risk misjudging again, for this time she would be attached to a man for the remainder of her life. She wanted a good man, an honest man, a man willing to be her hero even when she wasn't in need of one.

Sitting at the breakfast table the following morning, Grace could not help but be amused that, just as she'd predicted, an abundance of flowers began arriving before she cracked the top of her soft-boiled egg. She supposed she should have been giddy with excitement, but she was quite simply too practical for such nonsense. It was a result of her upbringing, she speculated, or more to the point—her mother's.

It was no secret that Frannie Mabry, Duchess of Greystone, had grown up on the streets under the care of a kidsman who taught her to survive by cunning, thievery, and fraud. Grace had listened to her stories with fascination, and as she moved toward womanhood gained an immense measure of respect for her mother. She also gained an unbridled belief in love, having witnessed it firsthand. Against all odds and her sordid beginnings, her mother had won the heart of a duke.

Grace dearly wanted the sort of love they shared: one of adoration, respect, support. For many years her mother continued to manage the books at Dodger's Drawing Room. She was part owner of the gentlemen's club, and her husband took great pride in her accomplishments and independence. They worked with common purpose to improve the plight of orphans. They shared goals, triumphs, and failure. But nothing deterred them from reaching for what they sought to obtain. Grace was convinced that in all aspects of their life they had achieved success and happiness because their relationship was built on a foundation of love.

While she might have asked her parents to help her determine if a gentleman truly loved her, neither of them thought any man worthy of her.

"Another morning filled with flowers, I see," her father mused as he wandered into the breakfast dining room and headed for the sideboard where an assortment of Cook's best fare awaited him.

Grace only recently learned of his failing eyesight, although it had apparently plagued him for years. He'd hoped to keep it a secret from his children for much longer, but as he had taken to leaning more on their mother, his steps became more cautious and he tended to squint more often, even though that action did nothing to widen a world that was slowly going dark.

Grace wanted to marry before he was completely blind. A silly reason, she knew, but she wanted him to see that she was gloriously happy.

"Do you suppose I should let it be known that I much prefer a gent make a donation to a children's home?" she said in response to his comment about the flowers. "It doesn't even necessarily have to be one of ours."

Her parents had built three homes for orphans and one for unwed mothers. Grace had always been aware that some people were less fortunate, and she was brought up to believe that she had both an obligation and a duty to help where she could. She wanted a husband who also believed in good works, not one who would squander her dowry. She really wasn't asking for much, was she?

Her father joined her at the table, sitting in his usual place at its head, while she had always taken a chair to his right. "Those who are in the flower trade have bills to pay as well."

"I suppose that's true enough. It's only that flowers wilt; they don't last."

"So we must enjoy them while we can."

Her stomach tightened with the realization that shortly he would be able to only enjoy their fragrance, not their vibrant colors, the shape of their petals.

"Most girls would be delighted to have a man shower them with flowers as a way of giving them attention," her father said.

"But then I am not most girls."

He smiled. "As I'm certain the gentlemen are coming to realize. How was the ball? Did anyone strike your fancy?"

Her parents seldom attended soirees any longer, as her father could no longer tolerate crowds. He had too much pride to be caught knocking into someone he couldn't see.

"A few gentlemen engaged me in interesting conversation. Lord Somerdale is quite fascinated with the pollination capabilities of bees. Tedious process."

"Equally tedious to hear about, I venture."

She laughed. "Immeasurably tedious. Lord Amber's bones creak when the weather grows cold. He lives in the North, which means I would forever be hearing his bones creaking. Not very appealing, really."

"No." Her father creased his brow. "You are talking about the fifth Lord Amber."

"No, unfortunately. The fourth."

"I thought he'd died some years back."

"Not quite." White-haired, he held a horn-shaped instrument up to his ear in order to hear. He didn't dance. He simply tottered about. "He doesn't need an heir. I think he's just lonely."

"Yes, well, you can mark him off your list. The whole point in giving you an ample dowry was so you would have an abundance of choices and wouldn't have to settle."

"I fear it's given me far too many suitors. I'm finding it a bit difficult to weed out the sincere from the insincere."

"Trust your heart."

She began slathering butter on her toast. "Yes, that's what Lovingdon said."

Not that his advice had been any help at all.

Her father stilled, his teacup halfway to his mouth. "When did you see him?"

She lifted a shoulder. "Oh, recently our paths crossed."

"Last night, perhaps?"

Now she was the one who froze, her lungs refusing to draw in air.

Before she could deny it, he said, "Your maid returned to the residence at half past eleven. You didn't seem to be about."

She should have known he'd be alert to her not arriving. She was surprised he hadn't been waiting in the foyer when she did finally get home. But then, her father was accustomed to her spending nights at the foundling homes. "I went to see him, yes, to ask his opinion about some of the gentlemen courting me."

"Grace, a young lady does not go to a bachelor's residence at all hours of the night."

"It wasn't all hours. It was only one: midnight. He was unhelpful and I promptly took my leave."

"You are missing my point."

"You know Lovingdon wouldn't take advantage. He sees me as a sister." She hated the disgust that wove through her voice with the final words.

"And you wish he considered you as more."

It seemed her father saw far more with his limited vision than most did with all their eyesight intact.

"Once, I admit, when I was a young girl I was infatuated with him, but now he just angers me. He no longer moves about in Society, and I've heard the rumors regarding what a wastrel he's become. It's very disappointing, and sets such a bad example.

Still, I must confess that I had rather hoped, when he saw me in my evening attire, that he would cease to think of me as a child."

Her father placed his hand over hers. "I don't think anyone would mistake you for a child. You've grown into a remarkable woman. You deserve a man who will love and appreciate you. As much as I hate to say it, I don't think he can love or appreciate anyone anymore."

"I fear you're right. He's breaking his mother's heart."

"Olivia can take care of herself. And I won't have him breaking yours. Now," he said, returning his attention to his breakfast, "no more of these late night excursions. I don't want to have to lock you in your room."

She gave him an impish grin. "As though you ever would."

"I will do whatever is necessary to see you safe and happy."

"Well today, happy is a new gown." She rose from her chair, bent down and kissed his cheek. "I love you, Papa."

"Someday, when you least expect it, sweetheart, love will arrive and it will not be at all as you imagined."

"Is that how it was for you?"

"It was so much more."

She retook her seat, threaded her fingers through

his and squeezed. "But at what point do I reveal the truth about my...situation?"

She could see the sadness and sorrow woven in the depths of his blue eyes.

"You leave that to me. I'll take care of it when they ask for your hand."

"While I appreciate your willingness to stand as my champion, I believe most strongly that the news should come from me. Sometimes I think I should take out an advert. 'Beware! Lady Grace Mabry may come with an immense dowry, but she is far from perfect.'"

"I was far from perfect. It didn't stop your mother from loving me."

"But I think it will take a very special man indeed to accept my imperfection."

"Not so special as you might think."

Lovingdon traveled through the London streets with the coach's shades drawn. He had an ache behind his eyes brought on by too much liquor and the smoke of too many cigars. The disadvantage to playing cards in a room without windows was that one was not able to see night giving way to day.

After Grace had left the evening before, he'd sent the woman in his bed on her merry way with a hefty pouch of coins, while he'd gone in search of liquor and gambling. Those he played with on a regular basis were very skilled, and winning against them required focus, which he had hoped would serve as adequate distraction. But Grace continued to intrude on his musings. She deserved love. He could think of no one who deserved it more. But he couldn't quite wrap his mind around her dilemma. She was sharp, clever, spirited. Surely she could tell if a man's affections were true. Something was amiss but he wasn't quite sure what it was.

Besides, a man would be unwise to play her for a fool. It was no secret that her parents' friends and their family members would defend her to the death. But she could have gone to anyone for assistance. Truth be told, anyone would have been a better choice, as he no longer frequented Society, avoided the trappings of polite merry-making like the plague.

His coach rolled to a stop. A footman hastily opened the door. Sunlight scalded Lovingdon's eyes, but he merely squinted against it as he exited. He wanted a bath and then a bed.

He strode up the steps. Another footman opened the large, thick wooden door for him. He marched through and was accosted by the heavy fragrance of flowers. Little wonder as an absurd amount of blossoms filled the entryway. All colors, all varieties, shapes, and sizes. Nauseatingly sweet.

"Welcome home, Your Grace," his butler, Barrow, said, appearing from down a hallway.

"What's the meaning of all this?"

"They arrived an hour ago, with this missive." Barrow held out the folded parchment.

In spite of his resounding headache, Lovingdon

took the paper, unfolded it, and narrowed his eyes at the words.

*This morning's arrivals. However is a lady to decide?*

He scoffed. Grace, not giving up on acquiring his assistance, it appeared. So like the stubborn little minx.

"What shall I do with them, sir?" Barrow asked.

"Send them back to Greystone's with a message that simply says, 'No.'" He started up the stairs, paused. "On second thought, send them 'round to a hospital or someplace where people are in need of cheering." He had already won the battle. No sense in engaging in further combat. He didn't want Grace bloodied. She would get his message quickly enough when she realized he was ignoring hers.

He had traversed three more steps when he abruptly reversed direction and headed back down. Barrow still stood at attention, as though he'd known Lovingdon was not quite yet finished.

"I'll be sending a missive 'round to Mabry House."

## Chapter 3

One did not complain about having in abundance
that which others wished desperately to obtain.

So Grace did not complain about her aching toes,
because they were the result of enjoying far too many
gentlemen's attentions. She merely settled herself
on the plush ottoman in the ladies' retiring room
and lifted a swollen foot, so her lady's maid could
replace her worn-out slippers with new ones. It was
the second time this evening that she'd had to retire
from the ballroom, promising a disappointed gentleman that she would be more than happy to entertain
him in her mother's parlor the following afternoon.
She did not reveal that he wouldn't be the only one
in attendance. She tried to leave a few dances open
so she could have a moment's respite, but the gentle-

men were simply so frightfully insistent that their night would be incomplete without a turn about the ballroom floor with her in their arms.

So she succumbed to their charms.

And they were charming. Every last one of them. Which was part of her dilemma. How to separate charm from con.

She had spent a good deal of the night searching the shadows for Lovingdon, but as far as she could tell, he had not come. The message that he sent a few days earlier—*He'll know your favorite flower*—had given her hope that he would be on hand at Claybourne's ball to assist her in discerning who was a fortune hunter and who was not. She couldn't assume that just because a man's coffers were empty he was only after her fortune. On her own she had eliminated some of the men who were. They always had greedy little eyes and spoke of all the things they could accomplish with her dowry in hand.

A rather poor courtship technique.

But most of her suitors were not as overt and rarely mentioned her monetary assets. Courtship was an art, and they had perfected it. As she was the lady of the Season with the largest dowry, she drew the most attention—which did not endear her to many of the other ladies. They knew they would be getting the cast-offs.

With a sigh, she stood. "Thank you, Felicity." While most in the aristocracy did not usually thank servants for doing their tasks, Grace had grown up hearing her mother constantly thanking servants. A product of the streets, her mother took nothing for granted and treated everyone as though they mattered because to her they did. She'd passed that attribute on to Grace.

Felicity helped to straighten her hair, to repin what could be contained. Grace's hair was so curly that the strands were often escaping their constraints. With a last look in the mirror, Grace turned and nearly ran into Lady Cornelia. The woman possessed all the curves that Grace didn't.

"Please release Lord Ambrose from your spell," Lady Cornelia whispered.

"Pardon?"

Lady Cornelia glanced around as though she expected demons to be lurking in the corners, but the only other two ladies in the room were busy chattering while their maids repinned their hair.

"Lord Ambrose—if you were to let him know that he had no chance of gaining your favor—he might look elsewhere for the funds he needs in order to continue raising his horses."

"You fancy him?" Grace asked.

"He is not so hard on the eyes. I will admit to favoring him. And I'm terribly fond of horses. His in particular, as they are the most beautiful thoroughbreds. And he has a lovely estate. I would like very much to be his countess."

Although love was woefully absent from the lady's reasons, Grace studied her card. It wasn't her place to judge what someone else desired for happiness. "Who do you have for the fifteenth dance?"

"No one. I've had all of three dances claimed. My dowry is nowhere near as large as yours, my father is not as powerful. I have atrocious black hair and am as white as my mother's tablecloth. My brother says I look like a ghoul."

Grace smiled. "Brothers are hideous, aren't they?"

"You're lucky yours aren't about this Season."

"I'm very lucky indeed." Striving to strengthen the bond between them, Grace wrapped her fingers around Lady Cornelia's arm. "Just before the fifteenth dance, meet me by the doors leading onto the terrace. I suspect my feet will be aching too badly for me to enjoy the quadrille. Perhaps you would be kind enough to dance with Lord Ambrose in my stead."

Lady Cornelia beamed, and Grace didn't think she looked at all like a ghoul. She thought she more closely resembled an angel. "The other girls are jealous of the attentions you get, you know."

"I know. But we always want what someone else has."

"What do you want?"

Grace gently squeezed her arm. "I want you to have Lord Ambrose."

Before Lady Cornelia could pepper her further, Grace walked from the room. She wasn't about to admit to anyone—other than Lovingdon—that she desired love. She didn't want to be painted as a pathetic creature who doubted her own self-worth, but there were moments when she feared love would be denied her.

She glided down the stairs that led to the first landing. Lord Vexley was standing there, his elbow resting on the first baluster. He was quite possibly one of the most handsome men she'd ever known. His black hair was styled to perfection. Unlike hers, none of the strands ever rebelled. His deep blue eyes sparkled, his smile was broad and welcoming.

"I was afraid I was going to have to go up those stairs and drag you out of that private room where ladies secret away to do and say who knows what," he teased as she neared.

"You're waiting for me?"

"I am. The next dance is mine, and unlike some of the other gents, I'm not willing to give up a waltz with the most beautiful woman here." He extended his arm as she moved off the last step.

She placed her hand in the crook of his elbow. "You flatter me, my lord."

"I believe we would make a remarkable pair."

He escorted her into the ballroom just as the music was drifting into silence. Very well-timed planning. And he was so deuced handsome. She did wish she felt more for him than mild pleasure at being in his company. Unfortunately none of the gentlemen courting her stirred her heart. It beat its same constant, steady rhythm whether she was thinking about them, dancing with them, or conversing. Nothing was terribly wrong with any of them, but neither was anything terribly right.

"Did my tulips arrive after Ainsley's ball?" he asked.

"They did." Not her favorites, but a close second. "As did the chocolates." She had not bothered to send those around to Lovingdon. She was willing to go only so far to convince him she was in need of his assistance, and giving up chocolate was one step too far. Although she wondered if they may have made a difference toward securing his cooperation. In his youth, chocolate had been his favorite treat, but then he was not who he had once been. If he was, he would have put her needs above his and been willing to assist her. On the other hand he had responded to the arrival of the flowers, although not to the extent she would have wished, but better than not at all.

It occurred to her that in order to gain further help from him, she was going to have to take more drastic measures.

Although it was long past midnight Grace walked with confidence along the dimly lit narrow corridor, her skirts rustling over the thick carpeting. She expected that her arrival would be frowned upon by those she would soon be encountering, but then she'd never cared one whit about obtaining their approval. Neither had they cared about gaining hers. They did as they pleased, when they pleased, with whom they pleased. While they might not want to have anything to do with her, she was not going to give them a choice. Not tonight anyway.

They were men, after all, and as she'd recently learned, a practiced smile accompanied by a fluttering of the eyelashes could turn the most intelligent of men into mindless dolts, who could be led wherever a lady wished to lead. Her problem, however, was that she didn't want a man who was so easily controlled, nor did she want one who sought to control her. She wanted a partner in life, one who saw her as an equal, even if the law didn't.

She finally reached the door located within the darkest of corners. Against the thick mahogany, she delivered three sharp knuckle raps, a pause, and two more, the last dispensed more quickly than the first set. At eye level a tiny door, a small opening in the much larger door, creaked open. A man peered out. The shadows effectively hid from her the details of his face. She would not have been surprised to find him wearing a mask.

Much ado was always made about secretive meetings.

"Only those knowing the special word may pass through here," he growled, his voice deep and rumbling, as though he were auditioning for the role of ogre in a child's fairy tale.

Ah, the dramatics. She was allowed to come and play here on her birthday, and so she knew how to gain entry.

"Feagan."

Homage paid to the kidsman who had once managed the den of child thieves that included her mother.

The oaf barring her way grunted. A lock clanked as it was released, then he swung the door open and Grace waltzed past him through the narrow portal. He was a big, hulking brute whom she had never encountered before. She suspected his size alone intimidated quite a few, and his large meaty fists would intimidate anyone else.

"I'll take you to the others—" he began.

"No need."

She moved on, parting heavy velvet draperies that appeared black with the absence of light, though she knew they were a deep, rich burgundy. Sitting areas and tables adorned with decanters were in this section, but no one was making use of the lounging area in which to sulk, which meant that in all likelihood the games had not been going on long enough for anyone to have been separated from too many of his coins. Parting another set of draperies, she glided through—

"No! God, Grace, what are you doing here?" Drake Darling came up out of his chair at a large round table covered in green baize. It appeared he had repeatedly tunneled his fingers through his dark hair, a sign that the evening was not going his way. He managed Dodger's; she suspected a day would come when he would own it.

Her eyes momentarily stung in the smoke-hazed

room. Tables with more decanters lined the walls. Servants liveried in red stood at the ready. One tall fellow moved toward her. Drake held up a hand to stay him.

"I've come to play," she stated succinctly.

Viscount Langdon, son to the Earl of Claybourne, groaned while glaring at her. "I'm not in the mood to lose tonight."

"Then give up your chair and be off," she said. Knowing that Langdon would do neither, she signaled to the nearest footman, whom she recognized from earlier visits. Without hesitation he brought her a chair, apparently well aware which side his bread was buttered on.

Amidst grumbling, three of the gents at the table scooted their chairs over to make room for her. The fourth moved nary a muscle, merely focused his amber gaze on her as though he could see clear through to her soul. His perusal caused an uncomfortable knot to form behind her breastbone. His dark blond hair curled where neck met broad shoulder. The darker bristle shadowing his jaw made him appear dangerous. She had the uneasy feeling that he knew exactly why she was there and the game she was about to play. "Lovingdon."

"This particular game is invitation only."

His rough voice washed over her, fairly skittered along her flesh. Why was it that no other gentleman's voice had quite the same impact on her?

"As my mother is part owner of this establishment, I believe the invitation is implied."

Grace settled into the chair, which put them at eye level or nearly so. She was relieved to find him here, though the men within this room were men not so different from him. They played by special rules. Jackets, waistcoats, neck cloths were discarded. Sleeves were rolled up past elbows. She was astonished that they didn't insist upon playing without shirts. They were all skilled cheaters, their upbringing influenced by at least one person who had survived the streets. They had all grown up fascinated by cons, dodges, sleight of hand, and misdirection. Among the aristocracy, they were uncommon, but among themselves—regardless of title, rank, or heritage—they were equal.

Well, almost so. Lovingdon, she'd always felt, was a cut above. She could not help but notice now the firm, solid muscle of his forearms that hinted at firm, solid muscle elsewhere. She suspected he could pick her up with very little effort. Not that she wanted him to. All she wanted was for him to guide her toward love.

"How did you know we were here?" the Duke of Avendale asked.

She turned her attention to the dark-haired, dark-eyed man sitting beside her. Like Lovingdon, he'd inherited his title at a tender age. His connection to her family came through the man who had married his widowed mother: William Graves, one of London's finest physicians. "None of you were at Clay-bourne's ball. What else was I to think?" A heartbeat of silence before she continued. "You do realize, do you not, that with your absence you are breaking the heart of many a mother—and daughter, for that matter?"

"There are many lords in need of a wife. I'm certain we're not missed."

"But none come from such powerful and wealthy families as you lot." Her gaze skipped back over to Lovingdon. Focusing his attention on the center of the table, he rolled a silver coin under and over his fingers, creating an undulating wave of light and dark again and again. She wondered if he was remembering when he had attended balls, when he had fallen in love.

The joy of it, the magic of it.

She desperately yearned for that joy, that magic. It had been sorely absent last Season, and this Season so far was little more than a repeat of the last.

"You're not here to play matchmaker, are you?" Langdon asked. He had his father's black hair and silver eyes. Every Earl of Claybourne had looked out at the world through eyes of pewter.

She laughed lightly. "No, I'm here to win your money. I'm in need of funds for one of the foundling homes."

The coin rolling faster over his fingers, Lovingdon grumbled, "I shall gladly make a donation if you'll but leave us in peace."

She gave him a cocky smile. "I'd rather take your money." And with any luck would take a great deal more than that. "It's such fun to beat you all, and I'm in need of entertainment this evening. I found the ball rather dull."

"My mother will be disappointed to hear that," Langdon said.

"It wasn't her fault I assure you." She eyed him. "I'm rather surprised she let you get away with not attending."

"I feigned illness."

"Well, she shan't hear the truth from me, unless of course I find myself ousted from here."

He bowed his head slightly. "You may play as long as I have coin."

Considering that his father was also part owner of Dodger's, she suspected he had a good many coins. She reached into her reticule, withdrew her blunt, housed in a red velvet pouch, and set it before Drake. He had grown up within the bosom of her family, was more brother than friend, but he studied her now as though he didn't quite trust her. She knew she was rather skilled at appearing innocent when she wasn't. It was the reason that the blame for little pranks—which she usually initiated—fell to her two older brothers and not her, the reason they suffered through punishments while she went blithely on her way. She was the one who had inherited their mother's quick mind and nimble fingers. Her brothers had inherited their father's cunning—and they always found a way to get even with her for causing them trouble. But as she was the youngest, they loved her all the same. And she adored them.

As they were presently traveling the Continent, they would not be interfering with her plans. Drake, however, was another matter entirely.

He finally pushed a stack of colorful wooden chips her way. Leaning forward, she scooped her hands around them and—

"You're not serious about allowing her to stay," Lovingdon said.

"She's as fine a gambler as you are," Drake replied, "and her money spends just as easily."

"If I wanted a woman's company I would seek one."

"Pretend I'm simply one of the boys, Lovingdon," Grace put in. "You seemed to have no trouble accomplishing that goal when I was younger."

His gaze took a leisurely sojourn over her, and she cursed the tiny pricks of pleasure that erupted along her bared skin. She wanted to be unaffected by his perusal. Instead she found herself shamelessly wishing to reveal more, to bare everything, to see a look of adoration in his eyes, when she feared that what she might very well see was revulsion. His first wife had been perfection. There had not been a handsomer couple in all of Great Britain.

He reached for his tumbler of amber liquid, his grip so hard that she could see the white of his knuckles. "Fine," he ground out. "But don't expect us to cease our smoking, drinking, or swearing because you're here."

She tilted her chin at a haughty angle. "Have I ever?" She glanced around the table. "So, gentlemen, what are we playing this evening?"

And with that, she began rolling her kidskin glove down from above her elbow to her wrist, where her pulse thrummed.

She was up to something. Lovingdon wasn't certain what, but he'd bet his last farthing that she had some scheme in mind.

Very deliberately, very slowly, her eyes never leaving his, she tugged on each fingertip of her glove and leisurely peeled off the kidskin, exposing her wrist, her palm, her fingers. So slender, so pale. It had been years since the sun had kissed her skin. He wondered if any gentlemen had this evening.

She moved her bared hand over to the other glove, and he cursed her actions and his fascination with the gathering of material, the revealing of skin. Bloody Christ. It was only an arm. Her pale blue ball gown with blue piping and embroidered roses left her shoulders and neck enticingly bare, but the upper swells of her breasts were demurely covered, and yet he found the unrevealed more alluring than everything revealed by any courtesan he'd visited of late.

His world tilted off its axis.

Even when she'd come to see him the week before, he'd still gazed upon her as a young girl, not a woman. But it was a woman whose sultry eyes met his, whose pouting mouth was waiting to be kissed.

With a great deal of effort, he righted his world, setting it back properly on its course, and mentally kicked himself for even being intrigued by that show of flesh. She was a dear friend, no more than that. He shouldn't find anything about her desirable. His younger version would not have noticed. However, he knew he was no longer who he had once been.

But then apparently neither was Grace. She could have taken the time to change into something less enticing before beginning her journey to the club. They would no doubt be here all night, which she would have known. She knew their habits, their sins, as well as they did. But she had chosen instead to make a grand entrance.

For what purpose?

He knew she had an aversion to losing, but was she really here to gain funds for a foundling home? He doubted it immensely. All she had to do was ask and they'd each reach into their pockets to find their last coin. No, something else was afoot, and he suspected it had to do with her midnight visit to his residence last week.

Realizing that he'd been studying her for too long, Lovingdon lowered his eyes to his two cards, one down-turned, one up, that had been dealt as soon as her gloves were secure in her reticule. With this lot, no hiding places were allowed. They were playing stud poker. Grace's brothers had taken a voyage to

New Orleans and discovered it while there. When they returned and revealed the intricacies of the game, it became a favorite among their friends and added to the repertoire of entertainments at Dodger's Drawing Room.

Downstairs, however, it wasn't nearly as cutthroat, nor were the stakes as high. He wondered if he should mention to Greystone that he was giving his daughter far too much allowance if she had enough blunt to allow her into their private games.

More cards were dealt, more wagers made, until Grace won the round. Her smile of victory was bright enough to light the room without the gaslights burning. The others groaned, which only caused her lips to widen further in triumph. "You never know when to stop betting, Langdon," she said, her voice laced with teasing that skittered down Lovingdon's spine. When was the last time he'd laughed, or even smiled, for that matter?

"You should play my father," Langdon replied. "I hear he never loses at cards."

"Grace seldom does either," Drake said, beginning to deal the next round. "Even when she played silly card games as a child that required little more than matching two pictures, she always managed to beat me."

"All these years I thought you let me win."

Drake did little more than wink at her. He had begun his life as a street urchin until he was brought into the bosom of Grace's family. He never spoke of his life before, but there were times when Lovingdon could see that it weighed heavily on him. He was devoted to his work here, ensuring that the gaming hell made a tidy profit, his way of repaying those who had given him so much.

"Anything interesting occur at Claybourne's ball?" Avendale asked.

Grace lifted one slender alabaster shoulder. "If you want to know what happens at the balls, you should attend."

"I don't truly care. I was simply trying to make polite conversation."

"Trying to distract me from noticing the cards dealt, more like. Although I did hear that a certain young lady was spotted in the garden with a particular older gentleman."

"Who?"

She gave him a pointed look. "I'm not one to gossip."

"Then why even mention it?"

She smiled, that alluring smile that Lovingdon suspected brought some men to their knees. "To distract you. Now you'll be wondering if perhaps it was a lady who might have made you an excellent duchess."

"I have no interest in marriage. I daresay none of us at this table, with the exception of you, do."

"You all require heirs."

"There's no rush," Lovingdon said laconically. "My father was quite old when he sired me."

"Which left your mother a young widow."

"Marrying young is no guarantee that you won't be left alone." As soon as the words left his mouth, he regretted them. After two years the bite of loss was still sharp. His mother encouraged him to move on. She had done it quickly enough after his father died, but then theirs had not been a love match. No, she had not known love until Jack Dodger, the notorious public owner of Dodger's Drawing Room, had been named Lovingdon's guardian.

Grace blushed, and he suspected if she still possessed her freckles that they would have disappeared within the redness of her face. "Of course not. I'm sorry. I…I was thoughtless there."

"Think nothing of it. My words were uncalled for." Tension descended to surround them. No one ever spoke of Juliette. Sometimes it was as though she had existed only in his mind. Of late he found it increasingly difficult to recall her scent, the exact shade of her hair, the precise blue of her eyes. Had they been a sky at dawn or sunset?

Grace turned her attention to her cards, and he found himself watching as her bright blush receded. Her face would be warm to the touch, but then he suspected all of her would be warm. He should leave the cards and find himself a woman, but tonight he had no interest in the women he'd been visiting recently. Yes, they brought surcease to his flesh, but he failed to feel alive when he was with them. He went through the motions, but it seemed for the past two years, in all aspects of his life, he'd merely been going through the motions. Putting one foot in front of the other without thought or purpose. He refocused on his pair of jacks, holding dark thoughts at bay.

It came as no surprise to him that neither he nor Grace won that hand. The game seemed trite and yet it was a relief to concentrate on something that didn't truly matter. He had enough money in his coffers that losing was no hardship. He had been brought up to adhere to his father's belief that debt was the work of the devil. A man paid as he went. He never owed another man anything because debts had a way of bringing a man down when he least expected it.

The night wore on, conversation dwindling to nothing as everyone concentrated on the cards they were dealt. Lovingdon watched as half his chips made their way into Grace's stash. It should have irritated the devil out of him, but he was intrigued by the glow of her cheeks and the sparkle of her blue eyes with each round that she won. That she cared so much about something so trivial when he cared not at all about the most important things...

The present hand showed Grace with two queens and a jack, while Lovingdon showed a king, a ten, and a nine. Drake and Langdon had withdrawn from the round earlier. The final cards were now placed facedown in front of the remaining players.

Graced tapped her finger on a card. "I shall bet fifty." She tossed her chips onto the pile in the cen-ter of the table as though the amount was of no consequence, but then it wasn't really the money that enticed any of them into playing. It was the thrill of beating the others. The chips simply served as a measurement of success.

"I believe I'm finished for the night," Avendale said, turning all his cards facedown.

Lovingdon peered at his last card, shifted his gaze to Grace. She wore confidence with the ease that most women donned a cloak. He met her fifty and raised her fifty more.

Without hesitation she met his fifty. "I want to increase the pot," she said.

"Then do so."

"I wish to wager something a little different."

He wasn't the only one who came to attention at that. He could fairly feel the curiosity and interest rolling off the others. He hoped he had managed to keep his own fascination from showing. "Explain."

She licked her lips, the delicate muscles of her throat moving slightly as she swallowed. "We each wager a boon. If your cards beat mine, you may ask anything of me and I shall comply. If my cards beat yours, you will honor my request."

"Don't be ridiculous," Drake said. "That's not the way the game is played. Use your chips or forfeit."

"Hold on," Lovingdon drawled, studying her intently. The glow that alighted in her eyes, the fine blush beneath her skin. "I wager she's been waiting for this moment all night. I say we let her have it."

"Why do I feel as though I've stepped into the

middle of some muck here?" Drake asked. "Do you
know what's going on?"

Lovingdon rolled his lucky coin over and under
his fingers. "I have a fairly good idea."

He had to give her credit: she didn't flinch, but
met his gaze head on. So he was right. She planned
to win his assistance.

"You're not seriously considering calling her on
it," Drake insisted. "You have no idea what she'll
ask."

"I doubt she'll ask anything that I would find re-
volting. The danger is to her, for she knows not what
I might ask, and my standards are not as high as
hers."

"You can't ask anything that would be unseemly
or might put her reputation at risk," Drake insisted.

"Are there rules to this wager?" Lovingdon asked
her.

She angled her chin. "None at all."

"I won't allow this," Drake said.

"The lady is willing to suffer the consequences of
so rash an action, so you have no choice," Lovingdon reminded him.

"I rule here. It's my gaming house," Drake insisted.

"It's not actually. It's owned by my stepfather,
Langdon's father, and Grace's mother. As much as I
respect how well you manage it, I must also respect
that the lady has the right to wager as she wants. As

long as she understands that she will not be at all pleased with my request should I win."

Drake leaned toward her. "Grace, this is an unwise course of action. You have no earthly clue what he might demand of you."

Never removing her gaze from Lovingdon, she smiled, and the slight upturn of her lips nearly undid him. She was daring him to do something wicked. Oh, he thought of the fun he could have teaching her the ways of men with scandalous reputations—

His thoughts slammed to a halt as though he had hit a brick wall. She was Lady Grace Mabry, lover of kittens, thief of biscuit tins, and climber of trees. What the devil was he doing thinking of her wrapped in silk sheets? He should have his back flayed, and he suspected Drake would be more than willing to do just that if his friend realized the journey his wayward thoughts had just taken.

"That you would think he might do something dastardly has piqued my curiosity beyond all measure," Grace said. "Still, I'm willing to wager a boon as long as you, Lovingdon, understand that you will not be happy with what I request, but you will be obligated to fulfill it until I am satisfied with the outcome."

He almost purred that he could most certainly satisfy her. He felt a thrumming of excitement, the first bit that he'd felt in a good long while. It was odd to think of all the drinking, gambling, and bedding he'd done, and the thrill of it paling in comparison to this one moment, the possibility of beating her…and the chance he wouldn't and that her request would no doubt set his blood to boiling, because he had a damned good idea what she wanted of him. It was strange to be so alert, so on edge after being in a fog for so long. He nodded with certainty. "By all means. I call your wager."

Bless her, but she looked triumphant and he knew what she held, before she turned up the first card she had received and the queen of hearts winked up at him. "Three queens."

"I can count, my lady." He flipped over both of his downturned cards and watched as her face drained of all color. Three kings sealed her fate.

"I see." She lifted her sapphire gaze to his, narrowed her eyes, licked her lips. "That is quite astonishing."

"I tried to warn you off."

She nodded, her jaw so tight that he thought she might be grinding her teeth down to nubs. "Your request of me?"

He would not feel guilty, because the cards had favored him and not her. He would not. He was well aware of the other gentlemen waiting on bated breath for his pronouncement. While he was known to take advantage of situations, it irked him to realize that they thought he would take advantage of her, a girl he considered a sister in spite of the fact they shared no blood. "You know what I require."

"And what exactly is that?" Drake asked.

"Something quite innocent, I assure you," she said as she stood, as graceful and proud as a queen who had been disappointed by her minions but refused to succumb to tears. With the exception of Lovingdon, all the gentlemen stood as well. "Drake, will you see about arranging a carriage for me? I sent my driver home earlier."

"I've had quite enough of the evening," Lovingdon said, shoving back his chair and coming to his feet. "I'll see you home."

# Chapter 4

The coach rattled through the streets. Inside, the silence was as thick and heavy as the fog settling in. Lovingdon sat opposite Grace. While she stared out the window, she could feel his gaze homed in on her. "You cheated," she said softly.

"So did you."

She didn't bother to deny it. It was one thing to cheat, another to lie.

"Then I should not have to pay the boon," she said.

"Would you have been so gracious if the circumstances were reversed?"

Her sigh was one of impatience, a bit of anger. She had expected him to play as a gentleman, not a scoundrel. She shouldn't be surprised. The rumors she'd heard that he had lost his moral compass were apparently true. And damn him. Even if she had won unfairly, she would have required he pay the boon.

"No, you're quite right. We were evenly matched, regardless of the outcome." Turning her head slightly to peer at him, she rubbed her hands up and down her arms. "Thank you for not telling them what it was I wanted."

He shrugged out of his jacket, leaned across the distance separating them and settled it around her shoulders.

"So warm," she murmured, inhaling the scent of cigar, whiskey, and something deeper, darker, unique to him. "It smells of you."

"You'll not distract me from my purpose here. I want you to get this absurd notion out of your head that I could assist you in any conceivable manner regarding your quest for a grand love. You must know what qualities you seek in a man. Finding love is a personal journey, Grace."

"I know." She sighed, nodded, glanced back out the window. "Lord Bentley, I should think."

"What of him?" His words were terse.

"I believe his attentions are sincere. He has told me that I am beautiful, that he carries me into his dreams every night."

"But then so do I."

Her heart thundering, Grace jerked her head around to stare at Lovingdon's silhouette. She wished she could see his eyes. They were lost in the shadows. He moved. Smoothly. Swiftly. Until his hand was caressing her cheek, a light touch that was almost no touch at all, yet still it almost scorched her flesh.

She inhaled his rugged masculine scent. Hardly a hairbreadth separated them.

"You are so beautiful." His voice was a low rasp that sent tiny shivers of pleasure coursing through her. "I've long thought of confessing my infatuation, but we have been friends for so long that I thought you might laugh—"

"No. Never."

"In my dreams, we're on a hillock, lying upon the cool grass, our bodies so close that they provide heat as warm as the sun bearing down on us."

"Lovingdon—"

"Were Bentley's words as sweet?"

"Not quite, but near enough."

"And you believed such poppycock?"

She stilled, not even daring to breathe. "You think he lied?"

He leaned away. "All men lie, Grace, to obtain what they want."

Lovingdon's sweet words had meant nothing. What a fool she was to have been lured—

She lashed out and punched his shoulder with all the strength she could muster. "You blackguard!"

His laughter was dark, rough, as he moved back to his seat across from her. "You deserved it. In the space of a sennight you've ruined two of my evenings."

"Why? Because I gave you a challenge tonight? No one plays cards as well as I do."

"No one cheats as well as you do."

"Except you." And that knowledge irritated her because like Drake he'd always let her win, but in her case she thought she'd bested him. The blighter. "So tell me, regarding Bentley, how can I determine truth from lie?"

"If the words are too sweet they are insincere."

"Always?"

"Always."

"So if a man tells me I am beautiful, I am to discount him as a suitor?"

"It would probably be wise to do so, although I suppose there are exceptions."

"Do you tell women they are beautiful?"

"All the time."

"And you never mean it?"

His harsh sigh echoed through the confines of the coach. "The words are designed to make a woman feel treasured, to seduce her. To make her believe that she alone holds my interest—and for the moment she does. But she will not hold me for long."

"So you'll break her heart."

"I'm honest, Grace. The women in my life have no false expectations."

"I think you're mistaken about Bentley."

"Ask around. I'm sure you'll find he's used the words on others."

"Oh, yes, by all means, allow me to be seen as a

fool." Beneath his jacket, she rubbed her arms. She was suddenly quite chilled again. "What else must I look out for?"

"False flattery is usually poetic, ridiculous, flowery. At least mine is."

"You never flattered Juliette?"

"We will not speak of my courtship of Juliette. Ever."

"I'm sor—"

"Don't apologize for it. Just heed my words."

"As you wish. Back to the matter at hand, then, the lesson you sought to teach. I feel like such a ninny. Here I am with so many men declaring their affections, yet I am unable to discern their hearts. Even though you instruct me to trust mine."

"Bentley is not for you."

"As you refuse to assist me, I'm not sure I can value your opinion on the matter."

"It's not opinion. It's fact."

The horses slowed as the coach turned onto the circular drive. Soon the driver brought the vehicle to a halt. A footman opened the door. Lovingdon stepped out and then handed her down. Offering his arm, he escorted her up the stairs.

"How can you be so sure about Lord Bentley?" she asked.

"I know Lord Bentley."

Turning to face him, without thought she reached up and brushed the thick strands of blond hair from his brow. "Can a man not reform?"

"You deserve better than a man who requires re-forming."

Laughing lightly, she gave her hand leave to fall softly onto his shoulder, to feel the firmness there, the sturdiness, the strength. "Now I am suspect of all praise."

"I would never lie to you, Grace."

Her hand slid down a fraction, to his chest, to where his heart pounded so steadily. But he appeared not to notice. "Yet, you did. In the coach."

"That was merely a lesson, one I hope you took to heart."

"You're an abominable teacher. You might as well have taken a switch to my palm."

"It was not my intent to harm you, but to spare you from harm."

With a quick release of breath, she stepped back. "So in the future I shall not take flowery words to heart." She glanced up at the eaves. "Unless, of course, I know him to be a poet."

"Not even then, Grace."

"We shall see what my heart says. One more question."

"There's always one more question with you."

She ignored the irascibility in his voice. "Do you think you might see your way clear to coming to the Midsummer Eve's celebration that my family hosts?"

"Probably not."

She nodded, bit her lower lip, debated—there was always so much left unsaid between them. "I remember watching you dance with Juliette at the Midsummer Eve's ball, the summer before you married." He went so still, she wasn't even certain he was breathing. "Does it hurt when people speak of her?"

"Sometimes. It's equally hard, though, when no one speaks of her."

"I'm always available to listen, Lovingdon."

He glanced down at his shoes. "We were so young, she and I. We met at the very first ball I ever attended. I've never been to one when she wasn't there."

With his admission tears stung her eyes and her chest tightened until it ached. "You think you'll feel an emptiness."

He lifted his gaze to her. "I don't know what I'll feel."

Nodding, she swallowed hard. "I've not experienced the kind of loss that you have. I can't know the depth of your pain. But I have suffered loss, and I have found it is easier to carry on if I focus on what I have to be grateful for."

He turned to face her fully. "What loss, Grace?"

She shook her head. "I don't wish to talk about it."

"Does it have to do with this fellow you loved? The one who married someone else?"

She released a quick bubble of laughter and lied, because it was easier than baring the truth. She wished she'd not traveled this path and wanted to get off it as quickly as possible. "Yes. Silly really.

To compare the two. Good night, Lovingdon. May you sleep well."

She was aware of his gaze following her as she entered the residence. She was grateful that he didn't pursue the conversation, although a part of her wished he'd called her back, wrapped his arms around her, and insisted she tell him everything.

Drake Darling made a final notation in the ledger. It was late, he should be abed, but sleep did not come easily to him. He always felt as though he had something to prove, something to make right, something left undone.

Closing the ledger and his eyes, he settled back and let his past have its way with him. He'd been born Peter Sykes, the son of a thief and a murderer, although that he was aware of the last was his secret. No one knew that he'd made his way to the gallows, watched his father swing for murdering his mother. Frannie Darling had thought she'd protected him from the truth. But he was a child of the streets. No matter what he changed, he could not change that.

When Miss Darling married the Duke of Greystone, she no longer had use for her surname, so Peter had taken it to use as his own in an attempt to wash off his father. When he was a lad, he'd sometimes pretend that Greystone was his true father. He'd had a dragon inked onto his back because the duke had one. When the duke pointed out the constellation Draco, Peter had insisted he be called

Drake, in honor of the dragon shaped by stars. Although he'd been embraced by the Mabry family, he'd always known he wasn't one of them. At seventeen he'd come to work at Dodger's, determined to earn his own way, to prove—

"Tell me what you know of Bentley."

Drake opened his eyes. A storm in the form of Lovingdon had just blown into his office. The man looked as though he needed to rip something—or someone—apart. They were close in age, had become fast friends as they'd traveled similar yet different paths. "Viscount Bentley?"

Lovingdon gave a brusque nod. "What is his financial situation?"

"I don't know all the particulars. He runs up a debt here, pays it at the end of the month, repeats the cycle. Boring, predictable really."

"Yes, boring, predictable." Lovingdon walked to the window, gazed out. "I don't understand what she sees in him."

"She who?"

"Grace."

"Sees in whom?"

"Bentley," Lovingdon snapped. "Aren't you paying attention?"

"Grace told you she has an interest in him?"

"In the carriage. She mentioned that he was reciting garbage."

"Garbage? And that appealed to her?"

Lovingdon glared at him as though he hadn't the

sense to come in out of a rainstorm. "She thought it was poetry, beautiful. But it was garbage—how he dreams of her and such dribble."

Why would Lovingdon care? Why would Grace confide in him? "What was her appearance here earlier truly about?"

"You'll have to ask her, and while you're at it, warn her off of Bentley."

He watched as Lovingdon charged from his office. Something very strange going on here tonight. Perhaps a word with Grace was in order.

"What are you up to, Grace?"

Within the duchess's sitting room, which looked out upon a rain-drenched garden, Grace lifted her gaze from *Little Women* to see Drake leaning against the doorjamb, arms crossed over his chest. "Surely you recognize a book and the act of reading."

It was early afternoon. She'd slept into the late morning hours and was still recovering from her clandestine adventure the night before. It did not bode well that Drake, who usually slept until early evening, was disregarding his own habits.

"Bentley?" Drake's voice dripped with sarcasm. "What of him?"

Drake uncrossed his arms, strode to the chair across from her and dropped into it. "You would no more consider Bentley a serious suitor than I would consider pursuing a March hare for a wife."

She smiled brightly. "Are you considering marriage? Mother won't be half pleased."

"Dammit, Grace."

"Who have you set your sights on?"

"Be forthcoming with me, will you?"

She settled back against the plush chair. "How do you know about Bentley?"

With dark eyes narrowing, he studied her long and hard. She refused to squirm. "Lovingdon returned to the club last night, asked after Bentley's debt."

She tried not to appear too satisfied with the knowledge that Lovingdon, for all his blustering that he didn't care whom she married, did in fact care.

"What dodge have you got going on?" Drake asked.

Like her mother, Drake had begun his life on the streets, and in spite of the years since he'd fought to survive on them, he still remembered the tricks of his trade. A dodge referred to a swindle. "Don't be silly."

Leaning forward, resting his elbows on his thighs, he scrutinized her as though he could see clear into her soul. "You're scheming something, and it has to do with Lovingdon. I'd wager that you lost that last hand on purpose."

"You'd lose that wager. My intent was to win."

"And the boon?"

Drake was as close to her as either of her brothers, more so. He was the one who had held her hand when they went to the country fairs, hoisted her upon his back when she grew too tired to walk, stolen pastries from the kitchen and given her half. He would not betray her confidence, even without a promise exchanged. "Men are swarming around me like bees to honey. I wanted him to help me determine if a gentleman truly loved me."

"You're too wise to fall for some man's ruse, and I'm too smart to believe that's all there is to your request." Drake's eyes widened. "You want him to be one of the bees?"

"Absolutely not. He's completely inappropriate." Setting aside the book, she rose to her feet and glided over to the window. Raindrops rolled along the glass, nature weeping.

"He won't marry again, Grace. Something inside him broke with the death of Juliette and Margaret. You can't put him back together, sweetheart, not the way he was."

"Were you not listening? I have no interest in him as a suitor, but that doesn't mean I shouldn't try. That we shouldn't. Try to put him back together, I mean. I don't care that he doesn't love me—but I do care that he is wasting his life."

"I've watched him for two years, Grace. Been his companion through the worst of his grief. If he mends at all, he'll still have cracks and jagged edges."

"We all have jagged edges." Hers more hideous than any Lovingdon might possess. Only when Drake came to stand beside her did she notice her own faint reflection in the glass.

"Those on the inside are much worse than those on the outside," he said.

"But those on the inside are not as ugly. They're invisible."

"Which is what makes them all the more dangerous." He sighed. "How long have you loved him?"

She shook her head. "I don't love him. Oh, I was enamored of him when I was younger, but that was little more than childish fantasy. I am not so dense as not to recognize it for what it was. Besides, I won't be a man's second choice, and I fear with him any other woman would always fall short. But he has knowledge that can assist me, and if in the process he becomes part of Society again, more's the better. He won't be vying for my attention, as he certainly has no need of my dowry."

"Neither do I."

Before she could read his expression, he turned about and was heading for the door.

"Tread carefully, Grace. If you place him in a position where he hurts you, I will be forced to kill him."

She should have gone after him. Instead, she sank down to the footstool. To her, Drake had always been an older brother. They were not connected by blood, but by their hearts.

What she had felt for Lovingdon when she was a child was far different. He stole her breath with a look, warmed her body with an inadvertent touch, caused her heart to sing with a single word spoken.

But he no longer had such power over her. He was the means to an end—one that mattered far more than she dared tell him.

She was grateful that he had given her a bit of advice regarding Bentley. But could she trust it? He had promised to never lie to her—

But what if the promise were a lie?

"Words that are too flowery," Grace said as she poured tea at the cast-iron table in the garden.

"Too flowery?" Lady Penelope, her cousin, and daughter to the Countess and Earl of Claybourne, asked. Grace had always envied her black as midnight hair because it made her blue eyes stand out.

"Yes, you know. Lots of adjectives and adverbs and pretty words."

"But I like pretty words," Lady Ophelia, sister to Lord Somerdale said. Her hair was a flaxen blond that reminded Grace of wheat blowing in a field. Her eyes were the most startling green.

"Yes, that's the whole point. That's why they use them, but if they do use them, then they don't truly fancy us."

"Where did you learn this?" Miss Minerva Dodger asked. As she was Lovingdon's half sister, Grace knew she couldn't very well tell her the truth. She would no doubt confront her brother and any hope Grace had of securing his assistance would be dashed. Minerva was not nearly as fair of complexion as Lovingdon. It came from having vastly different fathers, she supposed. Minerva's hair had the fine sheen of mahogany, her eyes were as black as sin.

"A gentleman told me."

"Which gentleman?"

"It's not important who. He's had a great deal of experience on the matter."

"Very well. I'll write it down, but it sounds like poppycock to me."

"You don't have to write it down."

"I thought we were going to publish a book to help ladies determine when a gentleman was merely after their dowry. *A Lady's Guide to Ferreting Out Fortune Hunters.*"

"Well, yes, but I don't know that we'll have enough material."

"I think we need to do it," Lady Ophelia said. "Even if it's only two pages. Look at Lady Sybil. Her husband nearly had her in tears last night at the ball with all his ranting just because she wore a new gown in the same shade as the one his sister wore. Why would he care? If you ask me he should put her ahead of his sister, tell his sister to go change her frock."

"I always thought he was so nice," Minerva said.

"We all did," Grace said with conviction. "Last Season, I was even considering him as a serious suitor, but then I realized that Syb was terribly fond of him. I feared I'd lose her friendship if I encouraged him. Now I feel rather badly that she's with him."

"It's not your fault," Lady Penelope assured her. "I

would have stepped aside as well in favor of a friend. Which is why we must help each other identify the worst of the lot, so we might all avoid a similar sorrow-filled fate."

"I've heard something rather disturbing," Lady Ophelia said, "but as it involves my dear friend Lady Chloe, you must not tell a soul."

"We never would," Penelope said. "This round table is like the one at King Arthur's court. We are honor bound to hold the secrets spoken here."

Minerva laughed. "You are always so dramatic. You should go on the stage."

"Don't think I haven't considered it. I don't think Father would mind. He doesn't care much what anyone thinks, but Mother is another matter entirely. She says our behavior reflects not only on our father but on our uncle." She gave Grace a pointed look.

"I doubt Father would mind."

"I'll think about it if I don't find a beau this Season. Meanwhile, Ophelia, tell us about Chloe."

"Well." She glanced around the garden. "She's making merry with Lord Monroe. She has been since last Season, but he hasn't asked for her hand in marriage. She'll be ruined if he doesn't."

"Surely he will," Grace assured her. "If they're… well, you know, being cozy and all, surely it's only a matter of time."

"I've thought about confronting him…"

"Bad idea, there. Don't want to get into the middle of it."

"Yes, I suppose you're right." Lady Ophelia gazed out over the lawn. "Finding a good husband should not be so difficult."

"Who are you going to choose?" Minerva asked Grace.

"Oh, I haven't a clue. The first one to send me my favorite flower, I suppose."

"Your favorite flower. What has that to do with anything?" Penelope asked.

"Something my elusive gentleman told me. A man who loves me will know my favorite flower."

"I'm going to jot that down as well," Minerva assured them. "Is this gentleman advisor of yours happily married? I'd like to know how he came to be such an expert."

"He's a widower."

She looked up. "He's old, then?"

Grace forced her expression not to give anything away. "Terribly old." To a child of two.

"I'd like to meet this mysterious gentleman of yours," Minerva said.

"I'll see what can be arranged, but I must confess that he is not one for going out."

"Decrepit as well, then. Does he still have his mind? Is he sharp enough to remember how he came to have his wife?"

Grace fought not to reveal any sorrow when she said, "He's sharp enough to remember everything."

# *Chapter 5*

Noon was far too early for a disreputable man to awaken, but when Lovingdon received word that his mother was waiting in the parlor, staying abed no longer seemed wise. She was not averse to barging into his bedchamber, and while his bed was empty of female companionship, she did not need to see him in his present state, when he had not shaved in eons, his eyes were red and puffy, and he reeked of tobacco and strong drink.

So he hastily bathed and shaved, donned proper attire, and went downstairs to pretend that he was glad she had come to see him.

Pouring tea, she sat in a green wingback chair, and it struck him with the force of a battering ram that she had aged considerably since he'd last seen her. He doubted any son loved his mother as much as he did, and if it made him a coddled mother's boy, so be it.

"Mother," he said as he strode across the room, then leaned down and kissed her cheek. "You're looking well."

"Liar. I look dreadful. I'm not sleeping much."

"And which of your children is to blame for that?" he asked, taking the chair near her and stretching out his legs. After she married Jack Dodger, she'd given birth to two sons and a daughter. Her lineage gained them entry into Society, while Jack Dodger's wealth made them acceptable. Lovingdon had no doubt that they would each marry someone who carried some aristocratic blood in their veins.

His mother said nothing, simply sipped her tea, and that was answer enough.

"You needn't worry about me. I'm fine," he assured her.

"It's been two years. You're not back into Society. You can't mourn forever."

He removed his pocket watch from his waistcoat. It had been his father's. Originally, it went to his father's bastard son, but Jack had given it to Lovingdon on the day he turned one and twenty. Inside the cover of the watch, his father had kept a miniature of a young woman, a servant girl whom he claimed was the love of his life. A girl who gave birth to Jack. Now there was a miniature of Juliette inside the watch. "Father loved only once. Perhaps I'm like him."

"He never tried to love again. Guilt held him back."

Lovingdon understood guilt. *Don't let us die.*

They never should have gotten sick. If only he'd stayed away from the slums like Juliette had asked, if only he hadn't felt the need to be a good Samaritan. If only he'd been content to provide the funds for clearing out some of the slums, if only he'd not felt a need to oversee the work. If only he'd sent his family away when he became ill. If only he'd died instead of them.

His mother set aside her teacup. "I'm not saying that you must love again, but I do think it would do you a world of good to immerse yourself back into Society."

"I immerse myself plenty," he said dryly.

"Yes, in women, I'm sure."

His jaw dropped and he almost had to nudge it to get it back into position.

She quirked a brow. "I'm married to a gambling house owner who shares everything with me. I have long since lost my innocence when it comes to wickedness."

He had to make his mind a blank slate so he didn't conjure images of his mother engaging in wicked activities. But then he supposed he shouldn't be surprised. It was Jack who had given him his first taste of liquor and tobacco. Jack who had taught him to curse and introduced him to cards.

She reached across and squeezed his hand. "Henry, I want you to be happy."

He shook his head. "Not yet, Mother. It's obscene to even contemplate it."

"Take a small step. The Countess of Westcliffe is having her annual garden party this afternoon. You should go."

"I can think of nothing more boring than swinging a mallet."

She furrowed her delicate brow. "I think you've forgotten how much you enjoy croquet. If you won't go for yourself, go for me. I shall sleep so much better if I know you're at least engaging with others."

"I engage—"

"Yes, I'm sure you do engage yourself with less reputable women, but that's not what I had in mind. Do something proper for a change."

"I'll think about it...for you."

"I suppose I can't ask for more."

"You could."

She smiled. "But I won't." She rose to her feet and he stood. "I need to be off making arrangements for Minerva's birthday party next week. You will come, won't you? It's only a small, intimate gathering. She'll be so disappointed if you're not there again."

He couldn't even recall how many he'd missed: one or two. Guilt pricked his conscience. He wasn't ashamed of his behavior but he had taken great pains not to flaunt his bad habits around his younger siblings. They'd always looked up to him. He recognized now that it was wrong of him to avoid them. He felt as though he'd been wandering through a fog and sunshine was beginning to burn it away. Although he didn't have a clue regarding what had caused the sun to appear.

"I shall try to be there."

She patted his cheek. "Do more than try for goodness' sakes. I don't ask for much."

No, she didn't. He walked with her into the entryway.

"By the by, have you seen Lady Grace this Season?" his mother asked. "I hear she's considering Lord Bentley."

"For what?"

"Why marriage, of course."

The Countess of Westcliffe was known for her garden parties, and Grace didn't think the lady could have asked for a lovelier afternoon. The sun was bright and joyful. It warmed the air and brought forth the fragrance of freshly cut grass. Most of the Marlborough House Set was in attendance. Some guests took refuge in the shade provided by canopies. Others played badminton or croquet. Many sipped champagne and nibbled on delicious pastries.

Grace sat on a stool beneath the wide full-leafed bough of an elm. Circling her, half a dozen gentlemen vied for her attention, and she was most grateful to see that Lord Ambrose was not among them. She was as charming as one could be under the circumstances, but she was not inspired to passion by any of the gents circling her. They all looked remarkably alike, desperate for her attention. She wanted someone who wasn't quite so needy, and yet she understood that the generosity of her dowry called to those in need. She did not hold their unfavorable circumstance against them. God knew she had been brought up to fully understand that not everyone was as well off as her family, but she preferred a man who was at least striving to make a go of it on his own.

Still, she smiled at Lord Winslow, laughed at Lord Canby's atrocious jokes, which held no humor at all, and listened with rapt attention to Lord Carlton's description of a babbling brook and how he had moved the stones around in order to make it sound different. She refrained from commenting that perhaps if he had assisted in moving stones from his land, the fields might have produced more grain and he wouldn't now be dashing off to fetch her more champagne in order to impress her.

It was a curse to have inherited her mother's knack for numbers, along with her penchant toward the sensible.

Lord Renken was a terrible stutterer and he said not a word. Grace didn't mind his affliction. She wasn't looking for perfection. She wanted love. Her mother had not held her father's approaching blindness against him. She could not have loved him more if his eyesight were perfect. But it was difficult to get to know a man if he never spoke.

Although, Lord Vexley was mute as well. He exchanged glances with her from time to time, secretive little looks that seemed to indicate he felt none of these gentlemen were competition for her affections. She couldn't deny that Vexley was handsome, intelligent, and easy to speak with while they danced. He seemed to appreciate *her* more than her fortune, but how was one to know for sure?

She cursed Lovingdon for not taking her problem seriously, but then she supposed it wasn't truly a serious problem. No one would go hungry, be without shelter, or die because of her choice. And if she didn't choose, her parents weren't likely to disown her. She supposed she could live very happily without a husband, but it was the absence of love that was troubling. As far as she knew, no one had ever been madly, deeply, passionately in love with her. She believed that a woman should experience the mad rush of unbridled passion at least once in her lifetime. Was she being greedy to want it permanently?

Lord Canby was beginning to recite another joke when Grace rose and shook out her skirts. He stopped mid-word, the expression on his face nearly making her laugh. Instead, she adjusted her hat to more effectively shade her eyes and said, "Gentlemen, if you'll be so kind as to excuse me—"

"I'll accompany you," Lord Vexley said, hopping to his feet.

She smiled warmly. "Where I need to go, ladies prefer to go alone. I shan't be long."

He bowed his head slightly. "As you wish."

His voice carried an undercurrent she couldn't quite identify. Disappointment? Impatience? She supposed it was much less frustrating being the pursued rather than the pursuer. She wasn't in danger of being rebuffed, while all these gentlemen were striving to impress. Perhaps she would assuage her guilt by trying to lead them toward ladies more likely to embrace their courtship with enthusiasm. It seemed to have worked for Lady Cornelia and Lord Ambrose.

Walking toward the residence, she was well aware of a prickling sensation along her neck, no doubt Lord Vexley's gaze on her back. She was so aware of his presence, his attentions…that had to count for something, didn't it?

As she neared the residence, out of the corner of her eye she spied Lord Fitzsimmons speaking to her dear friend Lady Sybil. They were standing at the far edge of the terrace, where several trees and bushes provided thick shade and coverage. She could not hear the words, but she could tell by Sybil's paling features that her husband was once again deriding her for something. It was no doubt some trivial matter that in the grand scheme of things held no consequence. The man was a toad. A prince who had turned into a frog instead of a frog who had turned into a prince. She knew it was none of her concern, that she should march on, but Sybil deserved far better.

Before she knew what she was about, she was striding toward the couple. Lord Fitzsimmons's nose was less than an inch from his wife's. His eyes were narrowed in anger, while she was cringing.

"My lord?" Grace called out. "My lord Fitzsimmons?"

Jerking his head around, he glared at her, the force of it nearly causing her to stumble back. If she were wise, she would walk right past. Unfortunately, a cowardly streak did not run through her veins and she tended to become stubborn when faced with bullies. It had to do with having older brothers and growing up playing with boys more than girls. She could hold her own in a pillow fight or when it came to playing pranks.

"I'm certain you didn't mean to embarrass your wife here," she stated succinctly, striving to edge her way in front of Sybil.

"Grace—" Sybil began.

"Lady Grace, this does not concern you," Fitzsimmons declared.

"I'm afraid it does. Lady Sybil is a dear friend."

He leaned toward her, his face a hard mask, his finger darting toward her nose. "Be on your—"

He yelped, and Grace was suddenly aware of a large hand holding that offending finger in such a way that it was nearly doubled back. Lord Fitzsimmons's eyes bulged. She had only to turn her head slightly to see Lovingdon standing there, his expression a barely contained murderous rage.

"If you ever point your finger in her face again, I shall snap it in two," he ground out.

"Your Grace, she was interfering—"

"Be grateful she did before I got here. I'd have used my fist rather than my words. You make a spectacle of yourself, man, when you treat your wife with such disrespect. I won't have it."

"You don't rule me— Ah!"

Grace realized that Lovingdon had yet to release his hold. It took only a bit of maneuvering for him to have Fitzsimmons bending his knees as though he would fall to the ground in agony.

"You will treat your wife better or you will answer to me. Have I made myself clear?"

"All marriages have discord."

"This isn't you, Fitz."

He jerked up his chin. "You don't know me, Lovingdon. Not anymore. We all change. You're certainly not the lad I knew in school."

"I'm not the one acting a fool here. Now apologize to your wife for not behaving as a gentleman."

Fitzsimmons hesitated, then said, "I'm sorry, m'dear. Won't happen again."

Lovingdon released his hold. "I suggest you take a brisk walk to cool off that temper."

"You don't control me."

Lovingdon arched a brow.

"But I can see the wisdom in your suggestion." With that he strode off.

Sybil looked first at Grace and then at Lovingdon. "Thank you, thank you both. I don't know what comes over him. As you say, Your Grace, it's absolutely unlike him to be so disagreeable."

"When did these bouts of foul temper begin?"

She lifted a delicate shoulder. "I'm not sure. Three or four months ago, I suppose. But no matter. I'm sure all will be well now."

Oh, Sybil, Grace thought, you are too much an optimist.

"If he should ever hurt you," Lovingdon said, "do not hesitate to send word 'round to me."

Apparently, he, too, had doubts regarding Sybil's optimism.

"He's a lamb at home. It's only when we're out in public. I don't understand it, but we'll be fine." Her cheeks flushing, she walked away.

Grace watched her go, wondering if she should go with her, yet reluctant to leave Lovingdon. She turned back to him. "Thank you for coming to my rescue."

"You could have handled him easily enough I suspect."

That didn't mean she didn't appreciate the steps he had taken to spare Lady Sybil any more embarrassment. Others around had noticed, yet no one else had bothered to step in.

"I didn't realize you were here," Grace said.

"Obviously."

"You're angry."

"I came very close to introducing him to my fist."

She smiled. "I was about to introduce him to mine."

She saw the barest hint of a grin before he brought it back into submission. "You're no longer a child. You can't get into tumbles."

She rolled her eyes at the absurdity of that conclusion. "Nothing wrong with a lady who isn't afraid to defend herself. You taught me how to beat up my brothers. It's a lesson I've never forgotten, and one that I see no reason to delegate to childhood."

He shook his head, and she could see the anger dissipating, perhaps in light of happier memories. Thanks to him, she knew how to hold her fist to minimize damage to herself while maximizing it to others. She knew how to hit hard and quick, how to fight dirty in order to win. Perhaps she should give Sybil a lesson or two. She sobered. "Do you think Fitzsimmons will take your threat to heart, that he'll treat her better? I fear she's being overly optimistic."

He glanced in the direction that Fitzsimmons had gone. "I'll have another word with him. Don't worry yourself over it."

"Difficult to accomplish when I love Sybil so." She studied him for a moment. "I would not have expected to see you at this garden party."

He shrugged. "I had nothing pressing this afternoon, so I thought I would stop by. I noticed you holding court."

She groaned at the censure in his voice. "I have little choice when so many come 'round. The alternative is to queue them up so they each have a few moments of my time, and I think that far worse."

His gaze slid past her, and she could see he was deep in thought. His brow furrowed slightly, and it was all she could do not to reach up and flatten the shallow creases with her thumb. She wanted to comb the locks off his forehead with her fingers. Silly things to want.

"None of those who were gathered at your feet will provide what you are seeking." His gaze came back to her, and in the amber depths, she saw the conviction of his words.

"How do you know?"

"A man who would love you would not have been content to keep his distance." He wrapped his hand around hers, and she was immediately aware of the largeness of his. While hers was slender and long, his was broader, stronger, more powerful. Gently, he tugged her nearer until they were both enveloped in the cool shade and his musky male scent won out over the sweet fading fragrance of the distant roses.

"He would want you near enough," he said, his voice low and raspy, "that when he gazed into your eyes he could see the darker blue that circles the sapphires everyone notices, the darker ring known to only a few. He would want to inhale your fragrance of rose and lavender, feel the warmth radiating off your skin. He would not be content to share you."

For the first time, she noticed the black ring that encircled the amber depths of his eyes. The discovery pleased her because everything else about him was so very familiar: the sharp lines, the acute definitions. When he angled his head just so, he appeared haughty, but at that moment he appeared enthralled, as though he had only just noticed every aspect of her, as though he were mesmerized to discover that she had grown to womanhood.

She was aware of their shallow breathing, of each forceful pump of her heart, the way his smoldering gaze roamed over her face until it settled on her mouth, her lips slightly parted, her tongue darting out in invitation—

Invitation for what, she wasn't sure, but she found it difficult to think, to analyze, to decipher all that was happening. The sun was making her far too warm. Or was it him, his nearness, his attention?

"He would stare at me?" she whispered, swaying toward him.

"He would touch you in ways he could not touch you with his hands—not in public. But images would be filling his mind. He would be unable to tear his gaze away." Clearing his throat, he broke the connection that was joining them and looked up into the trees. "He will look at you, Little Rose, as though you are everything, because to him you will be."

He lowered his gaze. The heat had been doused

and she wondered if it had ever been there or whether she simply imagined it. Embarrassed, hoping beyond hope that he had not been aware of the extent to which she'd been enthralled, she swallowed hard and turned her attention to the flowers. They paled in comparison to Lovingdon. She would much prefer watching him.

"It takes a while for love that intense to develop, doesn't it?" she asked.

Slowly he shook his head. "I fell in love with Juliette the moment I set eyes on her."

He stepped back as though he needed to distance himself from the memory.

"She wouldn't want you to be alone," she said.

He grinned, the cocky yet sad smile that had become such a part of him. "I'm hardly alone."

"Love, then. She wouldn't want you to go without love."

"Love is rare. There are those who never know it, but having known it"—he shook his head—"I have no desire to know it again. I could never love anyone as I loved her."

"I find that sad, and such a waste. You must have an heir."

"I can have an heir without loving the woman. My father did." His taut expression revealed that he regretted the words as soon as they left his mouth. "I've told you what you need to know to find the man who loves you."

Abruptly, he turned on his heel—

"Wait! One more question," she called after him.

He turned to her, his face without curiosity. He didn't truly care about her troubles or woes. Why had he come? Did it matter?

Biting on her lower lip, she took a step nearer. "If a gentleman is bedding a lady and has not asked for her hand in marriage, is it likely that he fancies her?"

"No."

He might as well have slapped her with the terse word. Something must have shown on her face, because he said, "Tell me who it is and I'll kill him for taking advantage of you."

She laughed lightly. "No one is bedding me. It's a friend. She thinks he loves her—"

"He might lust after her, but he doesn't love her. It would be prudent for her to end this relationship before she finds herself completely ruined."

"And you know this because you've been with ladies you didn't love."

"Not with a lady who has a reputation to protect. I've told you before, Grace, the women I frequent know the rules of the game I play. It sounds to me as though your friend doesn't—especially if she still expects marriage."

"Gentlemen don't play by the same rules as ladies, do they?"

"I fear not. We can be beasts when we set our mind to it. Warn her off." He retreated farther into the shadows, toward a side gate that would lead him into the street. She dearly wanted to go after him.

Did he have memories of his mother not being loved? Was that the reason he was here, offering advice, small as it was? She'd known of course that his father, much older than his mother, had married out of duty. It was a common practice among the aristocracy, although now love was more often beginning to hold sway and duty was less a factor.

Turning, she jerked back and released a tiny squeal at the sight of the man standing there, fairly hovering over her. "Lord Vexley, you took me by surprise."

"My apologies, Lady Grace. I saw an opportunity to have a moment alone with you. I could hardly let it pass." He stepped nearer, his gaze holding hers, his focus intense, almost captivating. "Lovingdon seems to have upset you."

"No, not at all. He was simply in the area, I suppose, and we had a little chat." She shook her head. "He hardly attends social affairs these days. I was hoping this one might do him some good."

"I feel sorry for any lady who might try to claim his heart. It is very difficult to live with a ghost."

"I don't think—"

"My mother was my father's second wife. She never held his heart. It made her a very sad woman. It is much better to be the first to claim a man's heart." He placed his palm flat against his chest and grinned at her. "Mine has yet to be claimed."

It was an invitation that she thought she should be delighted to receive, eager to accept, and yet she couldn't quite bring herself to do it. Instead she tried to make light of it without causing hurt feelings, as she couldn't deny that of all the gents vying for her affections, he was the one she most looked forward to spending time with. "I find it difficult to believe that your heart has not been touched by another when you are so incredibly charming."

"But I am not so easily charmed. You, however, my lady…" He looked toward the gardens. "Perhaps you would be kind enough to join me for a stroll about the roses."

"I should be most delighted." She placed her hand on the crook of his elbow. His words were not overly poetic, and he knew enough to take her through the roses. Now if he but knew which shade she favored.

"Red, I should think," he said, as though he'd read her mind. "Red roses are what I should send you tomorrow."

"Better to leave them where they are. They don't die so quickly that way."

"Ah, a lady who doesn't appreciate a courtship accompanied by flowers. What would you prefer, I wonder?"

She opened her mouth, and he quickly touched a gloved finger to her lips. "No, don't tell me. I shall deduce it on my own."

He gave her a warm smile, and she found herself wishing that her heart would do a somersault.

Having sent his carriage on its way, Lovingdon walked. He needed to walk. He needed his muscles tightening and aching, he needed the pounding of his heels on ground. He needed distance, distance from Grace, the dark blue rings that circled her irises, the damn freckle near the corner of her mouth. Why had it remained when all the others had disappeared, why did it taunt him? Why had he noticed?

The sun had kissed her there. Why had he wanted to as well?

He'd come because he simply wanted to observe, to make certain that Bentley wasn't monopolizing Grace's time. Step in if needed. He certainly hadn't expected to step into Fitzsimmons. What a scapegrace. If any man berated Grace in that manner, public or privately—

How the deuce would he know if it was happening privately?

She would tell him, of course. He'd have her word on it.

She would no doubt inform him it was no longer any of his concern, the stubborn little witch. If he wouldn't assist her in finding a man who loved her, he couldn't very well complain if she ended up with one who didn't.

He probably should have hesitated before stepping in to save her from Fitzsimmons. He would like to have seen the man's face when it met up with Grace's fist. Yes, she would have struck him. She was not demure, not like Juliette.

When Grace wanted something, she went after it, even if it meant asking a recent reprobate for assis-

tance. Which he was not so keen on giving. Whatever had possessed him to gaze at her as he had, to
draw her into gazing at him?

He never gazed into women's eyes anymore. He
never noticed freckles tucked in near to the corner
of a mouth. He didn't pay attention to quick breaths
or fingers lifting of their own accord to touch him.
He wondered if she'd even been aware of her action.
If he'd not moved, she would have touched him, as
she had the evening before—and it simply wouldn't
do to know the warmth of her again.

Her skin, her sighs, her heated glances would all
belong to someone else, someone with the wherewithal to love her as she deserved.


"You must tell Lady Chloe," Grace told Lady
Ophelia. After her walk with Vexley, she'd met up
with her closest unmarried friends near the rhodo-
dendrons. "He doesn't fancy her. He's never going
to ask for her hand in marriage."

"How do you know?" Ophelia asked.

"My gentleman."

"Vexley? Is Vexley your man? I saw you walking with him."

"No, he's someone else."

"Is he here?" Minerva asked.

"No, no. But he was most insistent that if a man
takes a woman to bed without asking for her hand
in marriage, it's only lust. And it makes sense. After

all this time, why would he ask her? He's searching for someone with a larger dowry."

"Blighter," Ophelia grumbled.

"You must do it."

"All right. All right. I'll talk with her." She opened her eyes wide and smiled brightly. "Ah, there's Lord Ambrose. Think I shall flirt with him a bit. Makes Lady Cornelia bonkers."

"Don't ruin things for her," Grace said adamantly. "I worked very hard to get them together."

"Did your gentleman tell you that Ambrose fancied her?"

"We didn't discuss them."

"Maybe you should. Would be interesting to know his opinion regarding all the various couples that are forming as you break one gentleman's heart after another."

"I'm hardly breaking hearts."

"We all break hearts; we all have our hearts broken. It's the way of things."

## Chapter 6

Slowly sipping his scotch and rolling a coin over, under, between his fingers, Lovingdon paid little heed to the men with whom he was playing cards—save one.

Fitzsimmons.

The man downed liquor as though he believed drinking enough of it would cure all ills, when in truth it was only adding to his troubles. Cards required that a man keep his wits about him if he hoped to have any chance at all of winning. Fitzsimmons's wits seemed to have deserted him completely.

He growled when Lovingdon had taken a chair at the table. Not that his behavior was particularly unusual. With the exception of Avendale, the other gentlemen had expressed their displeasure at his arrival by clearing throats, shifting in chairs, and signaling for more drink. Lovingdon was not known for his charity when it came to cards. He believed a man should never wager what he was unwilling—or could ill afford—to lose.

It seemed Fitzsimmons was of the opposite opinion. If this hand didn't go his way, he was going to lose all the chips that remained to him. And Lovingdon already knew Fitzsimmons wasn't going to win. He'd known three cards ago, and yet the man continued to raise the amount being wagered as though he thought continually upping the stakes would disguise the fact that the cards showing before him revealed an atrocious hand.

The final card was dealt facedown. Lovingdon set his glass aside, lifted the corner of his card—

Did not display his pleasure at what he'd been dealt. Fitzsimmons, on the other hand, looked as though he might cast up his accounts. Then in a remarkably stupid move, he shoved his remaining chips into the pile in the center of the table.

The gentleman to Fitzsimmons's left cleared his throat and folded. As did the one beside him.

Lovingdon didn't consider for one moment being as charitable. He matched the wager. Fitzsimmons was obviously on the verge of having an apoplectic fit, if the amount of white showing in his eyes was any indication.

To Lovingdon's left, Avendale folded.

Lovingdon held Fitzsimmons's gaze, watched as the man slowly turned over his cards.

"Ace high," Fitzsimmons ground out.

Lovingdon could feel the stares, the held breaths, the anticipation. It wasn't too late to gather up his cards without revealing them, to simply utter, "I daresay that beats me." Instead he flipped over his cards to reveal a pair of jacks.

Fitzsimmons appeared to be a man who had just felt the cold fingers of death circling his neck. "You cheated, damn you."

One man gasped, another scooted his chair back as though he expected Lovingdon to leap across the table and throttle the insolent Fitzsimmons.

"See here," Avendale proclaimed. "We're gentlemen. We do not accuse—"

"I'm not offended," Lovingdon broke in. "I'm amused. Tell me, my lord, how do I cheat when I keep my hands on the table, one constantly rolling a coin and the other occupied with drink?"

"I don't know." Fitzsimmons's voice was unsteady. "I don't bloody well know."

"I'm certain your credit is good here. You can get additional chips at the cage, although I would recommend against it. Lady Luck isn't with you tonight."

"Shows what little you know. She hasn't been with me in a good long while." Fitzsimmons scraped back his chair, stood, and angled up his chin, gathering as much dignity as possible into that small movement. "Gentlemen."

Then he headed toward the lounge, stumbling only twice.

"One should not mix drink and cards," Avendale declared. He shifted his gaze to Lovingdon. "As Lady Luck does seem to be with *you* tonight, and I have no interest in losing more coins, I'm off to Cremorne."

"You'll lose coins there just as easily."

"Yes, but to ladies who show their gratitude in more inventive ways. Care to join me?"

"In a bit, perhaps. I have another matter to which I must attend first." Lovingdon signaled to a young lad, who rushed over. "Those are my winnings." With a sweep of his hand over the table, he indicated all that belonged to him. "Disperse them evenly between yourself and the other lads."

"Thank you, Your Grace."

The lad eagerly set to the task of scooping the chips into a bowl. Lovingdon bid a good evening to the gentlemen who remained, then strode toward the lounge. He'd barely taken his place in a chair opposite Fitzsimmons before a footman placed a tumbler of scotch on the table beside him. Knowing each lord's drink preferences was a thirty-year tradition at Dodger's. Lovingdon lifted his glass and savored the excellent flavor.

"Come to gloat, have you?" Fitzsimmons asked.

"If I were going to gloat, I would have done it out there. Gloating with witnesses is so much more enjoyable." He tapped his finger against his glass. "You couldn't afford to lose tonight."

Averting his gaze, Fitzsimmons gnawed on his lower lip. Finally he murmured, "I've not been able to afford it in some time."

Placing his forearms on his thighs, Lovingdon leaned forward and lowered his voice. "I knew you at Eton. You weren't a bully—and God knows there were bullies. But not you. Why would you bully your wife? Lady Grace Mabry told me that Lady Sybil believed you loved her—"

"I do love her." Heat ignited his eyes, simmered, then was snuffed out. "I've not been myself of late."

"I've paid little attention to marriages the past few years, but I heard she came with a nice dowry."

"She also came with a penchant for spending. And I had not the heart to deny her the pleasure of it. I thought to increase my assets with investments. I chose poorly. I don't know why the bloody hell I'm telling you all this. Although it'll come out soon enough. I have nothing left. I squandered her dowry. I doubt she'll love me once she realizes the dire straits we're in. My ill temper with her—I think I wanted her to leave me so she would never learn the truth."

"She doesn't know?"

"Would you want your wife to view you as a disappointment?"

Lovingdon felt as though he'd taken a blow to the

chest. He'd disappointed Juliette in the worst way imaginable.

Fitzsimmons blanched. "Apologies. That was bad form to mention—"

Lovingdon held up a hand to stem further stammering. He didn't want Juliette's name echoing in this place. "Have you any funds left?"

Fitzsimmons slowly shook his head.

"Right, then. I shall provide you with capital and advise you on how to invest it wisely. You will return my investment with interest once you see an acceptable profit."

"Why would you do this? We're hardly the best of friends."

"Lady Sybil's happiness matters to Lady Grace, and Lady Grace's happiness matters to me. But understand that I can just as easily destroy you as assist you. Our goal here is to ensure you no longer feel a need to take out your frustrations on your wife."

"I won't. I do love her."

"Then treat her as such." He stood. "Be at my residence at two tomorrow afternoon and we'll work out the details."

Fitzsimmons shot to his feet. "I could be there at half past eight in the morning."

Such eagerness. He did hope he wasn't misjudging Fitz. He had known him as a good and honorable man, but he also knew what it was to have life's challenges divert one's course. "You won't find me available at that time of the morning. I intend to spend the night carousing. Tomorrow afternoon will be soon enough."

"I hardly know how to thank you, Your Grace."

"Be kind to your wife."

"I will be. You can count on it."

"And stay away from the cards, man."

"I will."

Lovingdon strode from the room. He decided that he'd head to Cremorne, where ladies and drink were in abundance. He was suddenly in want of both.

He'd known exactly where to find Avendale: at their favorite booth where ale flowed freely. Avendale spotted him, smiled broadly and extended a tankard toward Lovingdon. As soon as he took it, Avendale tapped his against Lovingdon's.

"I knew you couldn't stay away."

Not tonight. Tonight he needed…he wasn't certain what he needed. He knew only that he'd not found it at Dodger's. He emptied his tankard in one long deep swallow and called for another.

Avendale leaned back against the counter, placing his elbows on it and crossing his feet at the ankles. He looked to be a man entirely too comfortable here, but then his purview was sin. When they'd been younger men, he'd always sought to entice Lovingdon into joining him. It wasn't until after Juliette died that Lovingdon had finally accepted the invitation. It only took one night for him to wonder why he'd been so resistant in his youth.

Proper behavior was no way for a man to live, he reflected as he downed half the second tankard.

"What were you trying to prove with Fitzsimmons?" Avendale asked.

Lovingdon looked out over the crowd. Cremorne Gardens served two purposes. In the early evening it was for the respectable crowd. Until the fireworks. When they were naught but smoke on the night air, they signaled the beginning of the witching hour—when good folk left and the less reputable arrived. Swells were strutting about now, and buxom ladies were doing their best to entice them.

"Yesterday I witnessed him treating his wife rather poorly," Lovingdon explained. "He wasn't behaving as himself."

"As himself? Or as you remembered him from school?"

"As himself. It seems he's in a bit of a financial bind. Poor investments and all that."

"I suspect it's more than poor investments," Avendale said. "It's this damned industrialization, taking tenants from the land to the cities and factories. It'll be the death of the aristocracy. Mark my words."

Lovingdon chuckled. "Don't be such a defeatist. The aristocracy will survive."

Avendale straightened and lifted his tankard. "Survival is no fun. We want to flourish, have more coin than we'll ever need, so we are men of leisure with no troubles to weigh us down."

"I've never known you to be weighed down with troubles."

Something serious, somber, flashed across Avendale's face before he downed what remained in his tankard and set it on the counter. "What say we find a couple of willing ladies, whisk them off to my residence, and sample them until dawn?"

Lovingdon tried to recollect if he'd heard any rumors regarding Avendale's situation, but he couldn't recall anything. Their relationship was more surface than depth. "Is all well with you?"

Avendale laughed. "It will be once I find a willing wench."

His companion was on the hunt before Lovingdon blinked. After having his tankard refilled, he fell into step beside him.

"So I assume we're looking for our usual fare? Brunettes?" Avendale asked.

Lovingdon didn't answer. The question was moot, and well his cousin knew it.

"I understand you not having an interest in blondes," Avendale went on, "but gingers? They can be as fiery as their hair."

"I'll leave them to you." Juliette was the only blonde he would ever want. As for the reds, he wasn't certain why he didn't gravitate toward them. He supposed it had something to do with Grace and how she had despised her hair and freckles.

He was grateful that Avendale was not of a mind to take an interest in Grace. While he had no need of her dowry, Avendale was not one to remain faithful—or at least Lovingdon couldn't imagine him doing so. As far as he knew, the man had never even bothered to set up a mistress. Sameness bored him. He made a good friend, but as a husband, he would no doubt fail miserably.

Avendale drifted away when a woman crooked her finger at him. While Lovingdon intended to find company for the night, he found himself studying the gents who were about. Were any of them worthy of Grace?

She could be stubborn, and yet there was a softness to her, an innocence. She needed a man who wouldn't break her, who wouldn't berate her. A man who understood that sometimes she tended to behave in a way that wasn't quite acceptable. Coming to a man's residence in the middle of the night, drinking liquor, playing cards, cheating at cards, driving him to madness with her—

He staggered to a stop as he caught sight of red hair beneath the hood of a cape before the woman turned away. She was tall, slender…she couldn't be Grace.

"Hello, fancy man. What are you up to tonight?" A golden-haired vixen stroked his shoulder. He hadn't even realized she was near. He'd been so focused on the hooded woman, anyone could have fleeced his pockets.

"Pardon me," he uttered before striding away. Where the deuce was the woman in the cape?

It would be just like Grace to decide to come to Cremorne and make her own assessment of the suitability of gentlemen. Ah, there. There she was. He darted around one gentleman, then another. He edged around a large woman, moved aside a smaller one. She was walking toward the trees. Once she disappeared into the darkness, he'd lose her.

He quickened his pace. Grew nearer. Reached out. Clamped his hand on her shoulder, spun her about—

It wasn't Grace at all. Her eyes were the wrong color, her nose the wrong shape. Her chin was square when it should be round. Her cheeks were not high enough. Her hair…her hair was not the correct shade. It was a harsher red. It did not call to a man to comb his fingers through it.

Lovingdon looked into her kohl-lined eyes. No spark, no joy, no laughter resided there. He shook his head. "My apologies. I mistook you for someone else."

He backed up a step, and then another. What the devil was he doing thinking of Grace when he was here? She would never be in this part of London at this time of night. His entire evening had been about her, first with Fitz and now this.

He pivoted and went in search of Avendale. Perhaps he would venture away from brunettes tonight. Someone to take his mind off Grace, a place she should not be at all.

He spotted Avendale staggering toward him, a blonde on one arm, a dark-haired beauty on the other.

He whispered something to her. She separated her-self from him and strolled, her hips swaying entic-ingly, over to Lovingdon. When she reached him, she ran her hand up his chest, over his shoulder, and circled it around his neck. "His lordship tells me that you can remove my corset with one hand tied be-hind your back."

Lovingdon grinned broadly. "I can do it with both hands tied behind my back."

"Ah, you're putting me on now."

He leaned toward her. "I have a very talented mouth."

She laughed, a deep, full-throated laugh. "I'd like to see that."

"It will be my pleasure to demonstrate."

So for tonight, a brunette it would be.


"I had to speak with you before tonight's ball," Lady Sybil said, her arm wound around Grace's as they strolled through the Mabry House gardens.

It had been two days since the Westcliffe garden party, and Grace hadn't seen her friend since, al-though she had to admit that Sybil appeared more relaxed than she'd been then—but of course her hus-band wasn't with her at that moment, which could account for her ease. "Has Lord Fitzsimmons been unkind?"

"No. That's the thing of it. He's been terribly so-licitous."

"Well, then, I'm glad Lovingdon had words with

him at Westcliffe's." She had not heard from nor seen him since that afternoon. She'd decided to give up on his helping her. It was so obvious that he didn't want to be involved in Society any longer.

"I daresay, he did more than speak with him at the party." Sybil spun away, wandered to the roses and touched their fragile petals.

Something was amiss. Grace cautiously joined her friend. "Syb, whatever it is, you can tell me."

"Yes, I know, it's just so terribly difficult. I know you won't tell anyone, but…" She looked at Grace. "Fitz lost my dowry."

"How does one go about losing a dow— Wait, you mean he spent it all?"

"More like, I spent it. A good deal of it anyway. Then he made some bad investments—" She glanced quickly around before leaning in. "We're poor. At least for a time. Thank goodness I already have all my gowns for the Season, because Lovingdon gave us the most horrid rules for when we can spend money."

Startled, Grace stared at her. "Lovingdon gave you the rules? What has he to do with any of this?"

"I don't quite understand it all, to be honest, but apparently he's gone into some sort of partnership with Fitz, who is quite convinced that he shall recoup his losses and then some. That's the reason he's been so irritable. He's been under a great deal of strain, striving to pay our debts, and I wasn't helping at all."

"That's still not an excuse for how he berated you.

I'd have not put up with it, and you shouldn't have either."

Sybil shook her head. "I knew something was amiss. But he wouldn't talk to me. Pride and all that, I suppose." She grabbed Grace's arm and squeezed. "But I wanted you to know that all will be well. You'll see tonight at the ball. He's once again the man I fell in love with."

Grace hugged her, unable to embrace the optimism but hoping her friend was correct. "I'm happy for you, Syb."

When they drew apart, Sybil smiled at her. "Now we simply must find a gent who loves you, so that you can be as happy as I am. It would be so lovely if you were to receive a proposal at the Midsummer Eve's ball."

Every year, for as long as Grace could remember, her family hosted a ball at their ancestral estate to celebrate the summer solstice. Their guests always welcomed a few days away from the city. She'd often slipped out of her bed and secreted herself in a dark corner of the terrace where she could watch the merriment. She thought, then, that the time would never come when she would be old enough to attend. She'd always longed to dance with Lovingdon and never had occasion to do it.

But Fate seemed to have little regard for the yearnings of her tender heart. She'd been too young to attend balls and parties when he was old enough to make the rounds. When she was finally of an age where she could attend the social affairs, Lovingdon had become a widower and withdrawn from Society. Based on their recent encounters, she doubted he would come to her family's estate for the midsummer festivities.

"You seem to be narrowing your choices down," Sybil said.

Grace shook her head. "It's a decision that will affect the remainder of my life. I don't intend to make it in haste."

"Nor should you be overly cautious. You don't want to lose your chance at the perfect man."

"I assure you that I don't want perfect. Rather, I want someone who can appreciate the allure of imperfection."

There was something decidedly sinful in the way Lovingdon was sprawled over the bed. His hair was flattened on one side, sticking up on the other. His jaw was heavily shadowed, his face rugged, even in sleep. The hand curled on his pillow flinched, the one resting near his thigh didn't move. Nor did the rest of him. The sheets were pooled at his waist. He possessed a magnificent chest. While Grace had seen it before, she'd been distracted by other areas and hadn't given it the attention it deserved. A light sprinkling of hair in the center continued down, narrowed over a flat stomach, and disappeared beneath the covers.

She knew she should leave, but she couldn't quite

bring herself to do it. Surely he would awaken soon. And no doubt be furious to find her here. His fury would be justified. A man had the right not to be intruded upon while he slept, but she hadn't snuck in here. She'd knocked on the door several times, then marched in not bothering to soften her footfalls, but he'd barely stirred.

She sighed heavily. She would wait in the parlor, she supposed, as she was determined to speak with him. She spun on her heel and headed for the door.

"Grace?"

The word came out raspy and rough. She didn't want to contemplate that it was the voice with which he greeted his paramours in the morning. Glancing back over her shoulder, she saw his eyes squeezed shut, his brow furrowed, and his fingers pressed against his temples. "I thought you might—"

He held up a hand. "Shh. No need to shout."

If he were one of her brothers, she'd shout that she hadn't been shouting. But he'd done her a favor, so she lowered her voice to a soft whisper. "I prepared something for you." She walked back over to the bed. "It's a concoction that Drake puts together on occasion. Tastes ghastly but you'll feel better once you've had it."

He pushed at the air as though it were enough to physically remove her from the room. "Just go away."

"I can't leave you suffering like this."

"I suffer like this every day. Leave me in peace."

But that was the thing of it. He wasn't in peace and

well she knew it. She picked up the glass from where she'd left it earlier on the bedside table. "Humor me, Lovingdon. And then I'll go."

With a low growl, he rose up on an elbow and took the offering.

"Down it in one swallow."

"I know how to manage it," he grumbled.

In fascination, she watched his throat muscles working. Why did every physical aspect of him have to be so remarkably pleasing? Perfection, while she required a man of some imperfection. It would be easier to be accepted fully by a man who had not been chiseled by the gods. She wondered if he had any notion how fortunate he was to have been so carefully sculpted by nature's loving hand.

She took the empty glass from him and set it on the bedside table. "Just lie there for a bit. It won't be long before you're up to snuff."

He eased back down to the pillow, brought the sheet up and eased his right leg up, bending it at the knee, hiding from her view a rise in the covers that she'd noticed earlier but had fought extremely hard not to contemplate. He squinted at her. "What is it with you coming to gentlemen's bedchambers at all hours?"

"You're not a gentleman. You're a scoundrel."

"All the more reason you shouldn't be here."

"You won't take advantage."

"Maybe I should, just to teach you a lesson."

"You won't." She clasped her hands in front of

her to stop herself from reaching out and brushing the wayward locks from his brow. "I know what you did for Sybil."

"I don't know what you're talking about. And you need to leave. On your way out, tell the butler to send up some breakfast."

"Breakfast? It's half past two in the afternoon."

"It's my first meal of the day. Call it what you like. But leave."

"I need to speak with you."

"I'm not presentable," he barked.

"Judging by the volume of your voice, your headache is gone."

He rubbed his brow. "It seems so, yes, and as I asked for breakfast, my stomach is settled as well. Thank you for your witch's brew. Now be off."

"It's a warlock's brew, as it's Drake's recipe." She turned for the door. "I'll see to getting your breakfast, but make yourself presentable while I'm gone, as I fully intend to discuss some matters with you."

"Grace."

She spun around, and the sight of him raised up on an elbow, his other arm draped over his raised knee, the sheet gathered at his waist, nearly took her breath. She'd never given any thought to the fact that she might see her husband in this same position, that he would be as comfortable with his body and might expect her to be the same. "Please, Lovingdon, it won't take long."

He sighed heavily. "I'll meet you in the dining room."

"No need. The sitting area in here works fine. And you needn't tidy up completely. Just enough so we're both comfortable."

Before he could respond, she quit the room and went in search of the butler. She encountered a footman first and gave the orders to him. The butler knew she was in the residence, had assisted her by showing her to the kitchen so she could make her brew, but he'd been quite disapproving of her delivering it to the duke herself. She wasn't particularly anxious to have him scowl at her over her present request. The footman could see that food was delivered.

She returned to Lovingdon's bedchamber and knocked.

"Come!"

She opened the door to find him standing, shoulders bent as he grasped the edges of the table holding the washbasin. He wore trousers, a white linen shirt. No boots. Why did his present attire seem more intimate than seeing him in bed with naught but a sheet covering him? She approached cautiously. "Lovingdon?"

He peered over at her with bloodshot eyes. Droplets of water coated his face. His hair was damp. "I don't think I would have made it to the dining room."

"You made quite merry last night, it seems."

He shook his head. "I don't remember half of it."

"I don't understand the appeal in that."

"No, you probably wouldn't." He splashed more water on his face, then reached for a towel and rubbed it roughly over his bristled skin. She wondered what it might be like to shave him, to scrape the razor over the defined lines and strong jaw. Perhaps she'd shave her husband. It was a thought she'd never entertained before. After tossing the towel aside, he combed his wet hair back from his face and sauntered over to a sofa, his movements relaxed, loose-jointed. She had an odd sensation of being in his lair. Perhaps she should have accepted his offer to meet her in the dining room.

A rap sounded. She opened the door. While the maid set the tray of food on the low table in the sitting area, Grace walked over to the windows and drew back the draperies. He had such lovely gardens to look out on, and she suspected that he didn't even appreciate them. After the servant left, she took a chair near the sofa and began pouring tea.

"You don't have to wait on me," he said as he snatched up a piece of bacon with his fingers, then began to eat like a savage, as though there would be no formality in this room, as though it contained its own set of rules.

"Don't be so grumpy," she insisted.

"My house, my bedchamber. I can be as I want. If you don't like it, you can leave."

"I have no intention of leaving, and your foul mood will not send me scurrying away."

Slowly chewing, he studied her. "How did you know the miracle of Drake's concoction?" he finally asked.

With a smile, she set the teacup before him. "Because he prepared it for me once."

He raised a brow. "Lady Grace Mabry, three sheets to the wind? I would have liked to have seen that."

She chuckled softly. "No, I don't think you would have." It had been after a visit to Dr. Graves. She'd not been at all pleased by his diagnosis or his recommendation for treatment. And so that evening she'd indulged in a bit more liquor than was wise.

He nudged a platter of fruit, cheese, and toast toward her. "Eat."

She took a strawberry. "Are you always so pleasant upon first awakening?"

"My morning was disturbed."

"Again, it's afternoon." She finished off her strawberry. "Truly, Lovingdon, I appreciate what you did for Sybil. She came to see me this morning, explained the situation with Fitzsimmons and how you offered your assistance."

He shrugged. "I needed a new investment partner."

"Yes, but you're providing all the investment, from what I understand."

"Only until he gets back on his feet."

She shifted in her chair. "She said he's more like

himself, treating her as he did when they first married. Do you think it'll continue?"

He met and held her gaze, and she could see the conviction in his eyes. "He's not a bad man, Grace. I'm not making excuses for his behavior. It was deplorable. But sometimes when a man feels as though he's no longer in control, he can lose sight of himself."

She almost asked him if that was what had happened to him. This life he led now was so very different from the one he'd led before. He was so very different.

"I've known Fitz since my school days," he added. "His comportment in the garden was unlike him. We'll get his financial situation back in hand, and I'll teach him how to guard it better, and all should be well for Lady Sybil."

"You'd think he'd know how to guard his money."

"Unfortunately, Grace, sometimes when the coffers have been empty for a while and are suddenly filled, one can forget what is needed not to squander the coins. And if the coffers have been bare for a while, one may have never learned."

"Another reason that I prefer a man who isn't dependent upon my dowry."

"Then you need a man whose fortune is not tied to land."

He was lounging back, so very relaxed, like a great big lazy cat at the zoological gardens. Yet she had the sense that he was very much alert, could spring into action with the slightest provocation—or enticement, if the right woman walked into the room. She took another sip of her tea and set down her cup. "May I ask you something else, Lovingdon?"

A corner of his mouth quirked up. "As though my saying no would stop you."

Oh, he knew her well, and she loved when he teased her like that. No barbs were ever hidden within his words, even when he was put out with her.

"The night I came to ask for your assistance and you opened the door...you didn't resemble David."

He blinked. "David?"

"Michelangelo's David."

"Ah." He gave a brusque nod. "I should hope not. My hair is not nearly that curly."

She laughed in spite of the fact that he was deliberately making this difficult for her. "I wasn't referring to your locks, but rather lower. Were you aroused?"

He sounded as though he was strangling, and she wasn't certain if he were choking or laughing. He held up a hand. "I'm not having this conversation."

"I don't know who else to ask about these matters. Not my mother, surely. Minerva, I suppose."

"My sister won't know the answers," he said tersely. "Or at least she'd best not."

"So I must depend on you."

He scowled, and she feared his next words would be a command for her to leave. Instead he rubbed his bristled chin while studying her. She'd been glad that he'd not had time to shave while she saw to breakfast. She liked how dark and dangerous he appeared when he wasn't properly decked out. Three buttons on his shirt were undone to reveal a narrow V of chest and he hadn't bothered with his cuffs. Yes, there was no formality here.

"I had a woman in my bed, Grace," he finally said. "Of course I was aroused."

"A man's—" She pointed her finger at his lap, scratched her neck. "—it's quite a fascinating bit of anatomy. Can you control it?"

"A *bit*…of anatomy?"

She felt the heat suffuse her face. "Well, somewhat more than a bit, but you know what I mean. Can you control it?"

He rolled his shoulders as though they'd suddenly grown tense. She supposed she shouldn't continue with this line of questioning but she wanted some answers.

He cleared his throat. "Sometimes, sometimes not. Where are we going with this? For God's sake, hasn't your mother spoken to you about it?"

She shook her head. "As I understand it, it's a topic that only comes up the morning that a woman marries."

"Ask Lady Sybil."

"I have, but she's very vague. Here's my concern. If a man isn't aroused, then he can't make love or produce children, can he?"

He shifted his position as though he were exceedingly uncomfortable. "You have the gist of it, yes."

"Is love enough to arouse a man?"

He shifted again, leaning forward, planting his elbows on his thighs, bringing himself nearer to her. "Little Rose, are you worried that a man won't find you attractive? I assure you that you are in danger of having more children than you can count."

"You're only saying that because you're my friend. I'm thin. There are no paintings of thin women."

"What has that to do with anything?"

"Art reflects what one finds beautiful. Women without an abundance of curves do not find their way into art."

"Of course they do."

"Name one artist who portrays thin women."

He looked at his ceiling—

"Nymphs," she said, as though he'd gone blind. "Chubby nymphs frolicking in the gardens."

Scowling, he looked at the fireplace, at the window. Snapped his fingers and looked at her with satisfaction. "Monet."

"But the women are clothed."

His jaw dropped. "I beg your pardon?"

"In every painting, every statue, that I've seen of nude women, the subjects are plump, which leads me to believe that's what men prefer. What if a man doesn't find me enticing?"

She might have died if he'd laughed. She was certain any other gentleman would have, but ever since he'd discovered her weeping in the stables, he seemed to have an understanding of her insecurities, even though he had no knowledge of how they'd grown tenfold of late. He scooted nearer to her.

"Trust me, Grace, that is not something about which you need to worry. You are lovely beyond—"

"I'm not searching for compliments, Lovingdon. I'm quite disappointed in myself for needing reassurances, but there you are. I can be in a man's bedchamber and not entice him in the least."

Based on the way his gaze slowly roamed over her, she feared she might have overstepped the mark with that comment.

"Are you attempting to seduce me?" he asked in a silky voice.

"No, but I've always been able to talk with you as I can talk to few others. I thought if I understood men a little better, I might have more luck at securing that which I seek."

"Men are aroused by all sorts of things, Grace. For a man who loves you, the thought of being with you will be enough."

"Will it?"

"Of course."

She sighed. She didn't believe him. She'd caught sight of the courtesan in his bed. She suspected the woman's toes were even voluptuous. "I shall embrace your optimism."

"As well you should."

"I don't suppose you'll attend tonight's ball."

He slowly shook his head. "I intend to take a long soak in a tub of hot water that shall last the remainder of the afternoon."

An image of naked limbs, long and muscular, flashed through her mind. She really shouldn't have these sorts of thoughts where he was concerned. They only served to cause her stomach to quiver.

"So how will you spend your evening?" she asked.

"I shall join Avendale for an evening of merrymaking and a visit to Cremorne Gardens." He narrowed his eyes. "You don't go there, do you?"

"On occasion."

"But not after the fireworks."

Smiling mischievously, she half lowered her eyelids. "Perhaps."

The lounging duke was replaced by one who sat up stiffly and gave her his complete attention. "You've not been to Cremorne during the wicked hours."

She lifted a shoulder slightly. "Once."

"Do you have any notion how dangerous it is for a woman alone—"

"I never said I was alone."

His jaw dropped, although he recovered quickly enough and gave her a blistering glare. "Who was with you?"

"I can't tell you. You wouldn't approve."

He settled back, but he didn't appear nearly as relaxed as he had earlier. "Well whoever it was, you should no doubt marry him, as it's obvious you've wrapped him around your little finger."

"I never said it was a gent." She rose, and he came to his feet. "I must be off to begin preparing for the ball. I only stopped by to thank you for what you did for Sybil. It means a great deal to me. Enjoy your adventures this evening."

She could only hope that she would enjoy hers.

Lovingdon settled for a cold bath rather than a hot one because he was warm enough as it was. He'd had other women in his bedchamber, most with far less clothing than Grace, but he'd never felt so fevered. He was fairly certain she'd not meant to be a seductress, but when she picked up the strawberry, studied it as though it was the most interesting object in the room, and then closed her lips around it—

His body had reacted as though she'd closed her lips around him. And then when she began speaking about nude women in paintings, he'd envisioned her lounging over a bed, with sheets draped over her enticingly revealing just enough to set a man's blood to boiling.

He dropped his head back against the rim of the copper tub and stared at the nymphs cavorting over the ceiling. Surely they weren't all Rubenesque. When he realized he was searching for a tall, willowy one with long limbs and narrow hips, he cursed soundly, closed his eyes, and immersed himself in the frigid water.

Blast her! The girl had no sense whatsoever. Spending the afternoon in a scoundrel's bedchamber, licking strawberry juice from the corner of her mouth, touching her tongue to that damned little freckle, talking of nudity, conjuring up images of her in repose, flesh bared—

He came up out of the water and shoved himself to his feet. He had to get these thoughts out of his mind and had to keep them out. He needed her to stop showing up at his bedchamber. He needed her to leave him in peace.

Stepping out of the tub, he snatched up a towel. "Bailey!"

His valet rushed into the bathing room. "Yes, Your Grace."

"I need evening attire for tonight's outing."

Bailey looked as though he'd said he intended to dispense with clothing altogether. "Evening attire, sir?"

To be honest, Lovingdon realized he shouldn't have been surprised by the man's reaction. He'd not donned evening attire in more than two years. "Yes, Bailey, surely it's around here somewhere, buried in moth balls."

"I'm afraid, Your Grace, that it might be a bit outdated."

"I'm not striving to be named the most fashionably dressed man in London. Find it. Then have the carriage brought 'round."

"Yes, Your Grace. Are you celebrating something this evening?"

Bailey's ill-conceived attempt to get to the heart of the matter.

"No, Bailey, I'm determined to get a woman out of my life." Before he did something they would both regret.

## Chapter 7

Lovingdon wanted to bury himself in a woman, drown himself in drink, and show Lady Luck that no matter how atrocious the cards were, he didn't need her. He could make do very well on his own.

So other than cursing Grace, what the devil was he doing here? He'd expected the first time that he attended a ball after Juliette's passing would very much resemble taking a hard kick between the legs. He couldn't deny that when he first entered the ballroom, he'd glanced around, out of habit, searching for her.

But then his gaze was arrested by coppery hair held in place with pearl combs, and a smile that had threatened to steal his breath—even if it wasn't directed at him. With whom the deuce was she dancing? He didn't recognize the young upstart, but then he was obviously closer to Grace's age than his own. He'd have to ask around, he thought, then decided it was pointless to do so. Grace needed someone more established with a bit more maturity. That he'd fallen in love at nineteen had no bearing on the situation. Besides, he didn't like the way the lad looked, too moony-eyed.

He'd managed to slip in through the back gardens, through the open doors that led onto the terrace. To his immense satisfaction, he succeeded in observing the festivities unbothered. That had not been the case at the first ball he'd attended. There, the moment he'd walked through the door, he was pounced on by every mother with an eligible daughter. But he'd been a different man then. While he still had a respected title and a generous yearly income, his behavior of late made him less than desirable as a suitor. An eligible bachelor he might be, but husband material he was not.

Grace had spotted Lovingdon three dances earlier, while she was waltzing with Lord Edmund Manning, a second son who was looking to better his position in life through marriage. She did not consider him a serious suitor, but based on Lovingdon's scowling, she couldn't help but brighten her smile. He lurked in the shadows like some misbegotten miscreant. She couldn't deny the pleasure that swept through her at the sight of him, halfway hidden behind the fronds. He wasn't the shy sort, so she knew he was imitating a wallflower because he didn't want to deal with desperate mothers who might take delight in his presence. She could almost feel his gaze upon her, following her.

When the present dance ended, her latest partner escorted her from the dance floor.

"Thank you, Lord Ekroth," Grace said once she reached the sitting area where her maid waited for her.

"I hope at the next ball, you will be kind enough to reserve two dances for me." He lifted her hand to his lips, raised his gaze to hers. "And that I might call on you tomorrow."

"I can't promise you two dances, but I would, however, be delighted to have you pay a call."

"Until tomorrow, then."

He walked off and exited up the stairs, no doubt to join the gents in the gaming room. He had made it clear where his interest resided and that she was the only one with whom he would dance. He was tall with dark hair and swarthy skin. His mother came from Italy and had brought with her a small fortune. If rumors were to be believed, however, his father had not tended it well.

"I hope you're not considering him."

She swung her gaze around and smiled at Lovingdon. "Lord Ekroth?"

He nodded. "He doesn't fancy you overmuch."

She released a laugh of incredulity. "I daresay

you're quick to judge. I have it on good authority that the opposite is true."

"Well, then, if you have such good authority, you have no need of my observations." He turned to go. She grabbed his arm.

"Wait. I…" What could she say to hold him near? "I do value your opinion."

He gave her a dark smile. "As well you should."

She wanted to roll her eyes at his arrogance. Instead, she said with sincerity, "I didn't expect you to show."

"I decided that I can't avoid balls for the rest of my life."

"Actually, I suppose you could, but I'm glad you didn't. Has it been difficult?"

"Not as difficult as I thought. I've been concentrating on who is here rather than who isn't. Who was that child you were dancing with earlier? I daresay he's not taken a razor to his face yet."

Discreetly, she gave his arm a light punch. "Lord Edmund Manning. A second son who was honest enough to tell me that he is determined to better himself through marriage."

"I hope you informed him it would not be through marriage to you."

"I was not that blunt, but I doubt he'll send me flowers in the morning. So upon what do you base your opinion regarding Lord Ekroth?"

"Watching him dance with you."

"He was the perfect gentleman."

"Exactly."

She furrowed her brow. "All your cryptic comments will have to be discussed later. The next dance will be upon us soon and my card is full." A pity, she thought, wishing one spot remained for him.

"Let me see it." He held out his gloved hand.

"I've told you before that looking at the names—"

"I've observed several gentlemen dancing with you." He snapped his fingers. "Your card and your pencil."

He could be so irritating, and yet what she valued in him was his tendency to speak his mind. With a sigh, she handed over the requested items and watched in dawning horror as he struck through one name after another before handing the card back to her. The names of all the gentlemen with whom she'd danced had been obliterated. "All of them?"

"All of them."

She laughed caustically. "And Lord Vexley? You struck through his name, and I haven't even danced with him yet." At least not at this ball, not where Lovingdon could observe him. Out of the corner of her eye she saw him approaching to claim his dance. The music was starting up.

"He vexes me," Lovingdon said.

"He vexes you? He doesn't vex me."

"He should, if you have any sense about you. Besides, you'll be dancing with me."

Her heart tripped over itself. "I didn't think you

were interested in marriage, and based upon your reputation of late, you could very well ruin mine. You were only to observe."

He gave her a caustic look, as though she was perhaps *vexing* him. "Observation is not sufficient. You need a lesson. I intend to show you how a gentleman who fancies you would dance with you."

"But I promised Lord Vex—"

"I'll handle it." He took her arm and fairly propelled her toward the dance floor, passing Vexley on the way. "Sorry, old chap, but I'm claiming this dance."

Without a pause in his stride, he had her in the midst of the dancers before she could object further. And while she knew she should protest heartily, should leave him where he stood, she couldn't deny that she wanted to dance with him, wanted this moment. She might never have another opportunity. She placed one hand on his shoulder, while he held the other and pressed his free hand to the small of her back. Even with his glove and her clothing providing a barrier between their flesh, she could feel the warmth from his hand seeping into her.

"That was quite rude," she said.

"Unfortunately, the only way you would ever realize how much in my debt you should be would be if you were to marry the poor sod."

"I don't think he's as bad as all that. We've danced before and I find his conversation quite delightful."

"He talks while you're dancing?"

"Of course."

"Then he's not fond of you."

"Because we converse?"

"While dancing. The purpose of dancing is to provide an excuse for a gentleman to get very close to a woman, and if he has an interest in her, he is going to take advantage of that. The gents I crossed off your list spent their time looking about."

"So that we didn't run into someone."

"I've not taken my eyes from yours since we began waltzing, and yet neither have we stumbled into anyone."

As much as she wanted, she couldn't deny the truth of his words. "Loving—"

"Shh."

She almost blurted for him not to shush her, but the words that followed caused her heart to still.

"Pay attention to what we're doing."

She knew exactly what they were doing. She'd been doing it most of the night. Dancing. Waltzing, at this particular moment. But his hand holding hers tightened around her fingers and his eyes bore into hers. She became aware of his closeness, his bergamot scent. His legs brushed against her skirts.

"We're improperly close," she whispered.

"Exactly."

"We'll create scandal."

"If a man fancies you, truly fancies you, what will he care?"

"If he loves me, he'll want to preserve my reputation, ensure that his actions don't embarrass me."

"If he cares for you, he won't be glancing around, searching out his next dance partner—or striving to catch the eye of the woman with whom he wishes to have a tryst in the garden."

Her eyes widened. "Lord Ekroth…a tryst in the garden? With whom?"

"We're conversing far too much."

The change was subtle but there all the same. His fingers pressing more firmly against her back, tightening their hold on her hand, his gaze delving more deeply into hers, his legs in danger of becoming entangled with hers. The lights from the chandeliers reflected over his dark golden hair. He didn't smile, and yet those lips were soft, relaxed, as though waiting patiently for a kiss. Lovingdon captured her, drew her in, until she forgot that anyone else surrounded them. They moved with a harmony that required no thought. Her toes were safe with him, everything was safe with him.

Even as she had the thought, she knew it was a lie. He had no interest in marriage or love or her, for that matter, except as a friend. Which made him very dangerous to her heart, because it was not nearly as practical as her mind.

The final strains of the music lingered on the air. He ceased his movements but did not release her. She had the odd sensation that he was truly seeing her for the first time.

"He certainly wouldn't rush you off the dance floor," he said.

The words burst her bubble of captivity. "Pardon?"

"A gent who fancied you would be in no hurry to turn you over to another man." He tucked her hand within the crook of his elbow and began leading her from the dance area. Slowly, so very slowly, as though he could scarcely fathom the notion of leaving her. "Ekroth was fairly loping to get you to the chairs so he could make his rendezvous."

He had seemed rather anxious, now that she thought about it. She indicated a couple standing near the doors that led onto the terrace. "Lady Beatrix is certain Lord Winthrop is going to ask for her hand at Season's end."

"He's not."

"How can you be so sure?"

"Watch. See how his gaze keeps darting to those three ladies near that potted palm? He fancies Lady Marianne."

"Maybe he fancies one of the other two."

"Observe him through the remainder of the evening. I think you'll eventually agree I'm correct in my assessment."

Finally they reached the area where her maid awaited her, and Lord Canton was impatiently bouncing on the balls of his feet. The next dance was starting up, and Lovingdon had not struck the earl's name from her dance card.

"My lord," she said in greeting.

"Lady Grace." He tipped his head. "Your Grace. Odd seeing you here. I didn't think you were one to attend functions such as this."

"How else is a gentleman to have the honor of dancing with Lady Grace?"

Canton stilled in mid-bounce, which almost put the top of his head level with Lovingdon's shoulder. "You came here specifically for her?"

"Everything I do is specifically for her."

Had he not already demonstrated in the coach the other evening that his words were meant to toy and teach, were not spoken with true intention, she might have experienced a fluttering beneath her ribs. Instead, she unobtrusively slipped her hand free of his arm and extended it toward Canton. "I believe this dance is yours."

Offering his arm, he gave Lovingdon a final glare before escorting Grace back into the throng of dancers.

"You need to be careful of him," Canton said, his voice low, practically seething.

"I have known Lovingdon since childhood. There is little he could do that would take me by surprise."

Although he had surprised her tonight by coming here.

What the devil had he been thinking to dance with her?

Lovingdon stood in the shadowed corner of the

terrace, staring out on the gardens, rolling a coin over and under his fingers. Calming, bringing back a sense of balance. Jack had taught him how to use the coin to keep his fingers nimble. He doubted there was a gent in all of London who could get a lady out of her corset with the same swiftness that he could.

But dancing with Grace, he hadn't thought about doing anything with her quickly. Instead, he'd imagined going very slowly, painfully slowly, unwrapping her like a treasured gift, the joy in the unraveling as great as the pleasure of gazing on what was previously hidden.

"Have you an interest in Lady Grace Mabry?" Lord Vexley asked from behind him.

He didn't bother to turn around. "My interests are no concern of yours."

"She deserves better than you."

"The same could be said of you."

"At least I would be faithful to her. Can you claim the same?"

He no longer stayed with a woman long. They bored him after a time. A short time. He enjoyed sampling but not lingering. "I've already warned her away from you."

"If I understand anything at all about Lady Grace, it is that she is a woman who knows her own mind."

"And if I know anything at all about you, it is that you are in desperate need of funds." He did turn around then. Vexley was only a partial silhouette, most of him lost to the shadows. "She deserves better than a man who sees only a fortune when he gazes on her."

Until that moment he hadn't realized the truth of those words. She did deserve the love she so desperately sought. He'd come here tonight in an effort to rid himself of her, but he feared now that one night might not be enough.

"My coffers may be empty, but my heart is not."

Lovingdon nearly cast up his accounts at the atrocious sentiment. He had little doubt that Vexley would seek to woo her with such ridiculously scripted prose.

Before he even knew what he was about, Lovingdon grabbed Vexley's lapels and jerked him forward. The man's eyes grew so wide that the whites were clearly visible, even in the dimly lit gardens. "Seek your wife elsewhere. Grace is not for you."

"That is for the lady to decide. I was merely attempting to discern your interest in her. I like to know my competition."

"You overstate your worth if you think you could compete with me on any level, for anything."

"Ah, have you not heard, Your Grace, that pride goeth before the fall? Now if you'll be kind enough to unhand me…"

Lovingdon flung the man back as he released his hold. "Stay clear of her."

Without another word, Vexley walked off. Only then did Lovingdon become aware of the ache in his hand. He didn't know when he'd stopped rolling his coin about, but based on his tightly closed fist, knew that if not for his glove he'd have broken skin. Very slowly he unfurled his fingers.

He couldn't say exactly what it was about Vexley that vexed him. He'd never placed much stock in the rumors that Vexley had mistreated some girls, but when he thought of the man touching Grace—

Dammit all! When he thought of any man touching Grace, his blood fairly began to boil. He didn't want to assist her in her quest for a husband, but how could he live with himself if she ended up unhappily wed?

Later that night the woman sitting on Lovingdon's lap was all curves, not a sharp angle to be found. She was the sort in whom a man could become lost. She was scantily clad, a nymph who would dance through gardens. She'd loosened his cravat, unfastened the buttons on his waistcoat and shirt, and was presently nuzzling his neck with warm lips coated in wine. He should be focused on her, but instead men dancing with Grace paraded through his mind. More specifically, Grace was the center of his focus: her smile, her laughter, the way her eyes sparkled brighter than any chandelier.

He'd come to Avendale's in hopes of purging all thoughts of Grace from his mind, at least for an hour or so. Avendale was the most debauched of any man he knew. When he wasn't at Cremorne, his residence was populated with women of all sorts and sizes. Liquor flowed constantly, food was in abundance, bedchambers were open to one and all. The man believed in living life to the fullest without regret. Lovingdon had embraced his example.

At this moment he should be embracing Aphrodite. He doubted that was her true name. The women here called themselves whatever they thought a man wanted to hear. It was all pretense, nothing real about it.

"Perhaps you should give Persephone a go," Avendale said laconically.

Aphrodite halted her ministrations. Lovingdon lifted his gaze to Avendale, who stood before him holding a silver goblet no doubt filled to the brim.

"You look as though you're striving to solve a complicated mathematical formula," Avendale continued. "Or perhaps a physics problem."

Lovingdon patted Aphrodite's hip. "Sweetheart, fetch us some more wine."

Without a word or care, she scrambled off his lap and went to do his bidding. That was the thing of it. The women he'd had of late were so eager to please, which he supposed he should find appealing. Instead, he found himself thinking of Grace, too innocent one moment, too worldly the next. She had no qualms about castigating him, challenging him, revealing her disappointments in him. It would take a special man to love her as she deserved, to accept her forthrightness, to not strive to dampen her spirit in order to control her.

Avendale dropped into a nearby chair and stretched out his legs. "I hear you attended a ball tonight."

"Who told you that?"

Avendale shrugged. "I hear all sorts of things from all sorts of people. Are you going back on the marriage market?"

"No, God no. Assisting Grace. I told you that."

"I thought you'd decided to decline that responsibility."

"It's not a responsibility. It's…" Blast it. It was a responsibility, one he didn't want, but one he was feeling increasingly obligated to take on. He glanced around. "Do you ever get bored with all this?"

Tapping his goblet, Avendale shook his head. "Without all this to serve as a distraction, I'd go mad."

Lovingdon furrowed his brow and studied the cousin he'd only come to know well during the past two years. At least, he thought he'd come to know him. "A distraction from what?"

"Boredom, of course."

"I think you meant something else."

Avendale lifted his mug. "I'm not far enough into my cups to discuss it. I think I shall seek out some female companionship. You're not jolly enough tonight."

"What do you know of Vexley?"

"Hasn't two ha'pennies to rub together, from what

I hear. But he's handsome, titled, has three estates. What more could a woman with a dowry want?"

She could want a great deal more. Deserved it, even.

# Chapter 8

"There were fewer flowers this morning," Grace said, sitting astride her bay mare as it plodded along Rotten Row, keeping pace with Lovingdon's chestnut gelding.

"That should please you," he said. He'd arrived one hour before the respectable hour for a morning visit and suggested a ride through Hyde Park. As it was not the fashionable hour, few were about. "It's what you wanted, wasn't it? To separate the chaff from the wheat?"

"Yes, but I'm not exactly sure how it came about."

"Those who sent flowers yesterday but not today care more for your reputation than they do you."

"That's the reason you danced with me. You knew

that some men would be put off by my being in the company of a rakehell."

"Don't sound surprised. You're the one who pointed out that dancing with me might sully your reputation."

"But one dance? Not beyond repair, surely. Besides, you're a friend of the family. If you're in the midst of reforming, where better to begin than by waltzing with me?"

He laughed darkly. "I'm not reforming, Grace." Straightening, he took his gaze over her in a slow sojourn. "Is that what this little request of yours is about? Trying to put me back on the straight and narrow?"

"Absolutely not." *Well, maybe a little.* Not that she would confess that to him. "I care only about not making a ghastly mistake when it comes to love. Your appearance at the ball did me a great service. If I'm understanding correctly, a man who truly held affections for me wouldn't give a care who danced with me."

"Exactly."

"You're absolutely certain that you're responsible for my diminished number of suitors?"

"Without question."

"Thank God." She released a tight laugh. "I was fearful someone had seen Lord Somerdale kiss me in the garden and that—"

Reaching out, he grabbed the reins and jerked her

horse to a stop. Beneath his hat, his eyes were narrowed slits. "Somerdale kissed you?"

She wasn't certain why she experienced such triumph. He didn't seem to have a problem when his behavior was questionable. Why should she not be afforded the same consideration? "During the eleventh dance. He had claimed it, but suggested we cool off by taking a turn about the garden. Then he"— she felt her cheeks warming with a blush—"drew me into the shadows and kissed me. I'd never been kissed before."

She pulled the reins from his fingers and urged her horse forward. She was irritated by her reaction. He hadn't the courtesy to blush when he'd opened his door without a stitch of clothing. Why were men so much more comfortable with their bodies than women? He quickly caught up.

"Are you mad?" he asked. "If you want to marry for love, the very last thing you need to be doing is going into the garden with a gent alone at night. If you'd been caught in that compromising position, you would have found yourself at the altar with him."

Beneath her riding hat, she peered over at him. "Yes, I don't quite understand that. What in the world did I compromise? A kiss is pleasant enough I suppose, but hardly worth casting aspersions on a lady's reputation."

"Then Somerdale doesn't fancy you as much as you seem to think."

"I beg your pardon?"

"If he fancied you, he would have given you a kiss that would have had you understanding how one could damn well ruin your reputation."

She shifted her gaze to his lips, plump lower, thin upper. They appeared soft. Somerdale's had been chapped, rough, cold. Lovingdon's looked anything but. She swallowed hard. "But you don't love every woman you kiss."

"I've only ever loved one. As for the others..." He shrugged.

"So we're talking lust, not love."

A corner of that luscious mouth of his eased up. "What do you know of lust?"

That based upon the way she wanted to squirm in her saddle, she might be experiencing it at that very moment. She wanted to run her fingers through his hair, caress her hands over his shoulders, unfasten his shirt buttons and catch another glimpse of his chest. "I'm not so innocent as you might think. I have two older brothers. I've listened to some of their conversations."

"Unknown to them, I take it."

She despised hearing the censure in his voice. He was the blackguard here, not her. "As though you are without sin."

His smile faded, his face hardened. "We won't talk of my sins."

She would have taken back the words if she could, but more than that she wondered what had caused

his reaction. She suspected whatever he was referring to was darker, deeper than his current follies.

"Lady Grace!"

Glancing over, she saw Lord Somerdale sitting
astride a bay horse and trotting toward her. This
could prove awkward. "Please don't mention the
kiss."

"Not to worry. I won't allow rumors to propel
you to the altar."

She drew some comfort from knowing he was still
her champion, but she wondered why she didn't feel
content with the knowledge.

As Somerdale urged his horse around to the other
side of Grace, with little more than a curt nod as acknowledgment to him, Lovingdon wondered how
the earl would manage without his teeth. He was
contemplating knocking every one of them out of
his mouth. How dare the man kiss Grace?

When Grace had confessed about her encounter with Somerdale in the garden, the fury that shot
through Lovingdon had nearly toppled him from his
horse. It was one thing to watch men flirt and dance
with her, but to take it further? To woo her into a
darkened garden and kiss her—

That she would allow such liberties, that she
didn't realize the risk not only to her reputation but
to herself should a man take advantage was beyond
the pale. Some man would push her farther than he
ought. Vexley for example.

He crossed their path shortly after Somerdale's arrival. He didn't acknowledge Lovingdon, but damned if his cold glare when Grace wasn't looking didn't count as a challenge. He, too, had wisely sidled his horse on the other side of Grace, keeping a safe distance from Lovingdon, who wondered how Vexley would manage with a broken jaw. It was unlike him to have a penchant toward violence, and he certainly wasn't jealous of the attention they were giving her. It was quite simply that they were not the proper marriage material for a lady of her caliber. They were wasting their time, hers, and his.

Two other gentlemen came over on horseback, giving him a curt greeting before turning their full attention onto Grace. Their little entourage had come to a stop, and he was anxious to get them going again. It seemed Grace was not of a like mind.

"I'm going to sit beneath the tree for a while. You needn't stay, Lovingdon."

Was she dismissing him?

"I know my parents appreciate your serving as my escort." She glanced around and smiled. "Lest it not be clear, he is not a suitor."

A few nervous chuckles echoed around them while a couple of the gents eyed him warily. He supposed he couldn't blame her for wanting to lay out his position in her life so there would be no doubts, not that he thought anyone would see him as a serious suitor. He'd made it quite plain that he had no intention of marrying again.

"I've nothing else to do," he said. "I'll escort you home before I take my leave."

Without question she was capable of taking care of herself, but she was still somewhat innocent and naive. A man could take advantage. One no doubt would. Some gent was going to grow weary of competing with the others and seek to force her into marriage by compromising her. A man who was desperately in need of funds. Like the four flocking around her now. He knew their worth, not only in terms of money, but in terms of character. None of them was good enough for her.

But who was? There had to be someone with whom he wouldn't find fault, someone who would love her as she deserved to be loved. But for the life of him, he could think of no one.

While Lovingdon remained mounted, Lord Vexley dismounted quickly and fairly loped over to Grace, placing his hands on her waist—

Lovingdon's horse shied away and he realized he was gripping the reins, yanking them. After settling his gelding, he reached into a pocket, removed a coin and began weaving it through his fingers, seeking calm. Using his knees, he urged his horse forward, reached down and grabbed the reins to Grace's horse. He'd relegated himself to groomsman, but he certainly wasn't going to play the part of swain, especially after she'd already announced that he was nothing more than a family friend.

Lord Chesney came galloping over, a puppy nestled in his arms. He quickly dismounted, not at all hindered by the creature. As he handed Grace the squirming bundle of fur, she looked as though she would marry Chesney on the spot. Like his father before him, he bred dogs, had bred Lovingdon's most recent collie. That alone should have at least earned him some favor, but he couldn't see the man marrying Grace.

Grace's laughter wafted toward him. She was sitting on the ground, playing with the puppy in her lap while entertaining the gentlemen around her. He studied each and every one. In his more charitable moments he wished them each to hell. In his less charitable moments, he decided hell would be too good for them.

Grace shuffled into her bedchamber and looked at the bed with longing. It was wearying to be always smiling, to pretend to care about subjects that held no interest, to not want to hurt some gentleman's feelings because she knew with every fiber of her being that he was not the one.

Although she suspected her tiredness had to do with Lovingdon more than it did the other gents. He kept her alert, aware of every nuance of his movements, every tone of his voice. She'd been acutely aware of him watching her while she flirted with each of the lords who had joined her in the park today. She'd wanted to order him to get off his blasted horse and join her but refrained. If he'd barged into the midst of their group, she had little doubt the others would have scattered. But he maintained his distance, just as he had since Juliette's passing. Even when he was with her, it was obvious his mind drifted elsewhere.

Felicity entered and without a word began assisting her in removing her riding habit. She had left the dog with the boot boy. He would see to its needs until it learned not to make puddles in the house. It was such a sweet gesture on Chesney's part, but Lovingdon had grumbled on the way back to the residence, "A man who loves you would know that you prefer cats. Nasty vile creatures that they are."

He'd made her laugh, naturally and honestly, her first true laugh since Somerdale had arrived. It had felt marvelous to be carefree, to be herself. She never had to worry about impressing him. He'd always accepted her as she was. She was grateful that aspect to their relationship had not changed.

"I'm going to lie down for a while," she said, once all the outer garments were gone and only a layering of cotton separated her skin from the air.

"Are you feeling well, m'lady?" Felicity asked.

"Yes, just tired. Return in time to prepare me for dinner."

"Yes, m'lady."

After the maid closed the door, Grace walked to the bed, stopped, considered, then crossed over to the mirror. Very slowly, she unlaced her chemise. With her eyes on the mirror, she gingerly parted the cloth and, as she had a hundred times during the past two years, imagined her husband doing the same, tried to imagine herself through his eyes. Still, after all this time, when she was completely revealed she felt as though she were taking a punch to the gut. The familiar sight should no longer take her off guard, and yet it did.

"The scars aren't so bad," she whispered, but in her mind she heard a man's voice, deep and rich, roughened by passion. Her husband's voice, on their wedding night. Mayhap he wouldn't notice in the dark. She sighed. He'd notice.

Not bothering to lace herself back up, she wandered over to the bed and stretched out on her side. Her cat, Lancelot, leapt upon the counterpane, circled around, and finally nestled against her hip. She slid her fingers through his fur. "Don't worry, the dog won't replace you. I suspect he'll become Father's more than mine. They seem to have hit it off."

And then because Lancelot was the one in whom she had confided regarding her first love, her first heartbreak, she said, "What if the man I determine loves me doesn't love me enough to remain once he learns everything?"

Her scars were such a personal matter. No one outside of the family knew. Her mother insisted that there was no reason for anyone to know. It wasn't that anyone was ashamed. It was quite simply that things of this nature weren't talked about.

But Grace knew she would tell the man who proposed to her, on the day he proposed. She could not in all good conscience accept a proposal with secrets between them. But again she asked Lancelot, "What if he doesn't love me enough?"

She wasn't aware of going to sleep, but she opened her eyes to darkness warded off by a lamp on the bedside table, and a man hovering near the foot of her bed. William Graves, physician extraordinaire. When he wasn't serving the queen, he served the poor and those he considered friends.

Her mother sat in a nearby chair, hands folded in her lap, concern in her blue eyes. "Felicity said you weren't feeling well."

Grace rolled her eyes. "I was tired, that's all."

"Will you let Dr. Graves examine you?" her mother asked. "Please."

Dear God, she wanted to say no. He'd examined her so many times. But she understood her mother's fears. Reluctantly, she nodded. It was a small thing for her mother to ask. Swinging her legs off the bed, she sat up. Dr. Graves knelt before her, his pale locks curling around his head. She wondered if they would ever turn silver.

"You'll tell me if anything hurts," he ordered quietly.

Nothing had hurt before. That was the thing of it. Had Graves not warned her that eventually she would experience excruciating pain and eventual death, she'd have not believed it, but he'd been most adamant about the death part. So, yes, she understood her mother's fears.

Nodding again, she stared at the corner where shadows waltzed. The doctor was gentle, careful, but thorough. It seemed to take hours, but it was only minutes before he moved away.

"Everything appears to be all right."

The relief washing over her mother's face made Grace feel guilty for inadvertently raising an alarm. She'd only been tired. Reaching out, her mother squeezed his hand. "Thank you, Bill."

"Send word if you need me, Frannie. Any time."

With that, he quit the room. Her mother rose, wrapped her arms around Grace's shoulders, brought her in close to her bosom and rocked from side to side. "Thank God, thank God."

"Mother, I wish you wouldn't worry so. I keep a watch just like he taught me. I'd alert him if there was anything amiss."

Her mother kissed her forehead. "I know, but it is a mother's job to worry." Then she returned to the chair, while Grace retied her chemise. "How was your afternoon in the park with Lovingdon?" her mother asked.

"Lovely. Some other gentlemen caught up with us there, so we didn't have much time to converse about anything other than the weather."

"I doubt you discuss the weather with any of these gentlemen." Her mother studied her for a moment. "I was quite surprised he came to call."

"It's been two years. His mourning period has ended."

"Based upon what I heard, it ended some time ago. I'm also aware that he danced with you last night."

"I don't know why you're beating around the bush. I'm sure Father told you. I spoke with Lovingdon. I thought he could provide some perspective on the men who have been courting me."

Her mother flexed fingers that had once been nimble enough to pick pockets. "Grace, I'm very much aware that you were quite infatuated with him when you were younger."

"When I was a child," she said impatiently. "He can be quite charming. Or at least he was. What I feel for him now…" She struggled to find the correct word. "I suppose it's confusion more than anything. Sometimes I catch a glimpse of the young man from years ago, but mostly he's not there anymore. The person he is now is a friend, nothing more." She rolled her eyes. "Well, he's also an expert on rakehells. He's managed to give me some advice there."

"Are you certain you're not running a con, striving to snag something that has always been beyond reach?"

"Drake asked me the same thing. I'm not so desperate that I would try to trick a man into loving me. I'm insulted you would both think so poorly of me."

"Perhaps it is just that I fear a bit of the swindler resides in your blood."

"My grandfather, you mean. I do wish I'd met him."

Standing, her mother reached into her pocket and withdrew an envelope. "Lovingdon's man delivered a missive for you while you were sleeping. Take care, my darling. Games seldom end the way we imagined."

"I'm not playing a game, and I won't fall for him."

"Hmm," her mother murmured. "Funny thing is, I told myself I wouldn't fall for your father. The heart will have its way."

Grace waited until her mother left before opening the sealed envelope and removing the single sheet of paper. The message was short and to the point.

*Midnight.*
*The garden.*
*—Lovingdon*

The garden path was lit by gas lamps, and yet the darkness still dominated. Grace walked slowly, cautiously, searching through the shadows for a familiar silhouette. She wondered what Lovingdon wished to discuss with her and why he had chosen this setting rather than the parlor. He was always welcome in their home. He was well aware of that fact, although she did have to admit that the clandestine meeting appealed to her, the thought of doing that which she shouldn't.

And why so late at night? What was so urgent that

it couldn't wait until morning? She was not usually lacking in imagination, but she was quite stumped.

"Grace."

She swung around. In the darkest recesses of the rose garden, she thought she could make out the form of a man. Her heart was hammering so strongly that she feared it might crack a rib. "Lovingdon?"

She watched as the shadows separated and he strolled toward her. "I wasn't certain you would come."

"I'd never ignore a summons from you. What's this about? What's—"

His strong arms latched around her as he pulled her from the path, into a corner where light could not seep. Before she could scream or utter a word of protest, he latched his mouth onto hers with such swiftness that she was momentarily disoriented. His large hand was suddenly resting against her throat, tilting up her chin as he angled her head, all the while urging her lips to part. She acquiesced and his tongue swept forcefully through her mouth, as though aspects of it needed to be explored and conquered.

With a sigh and a soft moan, she sank against him. She had thought about kissing him for far too long to resist—and his skill made resistance unappealing. His other arm came around her back, pressed her nearer. As tall as she was, she supposed she shouldn't have been surprised by how well they fit together, thigh to thigh, hips to hips, chest to chest, and yet she was taken off guard by the intimacy, the heat radiating off him.

His roughened thumb stroked the sensitive flesh beneath her chin, near her ear. No gloves, just bare flesh to bare flesh. A slight alteration of position and his fingers were working her buttons. One loosened. Two. Three.

She knew she should pull back now, should insist that he stop, but when his warm, moist mouth trailed along her throat, she did little more than tip her head back to give him easier access. Another button granted freedom, and his tongue dipped into the hollow at her throat. Fire surged through her, nearly scorched her from the inside out. Desire rolled in ever increasing waves.

He groaned, low and deep, his fingers pressing more insistently into her back as though he wished for her to become part of him, as though he couldn't tolerate even a hairbreadth separating them.

He dragged his lips up her neck, behind her ear. Then he was outlining the shell of her ear with his tongue, only to cease those delicious attentions in order to nibble on her lobe. She was close to sinking to the ground, her knees growing weak, her entire body becoming lethargic.

"Do you understand now," he rasped, "how, when a man desires a woman, his kiss might very well ruin her reputation?"

He desired her. A sensation, rich, sweet, and decadent coursed through her. He desired her. The words echoed through her mind, wove through her heart.

"But he is not likely to stop here," he murmured.

*He? Who the devil was he talking about?*

"He will leave no button undone, no skin covered. He will remove your clothes, lie you down on the grass, and have his way with you. You will cry out with pleasure only to weep with despair because you're ruined. If you're discovered, you'll be forced to marry him. If not discovered—"

He gave her a tiny shake and she realized his fingers were digging into her shoulders, jerking her out of her lethargy. She opened her eyes, and though they were in darkness, she could still feel the intensity of his gaze.

"You play with fire when you go into gardens with gentlemen."

Abruptly he released her and spun away. Three steps later his silhouette was visible from the faint light of the lamps. She saw him plow one hand through his hair.

"You said you desired me," she whispered.

"I was demonstrating how a man who desired you would kiss you. If Somerdale didn't kiss you until your toes curled, then he doesn't desire you and it is very unlikely that he would ever love you."

"Demonstrating." Forcing her legs to regain their strength, she strode toward him. "How could you kiss me like that if you didn't desire me?"

"I've desired enough women to know the particulars."

Without thought, she swung her hand around and slapped him with all her might. He staggered back. Her palm stung. "How dare you! How dare you lure me out here and kiss me as though it meant something, as though *I* meant something."

"You need to understand the danger you place yourself in when you allow men to take liberties. And you need to understand that you will never be happy with a man who kisses you as Somerdale did."

"You place too much emphasis on his kiss. Perhaps he simply possesses the wherewithal to hold back his passions."

"Not if he loves you."

"You don't love me and yet you kissed me as though your very life depended on it. I should think that a man who cared deeply for me would be able to accomplish the opposite."

He sighed heavily. "Little Rose, I'm trying to impart a lesson—"

"Well I don't bloody well want your lessons." She hadn't gone to him all those nights ago to seek his assistance because she wanted his love, although perhaps her mother and Drake had the right of it. Perhaps she had been striving to rekindle what she had felt as a child. It had made her feel such joy, made her believe there was nothing she could not conquer. But what she had felt then was composed of childish things: simple and without basis.

She didn't love the man standing before her. She longed for the young lad of her youth, and he was nowhere to be found.

She marched past him. He grabbed her arm and she wrenched free of his hold. "Do not touch me when it means nothing to you, when I mean nothing to you."

"You mean…you mean a great deal to me. I want you to be happy, to have this man you want who will love you."

"Why can't it be you?"

The swirling shadows created an illusion of him jerking back as though she'd struck him again, but she knew her words meant little. He was helping her because she'd been insistent, not because he had any true desire to be of service. He didn't care what happened to her.

"I don't have it within me to love like that again." His voice was somber, reflective, filled with pain and anguish.

Although she knew the words would slice, she couldn't seem to hold her tongue. "Perhaps you never truly did love."

"You know nothing at all about love if you believe that."

Spinning on his heel, he disappeared into the shadows. She'd meant to hurt him, because he'd hurt her, the one person whom she'd thought would never cause her pain. Her father was right. She wasn't going to find love where she was looking for it.

So she'd damned well find it elsewhere.

Whipping around, she headed to the residence.

*Why can't it be you?*

What had prompted her to ask such an absurd question? He had only himself to blame for tonight's debacle. Meeting her in the garden had been a mistake. A colossal mistake. Five minutes after sending the message, he'd known it, and yet had been unable to not make the rendezvous.

From the moment he learned that Somerdale had kissed her, Lovingdon had thought of nothing except her lips, what it might be like to press his against them.

It had been unlike anything he'd ever experienced before. He was so young when he married Juliette, so untried, so blasted naive. He had been determined never to offend her with a man's lustful cravings. Oh, certainly passion had characterized their lovemaking. He had adored and desired her.

But with Grace it had been something else, something more. She responded with fervor that matched his own. And while his original intent had been to teach her a lesson, he feared he was the one tutored.

She held nothing back. As in all things, she was fearless.

Had she not been a friend, had he not cared about her, he would have done exactly what he'd predicted a man who didn't love her would—he would have taken her to the verdant grass and had his way with her. He would have slowly loosened her buttons, her ties, her bows. He would have bared her body—

His mind came to a screeching halt. *Grace.* These lustful thoughts centered on Grace.

She wanted love. He could give her lust in abundance, but not love. He had closed his heart to the possibility. He would never again experience the devastating pain of loss. He would not love. He would not.

*Perhaps you never truly did love.*

How he wished that were true, because he was so damned tired of the agony of loss. He never wanted to experience it again. It wasn't just losing the physical presence of Juliette and Margaret. It was losing the memory of them as well that tormented him. Sometimes he couldn't remember the exact shade of their hair or the peal of their laughter. Sometimes he would go days without thinking of them, and when he did, the guilt blasted into him because he was beginning to accept their absence. That hurt worst of all.

But he was thinking of Juliette now, with a vengeance, as he slowly sipped the whiskey while in a darkened corner in the sitting room at Dodger's. He'd considered returning to his residence, but he couldn't stand the thought of facing the many portraits of Juliette that adorned his home. She would look down at him from above the mantel and judge him, no more harshly than he judged himself.

In his mind she began to recede and Grace came

to the fore. Grace who had no qualms whatsoever about displaying her ill temper to him. Juliette had certainly never been angry with him. They'd never exchanged harsh words.

Grace frustrated him to no end with her quest for love. Did she think he could pull it out of his pocket and hand it to her?

"Contemplating murdering someone?"

Lovingdon jerked his head up to find Drake studying him intently. Drake was older by three years, and Lovingdon had once trailed after him like a faithful pup. Drake never seemed to mind, but he had taught Lovingdon some skills that he suspected his mother would rather he not know. He could pick a lock, lift a treasured piece without being caught, pilfer a pocket. With a sleight of hand, he could pluck out the cards that would ensure he won.

"Why would you think that?"

Drake lifted a shoulder. "I'm accustomed to your dark expressions, but this one seems to be almost black." He sat in the nearby chair. "Want to talk about it?"

Lovingdon shook his head.

"Doesn't have anything to do with my sister, does it?"

Lovingdon stilled. While Drake and Grace were not joined by blood, they were as close as any siblings who were.

Drake lounged back. "I thought so."

"She's trying to find love, and making poor

choices in the process. She's asked for my assistance, but I don't understand why she has doubts about her ability to recognize love when it arrives."

"She has an air of confidence about her that can be misleading." Drake scratched his thumb over the fabric, studying the motion as though it could help him gather his thoughts. "She's not certain that a man can truly love her. *Her, for herself.*"

"That's ridiculous. She has much to offer a man."

"While I agree—unfortunately she is not as confident." With a growl, Drake leaned forward and planted his elbows on his thighs, his head hanging as though the weight of his thoughts was too much. "Take care with her, Lovingdon. She's always admired you the most, thought you the smartest, the cleverest, the kindest. Without meaning to, you could devastate her."

Based on her reaction in the garden, the warning may have come a tad too late. "You could marry her."

Drake shook his head. "I was raised within the bosom of a noble family, but I am not nobility. I know my place in the world."

"It's standing beside the rest of us."

"I appreciate the sentiment, but you can take a boy out of the streets but you can't take the streets out of a boy. And our topic of discussion is Grace, not me. She's more vulnerable than you might think. Help her if you've a mind to. Otherwise walk away. I value your friendship, but I value hers more. I could destroy you within the blink of an eye."

* * *

Sitting in a rocking chair, cradling a sleeping infant who had been left on the foundling doorstep a month earlier, Grace relaxed into the rhythmic motion and gave her mind freedom to wander. As it most often did since the kiss in the garden four nights ago, she found herself thinking not only of lips but of every aspect of a man's mouth.

She had not expected a kiss to encompass so much. Somerdale's lips had been chapped and remained sealed as tightly as a lady's corset, not that she had attempted entry into his mouth—the thought had not even occurred to her. But now it was all she could think of.

Three of his teeth overlapped, which gave him an endearing grin. She imagined kissing him as Lovingdon had kissed her. She would notice the little imperfections, just as she'd noticed Lovingdon's perfections. His teeth were as disciplined as he, lined up perfectly.

She had never thought beyond the lips, but now everything seemed important: breath, tongue, size. Chesney's mouth covered the area of a small horse's. It would swallow her up. Lord Branson was fond of onions. She didn't think he would provide as flavorful a kiss as Lovingdon's, which was rich with the lingering taste of brandy.

Could she love a man whose kiss did not tempt her into kissing him again? She'd never wanted to break away from Lovingdon's mouth. She had wanted to stay there until the lark warbled and the nightingale went to sleep. She had wanted—

"Hiding out?"

She looked to the doorway. Lovingdon stood there in his evening attire, so blasted handsome that he fairly took her breath. She felt the unwanted heat sweep through her as she noticed his lips, as straight as a poker, not curling upward or downward, and yet so frightfully kissable.

"What are you doing here?" She was rather pleased that her voice didn't betray the turmoil burning inside her at the sight of him. She wanted to remain aloof, uninterested. She wanted to leap from the chair and throw her arms around him. She'd feared after their encounter in the garden, after her unkind words, that she'd never see him again. She'd written him a dozen lengthy letters of apology but none seemed quite right. In the end, she'd merely sent him a note that read:

> *I'm sorry.*
> —*G*

"Looking for you," he said. "Do you have any notion as to the number of balls I've slipped in and out of, searching for you?"

A spark of joy should not be rekindled by the words, and yet there it was struggling to burst into a full-fledged flame. "How many?"

"It seemed like a thousand."

The joy ignited and she smiled. "I doubt it even came close to that number. How did you know I was here?"

"Spoke with Drake. He said you spend considerable time at the foundling homes and orphanages your mother has built. Naturally you would be at the last one I visited."

"So what did you want?"

He studied his well-shined shoes. "To apologize for the kiss."

"No need. I thoroughly enjoyed it."

His head came up. "You slapped me."

"Because of the reason behind it. I don't fancy your lessons."

"I thought demonstrating would be more efficient than explaining. Why don't you put that little one to bed and I'll escort you home? We can discuss a different strategy on the way."

"What sort of strategy?"

"One that will ensure that you marry a man who loves you."

"I'm beginning to think that can't be assured."

"Only if you focus on the wrong man."

And that would be you, she thought.

He walked across the room and sat on the floor at her feet, but his attention was not on her, but rather the babe she held. Her heart lurched as he skimmed a long, narrow finger along the child's chubby cheek. As thin as the child was elsewhere, her cheeks had remained rosy and fat.

"I can't love again, Grace," he said quietly. "It hurts too damned much."

"I think it sad that you would go the remainder of your life without love. You are not old, Lovingdon, and you have years ahead of you, years to be lonely."

"Just because I don't have love doesn't mean I will be lonely." He lifted his gaze to hers. "I don't want for women."

"And I don't want for men circling about, but it's not enough. It's superficial, it's—"

"Undemanding."

"Juliette never struck me as demanding."

"She demanded that I not let her and Margaret die."

With that admission, her stomach fairly fell to the floor. She realized there was more to his change in character than loss. There was the burden of guilt, horrible guilt. It was a wonder he managed to get out of bed at all with the weight of it. "Oh, Lovingdon, do you not see? You could not have stopped their deaths. You're not God."

"I brought the typhus to them. Juliette asked me not to go into the poorer sections of London, but I felt I had a duty to help the less fortunate. I'd contributed money for improvements and felt I needed to over- see the work. In addition, I was striving to collect data, to provide reports to Parliament. I wanted to change things, I wanted to do something worthwhile. Instead I fell ill." His voice caught, turned ragged. "I should have been the one to die, but I survived. My darling wife and precious daughter died, because I put others before them."

"No, no." Her need to ease his suffering was a physical ache that threatened to crush her chest. "You don't know that it was being in the slums that caused your illness. Maybe you came too close to someone at the opera or your tailor or a man you strolled past outside your home. Maybe all three of you were at a park together. Someone, not realizing he was ill, stopped by to say good day. People fall ill for all sorts of reasons. Sometimes it's little more than Nature's cruel ways." She was far too familiar with the truth of those words. "You can't blame yourself for something that's not your fault."

"I can. I do." His voice sounded stronger, as though he'd found his way onto a path that he'd traveled far too frequently. "But I have an even greater sin." He gently, so very gently, combed his fingers over the infant's hair, as though the motion could calm his wretched soul. "I lied to Juliette, you see. She asked me to protect our child, not to let Margaret die. I promised her that I would do all in my power to see that our daughter got well." She saw tears welling in the corner of his eye. "I promised her, and in that promise resided my lie, because our daughter was already gone, and I hadn't the courage to tell Juliette, because I knew she would hate me and I didn't want her leaving this world hating me."

"Lovingdon." Grace wasn't certain how she managed it, but she slid from the rocker to the floor without losing her balance, without toppling over, and she carried the babe with her. Cradling her in one arm between herself and Lovingdon, she wound her other arm around him. "Courage had nothing to do with it. It was your love that stopped your words. You let Juliette go in peace, without having to grieve."

While the whole of the grieving was left to him.

She held him, listening to his harsh breathing, willing him to unleash the tears that she was certain he had been holding at bay ever since his wife and daughter died. She understood now the burden he carried, the life he led, the reasons behind his determination not to love again. Within her breast she wept for him, but she knew if he were aware of the secret tears she shed, he would distance himself further. He was too proud to welcome her sympathy. He was lost in guilt, grief, and remorse, and she didn't know how to convince him that he was forgiven.

Leaning back slightly, he cupped her cheek with his hand, his eyes reflecting his sorrow. "You deserve someone who loves you with every bit of his being. But he is not me. Still, if you wish me to assist you, I will do it with more enthusiasm."

She thought more enthusiasm might very well kill her if that enthusiasm included another kiss. She dropped her gaze to his lips. It was all she could do not to lean in, not to taste them one more time.

"Nothing improper between us," he whispered as though he read her thoughts.

The babe began to mewl and squirm, and she realized she was holding the girl much too tightly, that she had wedged her small body between hers and Lovingdon's. She welcomed the reprieve, the distraction.

She eased away, turning her attention to the child, so he wouldn't see the disappointment in her eyes. "Yes, I still welcome your assistance, along with your proper behavior."

He chuckled low. "You forget that I knew you as a child. Proper was not what you relished then."

"But now I'm grown."

She dared to look at him then, keeping all her yearnings buried. He would not love again. She was certain of it now. She did not agree with his reasons, but then it was not her place to agree. Unfortunately, as much as she cared for him, she thought too much of herself to settle for less than she deserved. She deserved a man who loved her wholeheartedly. "I believe my plan to approach you was misguided. I will truly understand if you prefer to return to your debauched life."

"Helping you doesn't mean I have to leave my debauched life behind."

Pushing himself to his feet, he helped her up. "Tomorrow we will begin our earnest quest for your love."

## Chapter 9

Glass. It was an exhibit of glass. Glasses. Things out of which people drank. Why would anyone bloody care?

Lovingdon could not help but recognize that of late there were exhibits on everything. Grace had been interested in visiting this one. He would have been more entertained by cow dung.

There was a reason he preferred nightly entertainments. The day ones were numbing, but apparently very popular. He could hardly reconcile all the people who were entranced with drinking vessels.

With her arm nestled in the crook of his elbow, she said, "Of the couples here, which of the gentlemen truly fancy the lady they have accompanied?"

"All of them. A man would have to be truly, madly, deeply in love to force himself through this."

She smiled and that deuced tiny freckle at her mouth winked. "You're bored."

"It's glass, Grace. Now if it had a pour of whiskey or rum in it…or God, I'd even be grateful for rye."

She laughed and he made a mental note that he shouldn't cause her to laugh. He loved the way her throat worked so delicately, the way her lips parted in merriment, the absolute joy that lit her eyes…over something as mundane as stemware.

"I don't think you're taking this outing seriously. We're a bit early so it's the perfect opportunity for you to provide me with some clues as to what I should look for. But soon the Set will be descending, because everyone knows that Bertie is keen to see the exhibit, and I will no doubt be swept away by numerous suitors. So that couple over there by the blue glassware. Does he fancy her?"

"He's here, isn't he?"

"You're here and you don't fancy me. Perhaps he's a relation. Is there anything that says he can't live without her?"

This was an idiotic exercise. He needed to see her suitors buzzing about her in order to know which ones she should avoid. But as they were here, and she had asked—

"He fancies her."

She jerked her head around to stare at him. "Oh, I think you're wrong, there. He can barely drag his gaze from the glass. Surely if he fancied her, he'd be looking at her."

"He touches her…constantly. Small touches. On the shoulder, on the arm, on the small of her back. That's the big one. The small of her back. Solicitous. Every time she speaks, he leans in so he doesn't miss a word. If he didn't fancy her, he wouldn't care what she said. He'd simply grunt or mutter something unintelligible, because women, bless them, don't care whether or not we listen. They simply want to speak. As long as we offer an occasional, 'Yes, dear, you're quite right, couldn't have said it better myself,' women are overjoyed—even when we haven't a clue as to what it was we couldn't have said better ourselves."

"No." She gave him a discreet punch in the side. "We talk because we have something of import to say."

"Something that a man generally has no desire to hear, and will hardly ever classify as important."

She stepped away from him, anger igniting her eyes into a blue that was only seen in the heart of a fire. "Is that how you feel about me?"

No words existed to describe how he felt about her. He wanted to see her happy; he wanted her to have love. He wanted to whisk her away to a tower somewhere so she would never know the pain of loss. It occurred to him at that moment that by helping her acquire what she desired, he was condemning her to unbearable suffering. He could only hope that she would be up in years and too senile to fully experience it. Yes, a love that lasted her entire lifetime was what he wanted for her. What he could not guarantee. *That* realization had him speaking a bit more testily than he might have otherwise. "No, of course not. You have things of interest to say, and I never know what is going to come out of that pretty little mouth of yours."

That pretty little mouth set into a stubborn line, and he knew she was trying to decipher whether he had just said something that was too flowery to be true. Therein resided one of the problems with giving women too much information. While most men wouldn't agree, he knew not to underestimate a woman's intelligence and reasoning abilities. He suspected if the gents of town discovered what he was revealing about their habits, they would hang him from London Bridge. He needed to get her thoughts elsewhere.

"I can also tell you that she is married to someone else, someone who probably doesn't fancy her."

She shifted her gaze over to the couple, her mulish mouth now a soft O. "They're lovers? How did you discern that?"

"Why else would they be at such a place where they are unlikely to be seen because no cares about glasses?"

The humor was back in her eyes. "They are likely to be seen, as there are several people here, and soon there will be a good deal more. You obviously don't appreciate the setting. Exhibits are designed as a way to expose us to the world. Here, come with me."

He shouldn't indulge her. To make his point, he should stay where he was, but she had piqued his curiosity. He followed her to a glass case that housed decanters in numerous shapes, all in various shades of red.

"Imagine what it took to create these," she said softly. "Heat, such immense heat, melting the glass, then a craftsman carefully gathering it up on a rod like honey."

He couldn't help but think of a woman's heat, a woman's honey. Nor did he seem capable of preventing his gaze from trailing over her, but she didn't notice. She was focused entirely on the goblets and pitcher in the case, and her mesmerized expression was almost as intoxicating as her words.

"Glass blown with care—just the right amount of breath, of pressure, of force. Heating, cooling, shaping, reheating. The red added. All the work, the artistry, the passion that must go into creating something so beautiful." She looked up at him then. "Can you imagine it?"

He could imagine it. Vividly. Too vividly. Her skin flushed with the fire of passion. Her lips plump from pressure. Her gaze smoldering with blazing desire. He imagined taking her mouth, burning his brand on her soul.

What the devil was wrong with him?

"How can you not appreciate a work of art, even if it is a common item?" she asked.

There was nothing common about it, about her. She shortchanged herself if she believed men were after only her dowry. Even if they didn't love her, they would gain so much by having her—a work of art herself—at their side. Her fortune, her land, paled when compared with her worth.

"I think what I like best," she said softly, "is that even its imperfections don't detract from its beauty."

"You say that as though you have imperfections."

"We all have imperfections." A sorrow and something that went deeper touched her eyes.

"They add character," he told her, mimicking words his mother had once told him.

She laughed lightly. "So my mother says."

He wondered if all mothers relied on the same counsel. He had a strong urge to want to make her believe the truth of them, if there was something about herself with which she found fault. He wondered if it was that small freckle, the one that had been left behind when all the others had deserted her. He remembered how much she had detested them when she was a child.

She turned her attention back to the glass. "Some of these items are hundreds of years old. They've managed to survive the centuries. If only they could talk. They were lovingly created by someone who is no longer here, being enjoyed by people whom the creator never met, would never meet because they were yet to be born."

"Perhaps they weren't lovingly created. Perhaps they were nothing more than a way to pay creditors."

"What a cynic you are. No, whoever made these cared about them a great deal. They would not be so beautiful otherwise. I won't accept any other answer."

"You're a romantic."

She laughed again. "Frightfully so. But then I don't suppose that comes as a surprise, considering the reason behind your presence here."

Before he could respond, a commotion caught his attention. A group of people was barreling down the passageway. Apparently, the Marlborough House Set had arrived.

They swarmed in, bees to a fresh dusting of pollen, and swept her away as easily as driftwood on an outgoing tide. It was rather amazing to watch, as though he weren't even there, as though it were impossible to conceive that they might have been together.

Jolly good for his reputation as a man who no longer had any interest in marriage.

He supposed he could have inserted himself, but she expected him to observe and share those observations later. Instead, his gaze kept drifting down to one of the vases. The red was muted, the shade of her hair, and he imagined the artisan blowing a soft breath into it, gliding his hands lovingly over it. He envisioned her as the inspiration for the piece, that somehow three, six, eight hundred, a thousand years ago another man had pictured her as he'd worked to create a vase that would outlast his lifetime.

Death had come, and yet the vase carried on. Whoever had served as the inspiration was gone as well. And yet, she, too, in an odd manner was still bringing beauty to the world.

The poetic nonsense of his thoughts could only be attributed to how ghastly bored he was looking at glass. Because on the heel of those musings he was struck with the uncanny certainty that they belonged elsewhere, and that he wanted them.

Exhibits were collections. Someone had put this one together. Someone owned these pieces. He wanted them. He intended to have them, regardless of the price.

It had been a long time since he'd wanted something this badly.


That evening, curled on a divan in the front parlor, Grace fought not to be disappointed that in the crush of admirers, she had lost sight of Lovingdon at the exhibit. His driver had alerted her that His Grace had taken his leave but left his carriage for her convenience. She supposed he had gotten rather bored with the glass and decided to go in search of a more interesting activity.

She was presently in search of entertainment as well. Undecided regarding how she would spend her evening, she sorted through various invitations. No grand balls tonight. Instead it was a night for small affairs. A reading at Lady Evelyn Easton's. A concert at Marlborough House. A dinner at Chetwyn's. The gentlemen had tried to tease her into revealing where she'd be tonight, but she hadn't a clue, so it was easy to tell them the truth.

She wondered what plans Lovingdon had for the evening and if he would be in the back room at Dodger's. Her fingers itched for another round of cards, a chance to get even. How the deuce had he cheated anyway? She kept careful watch of his movements. How had he known she'd cheat?

Because she always had. It was unseemly, but the lads had always bested her at so much. Swindling them had been her small victory.

She heard the doorbell. A caller. She wasn't up to it. Besides, Lovingdon would probably tell her that a gentleman who bothered calling wasn't truly interested. It seemed all his examples involved the various ways that demonstrated when a man didn't fancy her. How would she know if he did?

*He'll know your favorite flower.*

There had to be more to it than that.

She looked up as the butler walked in carrying a large box.

"The Duke of Lovingdon's man just delivered this package for you."

It was a large box, plain as a dirty road, not wrapped

in fancy paper or decorated with ribbons. He set it on the small table in front of her.

"Whatever could it be?" she asked.

"I'm certain I don't know, m'lady."

"What have we here?" her mother asked as she glided into the room. "I heard the bell—"

"A gift from Lovingdon."

"Fancy that. Whatever prompted such a gesture?"

She laughed self-consciously, because she wanted the gift to mean something when she knew that it probably was merely another lesson to be learned. How would she explain that to her mother? "I haven't a clue."

"Shall we see what it is?"

"I suppose we should."

She lifted the lid, set it aside. Amidst black velvet rested red glass. Very gingerly she lifted out the pitcher.

"Oh my word. Isn't that's lovely?" her mother asked.

"I saw it at the exhibit today." Overwhelmed, she didn't know what else to say. The goblets were also there but it was the pitcher that had arrested her attention. She held it up toward the gas-lit chandeliers and the color lightened, glimmered. So magnificent.

"Is there a note?"

"What? Oh." Moving the velvet aside, she saw the parchment, pulled it out and read the neat script.

*For your future household. I suspect the artisan would rather it be used than collecting dust in an exhibit.*

She supposed she would forgive him for not appreciating the exhibit, when he had managed so successfully to touch her heart. Water served from this pitcher would taste incredibly sweet, and she would never be able to sip it without thinking of him.

"He's optimistic at least," her mother said after reading the missive.

"Optimistic that I'll find a man who loves me. He knows I won't marry one who doesn't."

"I suspect it's been a long time since he's been optimistic about anything. Perhaps it's not such a bad thing that he's been coming around."

Not a bad thing at all.

## Chapter 10

Lovingdon couldn't recall how he'd come to be on the floor of his library. He thought after he retrieved his last bottle of whiskey that he'd been heading for the chair. But here he was with his back against it and his bottom on the floor. Which worked well, because it gave him a sturdy place to put the bottle when he wasn't drinking from it.

It also gave him a lovely angle from which to gaze at the vase. With the lamp on the desk off to the side, it cast a halo around the glass container, changed the way it looked. Shadow and light. Copper and red.

"I expected to find you at Dodger's."

Grace's sweet voice filled his ears. He lolled his head to the side. Shadow and light. Copper and red. "I really must talk with my butler about his penchant for allowing you to wander through my residence unannounced."

She glided nearer, no provocative sway to her hips, no enticing roll of her shoulders, no flirtatious lowering of her eyelids, yet he considered her more alluring than any woman he'd known of late.

"He understands that I'm practically family."

"I suspect it more likely that he understands your nature to do as you please."

She grinned. "That as well."

"I didn't think you had any plans for the night."

"I didn't, but I wanted to thank you for the lovely glass. I suppose you were demonstrating another rule. If he loves me, he'll know when I covet something."

He couldn't stop himself from smiling. He did hope he didn't look as silly as he felt. "It pleased you?"

"Very much." She was standing over him now. "Would you like me to help you into a chair?"

He shook his head. "No, I'm where I want to be."

"Not very high standards." She turned, came up short. "You bought the vase as well."

"It appeared lonely with all the other red pieces gone."

"Careful there. You're almost sounding poetic."

"Never."

He watched as she strolled over to his decanter table, grabbed a crystal carafe and glass, and walked back over to him. She settled onto the floor facing him, working her back against the chair opposite his, her legs stretched out alongside his.

"What are you doing?" he asked, his tone not nearly as firm as it should be, failing to convey the inappropriateness of her actions. "You shouldn't be here."

"It's bad form to drink alone. Besides, Mother and Father don't know that I'm here. They think I went to bed early with a headache." She poured—what was it she had? Ah, yes, the rum—into her glass. She lifted it a bit. "Cheers."

And proceeded to take a healthy swallow. No coughing or choking. She wasn't a novice to hard liquor, but he hadn't expected her to take so well to the rum.

"I have sherry, if you'd like," he told her.

"I prefer rum. Awful of me not to prefer the more dainty drinks, I know. I mastered rum because my brothers were drinking it. It's not fair that men go off to a private room to smoke and drink, and ladies sip tea. We should be able to end our evening with a hearty drink." She lifted her glass in another salute before sipping the golden brew. "So I came to a get a report."

"A report?"

"Yes, about what you observed today. Anyone who doesn't fancy me."

"Bertie fancies you."

She laughed lightly. "The Prince of Wales?"

"Indeed, but you want to steer clear of married

men, especially one who might one day rule an empire."

"No worries there, as I have no interest in married men. Sort of defeats my purpose, since I am in search of a husband."

He studied her, sipped his whiskey. It was loosening his tongue. Probably not a good thing, but—

"Why the urgency, Grace? Why the urgency to marry?"

She ran her finger around the rim of her glass. "You won't understand."

"Whatever the reason, I promise not to judge you."

She sighed. "I probably shouldn't have had spirits tonight. It makes it so easy to talk, to say things that I wouldn't normally say. Why does it do that?"

She hadn't had a great deal yet, so maybe she wasn't as accustomed to it as he thought. "That's the whole point of it, to make you lose your inhibitions, to not give a damn one way or another. You can tell me because I'm so far gone that I probably won't remember in the morning what you said."

She tapped her glass, and he had an insane flash of her tapping that finger against his bare chest, of her running that nail down his breastbone, scoring his flesh. Yes, he should stop drinking now.

"My father," she said.

He blinked, fought not to look surprised. But he was off his game. He suspected he looked like a deer that had suddenly found itself crossing the path of a hunter. "He's forcing you to marry?"

"Of course not, but he's losing his sight. You mustn't tell anyone. He's so proud and he's hid it for years. I want him to see me as a bride, to know I'm happy. I want him to be able to dance with me on the day I marry."

There was little that he could imagine that was worse than going blind, unless it was to lose the one you loved, but he suspected that others could tell him something worse. Everything was perspective. Everything was subjective.

"I'm sorry," he said, words he meant from the depths of his blackened heart.

"I don't know if it's better to have been born blind and to never know what the world looks like or to have seen the world and then be condemned to blackness."

"It's rather like that question you posed the night you asked for my assistance: is it better to have loved and lost than to have never loved at all?"

"I would rather have love for a little while."

Because she'd never had it. Things that one never possessed always shined more brightly than the things that were held.

They sat in silence for several long moments, with the fire crackling, the clock ticking, his collie snoring in the corner. Her dress buttoned up to her chin. The sleeves were long. No need for gloves when she was here in such an informal capacity. She drew up her knees to her chest, wound one arm around her legs. She couldn't have had on more than one petticoat, because her skirt draped over her as though nothing existed between her and her skin. He wanted to touch her ankle, her knee, her hip, her shoulder, her chin. Light touches.

Sometimes they could be the most intimate.

Oh, but he needed to get his thoughts onto something else, so he said, "The couple at the exhibit, looking at the blue glass—I had it wrong. They were married to each other."

She perked up. "How do you know?"

"Because of the way he touched her. Without thought, without artifice. He wanted her to know he was there, enjoying the moment with her, but he was careful not to intrude."

Her brow pleated. "But you said they were lovers."

"They are. One does not exclude the other."

"But you were quite sure that she was married to someone else," she reminded him.

"I'm not perfect, Grace. I do know they have six children, and so they frequent exhibits in order to be alone for a bit."

"How did you acquire that information?"

"Spoke with him for a few moments when she went to the necessary room."

Smiling brightly, she settled back against the chair. "I'm glad they're married. That they're lovers, and in love. So if a gentleman touches me, he loves me."

"If he touches you without thinking, if he touches you simply because you're near."

Silence again. He didn't know if he'd adequately explained the sort of action to which he was referring.

"Why are you here alone tonight?" she asked quietly.

"Sometimes I need to be alone."

She craned her head back to see the portrait above the fireplace, the one of Juliette. "I was so young when you got married—too young for her and I to become dear friends. I wonder why I always saw her as so old, but never was bothered by the years separating you and I."

"Perhaps because I was always in your life, and she came into it later." Now he looked up. He couldn't see Juliette from that angle, which was a good thing. She'd never approved of his drinking, so he only had a glass on special occasions. She'd never even developed a taste for wine. She didn't like card games. Had she played, she certainly never would have cheated at them.

Unlike the woman across from him who was pouring herself more rum. She didn't chastise him for sitting here, three sheets to the wind. She simply grabbed a decanter and joined him.

"What are you smiling at?" Grace asked.

Jolted from his reverie by her question, he jerked his head back. "Am I?"

"I can't see your teeth, but your lips are curled up. I always liked your smile."

"Always liked yours."

"My teeth were too big for a bit there."

"I never noticed."

"Liar."

He thought his smile grew. He always felt comfortable with her, as though there were no judgments, no wrongs, no sins. But at that moment he wanted more with her.

Perhaps it was because he'd had too much to drink.

Perhaps it was because they were alone.

Perhaps it was the shadows promising to hide secrets.

Leaning over, reaching down, he wrapped his hand around her ankle and pulled her toward him.

Startled, she looked up, but she didn't resist, and he quickly had them hip-to-hip. He splayed his fingers along the back of her head, tucked the other hand beneath her chin, tilted her head up and sipped at her mouth. He circled his tongue around the outer edges of her lips before running it along the seam. An opening, a slight parting, an invitation.

He slid his tongue inside and groaned when he discovered hers waiting, ready to parry. No shy miss, his Little Rose.

She tasted dark, rich, and decadent. The rum added a tartness, a sweetness, a uniqueness. He swept his tongue through her mouth as though he'd never explored it before. Where in the garden there had been a hungry need, tonight the need was leashed. He didn't want madness or haste. He wanted to linger, to enjoy, to relish.

He felt her fingers scraping his scalp, combing through his hair. Touching, caressing. Marvelous, so marvelous. He felt like a cat stretching beneath the sun. It was so very long since he'd been stroked with such tenderness. So long since any woman had given to him as she was doing now. No frenzy, no hurry. Only savoring.

In the garden, he had taken her mouth on a rush of passion and the hard edge of something that resembled jealousy, although he'd never been jealous in his life, not even when it came to Juliette. He'd known she was his, that no one would take her from him.

Yet the Fates had.

But with Grace it was different. He couldn't define her or what he felt for her. It wasn't love, yet it was more than the hollowness that accompanied him when rutting. He wanted to kiss her. He'd wanted to kiss her at the exhibit when she rhapsodized on about silly glass. Her passion for the creation of the pieces had sparked a passion in him.

But tonight it was just his whiskey and her rum, and a darkness that said, *Taste, taste me again.*

She sighed and he was acutely aware of her falling into him. It was a good thing they were sitting, as he thought his knees might have buckled with the force of the desire that slammed into him.

He'd had far too much liquor to perform. That was a good thing. He wouldn't ruin her, but damn, she tasted so tempting, cream on strawberries, chocolate on cake. He didn't ever want to leave the little paradise that was her mouth—

And it was that thought that had him leaving it. She wanted a man capable of great love. She deserved that sort of man. And that wasn't him.

He pressed his forehead to hers, listened as she gathered her breath, enjoyed the sensation as she trailed her fingers across his shoulders, down his arms, leaving only the memory of her touch behind.

His chest tightened into a painful knot. With gentleness and his fingers, he brushed the strands of hair from her face. "Ah, Grace, I've always loved you. Surely you know that. I just can't love you with the depth of caring that you want."

"It's scary to love, isn't it? It doesn't seem that it should be so, but it is."

"Not always."

"You weren't scared when you fell in love with Juliette?"

He shook his head. He'd known no fear. He'd thought it marvelous, all the rioting emotions he felt.

"If you'd known on the day that you met her that you'd only have a few years with her, would you have still fallen in love with her?"

He didn't know the answer to that. Because he hadn't known, he'd gone into it with naive innocence. Innocence he could never regain. Now he knew that forever was a myth, and that "until death do you part" was not a promise of growing old together.

"It's bad form to speak of another lady when a man is kissing you," he told her.

"You're not kissing me at this precise moment."

"Perhaps I should remedy that." And he did, taking her mouth again, unhurriedly swirling his tongue through the dark depths until he'd had his fill of her, for the moment at least. "I've never kissed a woman who tasted of rum," he said quietly.

"What about the naughty women you visit?"

"I don't kiss them."

Jerking her head back, she couldn't have looked more surprised if he'd jumped to his feet and done a jig around the room.

"But you're intimate with them."

"I'm not intimate with them. I'm not making love to them. I'm rutting."

"It sounds so ugly."

He'd not wanted to travel there. He'd wanted to travel back to her mouth. "I ensure they are pleasured. They have a pleasant time. They are unaware that the only thing engaged is my cock."

And with the uttering of that word to a lady, he realized he was probably six sheets to the wind. "My apologies. I should not have—"

"No." She touched her finger to his lips. "I came to you, Lovingdon, because I knew you would be honest with me. Your words and sentiments might be crude, but you have never put a veil of protection between us. Your words reaffirm what I've believed all along. I don't want a man rutting over me. I don't want him thinking, 'Let's get on with this, I need an heir.' I want pleasure. I want him to want to come to my bed. I believe love is the key, which is why I want to find a man who loves me. I don't want to make a mistake, with which I would have to live for the remainder of my life."

He skimmed his fingers along the side of her face. "You won't. It would be a rather poor reflection on my knowledge of blackguards if you end up with a man who doesn't love you. Trust me, Little Rose. I can spot a blackguard a mile away."

"I do trust you."

More's the pity. Because at that moment his words were no more sincere than any of the dribble that Bentley had spouted. It was her lips, glistening and swollen, that prompted his wicked behavior. He wanted those lips, he wanted that mouth.

*Don't don't don't.*

But he was beyond listening to his conscience. Just one more taste, one more little sip. She tilted her face up slightly, the most beautiful invitation he'd ever received. He framed her face between his hands. "Just one more taste."

She nodded, her mistake, his undoing.

He started with the freckle, the one on the corner, the one that went into hiding when she smiled. He wondered if all the other lords had noticed it. He should tell her about it. *If he loves you, he'll no-*

*tice that you have the tiniest freckle at the corner of your mouth.*

*If he loves you, he'll be fully engaged in the kiss. He won't be thinking of other women or exhibits or laws that need to be passed. He won't be thinking of anything beyond the flavor and feel of you.*

But he was thinking of other things. He was thinking of fire molding glass, he was thinking of flames licking at red, he was thinking of hands fashioning and shaping—

Hands skimming over her from toe to crown. His hands wrapping around her small ankles, traveling over her slender calves.

He carried her down to the carpet. She didn't protest. She simply went, with the trust she had spoken of earlier. He wouldn't ruin her, but there were other lips to taste, other flames to fan.

*Don't don't don't.*

He didn't love her, he couldn't love her, he wouldn't love her—not in the manner she desired, not in the manner she deserved.

But she wanted lessons in blackguards, and tonight he was just drunk enough to give her one she wouldn't soon forget.

She knew there was danger in coming here so late at night when he'd no doubt be well into his cups, yet she'd not been able to keep away. When she walked into the library, she had felt the energy like a storm just before lightning struck. She should have said, "Thank you for the gift. I'll be on my way now."

But she had seldom been one for doing what she ought.

Life was too short. Life could be snatched away.

She needed his kisses the way she needed air. This kiss was different from the one before, gentler and yet hungrier. It made no sense. The other had seemed to be about possession.

This one was more about ownership. He was beginning to own her heart.

*Beware!* her mind cried. *Beware, beware, beware.*

She couldn't love him as a woman loved a man, not when he was unwilling to love in return. She was fairly certain this was another lesson to be learned, that when he was done he would reveal whether a man who worked his mouth over hers with such determination would love her.

Not that she cared at that particular moment. She loved the taste of whiskey on his tongue, loved the way her mouth molded to his.

He trailed his lips over her chin and lower, lower. She held her breath. His hot mouth closed over her right breast, and the heat of it shot straight into her core. It mattered not that she wore a dress and chemise, that she had left her petticoats draped over a chair in her bedchamber. She had chosen comfort over propriety.

It seemed he wasn't of a mood for propriety either. His hands bracketed her waist and he pushed himself down farther, rose up on an elbow and watched as his hand traveled over her hip, along her thigh. His gaze came to rest on hers, his holding a challenge that went unanswered.

She didn't know how to respond. Her body was thrumming with need, with something she didn't quite understand.

His large hand knotted around a section of her skirt, began gathering it up.

"Lovingdon—"

"Shh. You'll leave here a virgin, I promise you that."

She trusted him, but she wasn't ready for him to know everything. She doubted she ever would be, but neither was she quite ready to leave him, to lose these warm sensations that were purring through her. "Are you mimicking a man in love with me or a blackguard?"

He raised his eyes to hers. "A blackguard. Most definitely a blackguard."

"I should stop these advances," she said.

"Yes, for other blackguards. But don't you want to know what lies at the end of them? You'll spend the rest of your life with a gentleman. Why not know what it is to be with a scoundrel for a time?"

Her throat was tight, her heart fluttering, her chest barely able to take in a breath. She thought she nodded. Perhaps it was only that she didn't shake her head. Whatever, she'd apparently given him permission to go further.

He pooled the hem of her skirt at her waist. "Silk underdrawers," he rasped, his voice tight, controlled.

"I like the way they feel against my skin."

"I think you'll like more what I'm about to place against your skin."

He unlaced her drawers and began easing them down. Her face burned as she was exposed to him, and she thought of flames shaping the glass. She wondered what he was molding her into. A wanton, no doubt. Or a girl on the verge of truly becoming a woman. Would her husband touch her like this or was such behavior only the purview of rogues?

"Ah, Little Rose, red everywhere."

Especially her cheeks, her neck, her chest. The heat was consuming, and only grew hotter when he pressed his lips to the inside of her thigh.

She had heard about the dangers of rum, how it released inhibitions, made one not care. She knew she should clap her legs together, shove him aside. Instead she opened herself more fully to his questing mouth.

She would no doubt have regrets when she was sober, but for now the scrape of his shadowed jaw against her inner thigh was too tantalizing to warrant regrets. He moved up, half inch by agonizing half inch. She felt his breath wafting through her curls.

Lifting his head, he reached for the crystal decanter.

"What are you doing?" she asked.

"Tasting rum on lips, remember?"

Before she could respond, he poured the golden liquid over her most intimate region. She squealed, kicked ineffectually at him, an instinctual reaction.

He dropped his head back and laughed, a bold, joyous sound that reverberated around the room. Suddenly the sound stopped, but the essence of it continued to vibrate as though it had become a permanent part of the air surrounding them.

With a somberness that didn't seem to fit with what had just happened, he held her gaze. "God, I can't remember the last time I laughed." He laid his head on the pillow of rumpled skirts at her belly. "Damn, but it felt good."

"Laughter is a balm for the soul."

"Especially one as black as mine."

His eyes came to bear on hers again, and there was something different in them, something heated and dangerous. "It was a release, as good as any I've had with women of the night. You're deserving of one as well."

He lowered his head, and she felt his tongue lapping at the rum, lapping at her. Velvet over silk, and so much nicer than undergarments. She wouldn't mind having that sensation over her entire body—but then he would learn the truth, and while she trusted him, some things a woman simply did not share.

She shoved dark thoughts aside and instead focused on the pleasure, the laughter of her senses. Oh, he was wicked, doing things that she was certain no husband would ever do. It was so inappropriate, so naughty. It was not for the refined, for ladies.

It was decadence at its most decadent.

She knotted her fingers in his hair because she couldn't stand the thought of not touching him. Pressing her thighs against his shoulders, she wished she felt the silk of flesh there instead of soft linen. She should have asked him to remove his shirt. Had she known where he had planned to take her, she might have asked him to remove everything.

He kissed, he stroked, he suckled. He created sensations that were beyond description. Pleasure rolled through her in undulating waves that threatened to take her under, to lift her up. If she were glass, she would have melted by now.

Her breaths came in short gasps, her sighs evolved into ever higher pitches.

"Lovingdon—"

"Let it happen, Grace. Let your body succumb to the ultimate joy of pleasure."

Then there were no more words, only his tongue urging her on with its determined actions. Swirls of red spun behind her closed eyes. Faster, faster, a vortex that flung her over a precipice—

She screamed as her body tightened, her back arched, her fingers dug into his scalp. She shuddered and trembled, reached heaven before floating mindlessly back to earth.

There was silence in the coach. It wasn't heavy or awkward. It was simply present, because after that mind-shattering experience, Grace had been without words.

So had Lovingdon apparently.

Quietly, he had reassembled her skewed attire. With his hand on the small of her back, he led her to the coach and climbed in after her. It didn't seem to matter that it was her family's coach, that it would either need to return him home or he would have to walk.

Perhaps he was aware that she wasn't yet ready to be alone.

Otherwise, why would he be holding her now, his arm around her shoulders, her face tucked into the hollow of his neck? He smelled sultry and wicked. Every now and then she thought she caught a fragrance that might be her.

"I'm beginning to see the appeal of marrying a blackguard, whether he loves me or not," she finally said.

He chuckled darkly. "I thought you might."

"I suppose the best thing would be to marry a blackguard who loves me."

"Blackguards don't love."

"Pity that."

Silence again.

"I suspect," he began, "that I shall forever think of you when I drink rum."

Heat and pleasure swarmed through her. She would never again drink rum without thinking of him. "I fear your carpet is ruined."

"Simple enough to have it replaced."

She placed her hand on his chest, felt the steady pounding of his heart. "I'm not certain what I should take away from tonight's lesson."

"Not all men would have stopped where I did. Never allow a man to lift your skirts."

Pressing her lips to his neck, she tasted the salt of his skin. "Tonight I'm ever so glad I did."

She was aware of him stiffening, was certain he would regret his actions on the morrow when whiskey was no longer coursing through his veins. Perhaps she would as well, but she also knew that even a man who loved her might never make passionate love to her. When all was revealed, he might find bedding her a chore.

The coach came to a halt. Lovingdon leapt out, then handed her down.

"Your father is much too lenient, allowing you out at all hours."

"As I told you earlier, he doesn't know." Rising up on her toes, she kissed his cheek. "Thank you for the glass. That's all I intended when I came to see you, to thank you for the glass."

"Intentions—bad or good—have a way of going astray."

"Good night, Lovingdon."

She headed up the walk and heard the coach rattling away. At the top of the steps she turned back and saw Lovingdon walking down the drive, a solitary figure, encased in loneliness. She wanted to rush after him, return to his residence, curl up in his large bed and hold him. Just hold him. Have him hold her.

She waited until he was no longer in sight. Then she turned and pressed her forehead to the door.

Oh dear Lord, now she'd gone and done it.

She'd fallen in love with him all over again.

## Chapter 11

"If a man is keen on us, he will look us in the eye when we speak, and if we speak low, he will lean in to hear what we say. If he doesn't lean in, he doesn't fancy us." Grace was standing in a distant corner of Uncle Jack's parlor, speaking with Minerva and Ophelia. A small gathering of family and friends had arrived for dinner to celebrate Minerva's birthday.

She had hoped to see Lovingdon here, but he had yet to show. He'd not attended a family gathering in two years. She was disappointed tonight would be no exception. She knew Minerva was equally disappointed. It was not every day that a girl turned nineteen. Her oldest brother should be on hand.

"You know, my grandmother always insisted that

a lady speak extremely softly. I wonder now if this was her reasoning," Ophelia said.

"Oh, I've no doubt," Grace said.

"Did your gentleman tell you this?" Minerva asked.

Grace nodded perfunctorily.

"I suppose it should go on our list, but it seems that there should be more to it."

"How often have you spoken to a man, only to have him murmur 'Yes, yes' when you hadn't even posed a question?"

"Yes, but—"

"I say we test it tonight," Lady Ophelia announced with authority. "We have the perfect opportunity. The gathering is small, intimate. Several gentlemen are in attendance. We should be able to get results very quickly. We shall hold a meeting afterward in the garden."

"Yes, all right," Minerva agreed. "Although Lovingdon would be a perfect test sample. He cares not one whit anymore about love or women."

Grace felt her face heat up as visions of him caring about bringing her pleasure swamped her. She could readily recall every sensation he elicited with seeming ease. "A more accurate statement might be love or marriage. I'm sure he's not being celibate."

"Why would you think that?"

Experience. A recent ill-advised late night visit that left her lying in bed each night since wondering if she should pay another visit, but she thought it unlikely that she would find him at home, or if he were, alone. That time had been an aberration. He was very much in want of the company of women. "Celibacy does not a scoundrel make, or so I've heard."

*From your brother himself.*

"You're quite right," Ophelia confirmed. "Wine, women, and gambling, according to my brother."

"Lovingdon!" Minerva's mother called out.

Grace turned to see her embrace her firstborn child in the doorway, two footmen behind him holding a rather large box. More glass?

"He came," Minerva breathed, the delight in her voice palpable as she rushed across the room.

Grace hurried along behind her, not wanting to miss the welcoming. She knew he had distanced himself from his family after Juliette passed. Unfortunate timing, as she thought those who loved him could have helped him the most with his grief, could have ensured that his foundation didn't crumble.

Minerva stopped just shy of him. "I'm so glad you're here."

"It's your birthday, isn't it?" Lovingdon said. "I've brought you something. It's rather heavy. Lads, set it on the floor."

The footmen did as instructed. Minerva, in spite of wearing a dinner gown, knelt down and lifted the lid. "Oh, my word! What is it?"

Lovingdon signaled to the footmen, who worked to release it from the box and set it on the floor with a clunk. It looked to be some sort of machine with four rows containing oval disks, a letter marked on each one—

"It's a typing machine," he said. "You want to be a writer, don't you? You punch the letter you want and it prints it on paper that you put in the machine. I can show you later."

"It's wonderful."

"Well as I can barely decipher your handwriting, I thought it might prove useful. Don't want publishers attributing incorrect words to you."

"You're the best big brother a girl could have." Tears welled in her eyes as she flung her arms around his neck.

"I'm sorry, Minnie," he whispered. "Sorry, I haven't been here...for a while."

His gaze caught Grace's, and she saw the regret there, but more than that, she saw the gratitude, and her heart did three little somersaults, when it shouldn't be jumping about at all. Not for him. She couldn't help but believe that slowly, irrevocably, his heart was healing and that he might one day fall in love again. Not with her, of course. She was far too stubborn and bold for his tastes. She remembered Juliette as being extremely genteel and reserved. They could not have been more opposite in that regard.

When Minnie finally released her hold on him, he stepped over and shook Uncle Jack's hand. While Jack Dodger was not related to Grace by blood, he was dear friends with her mother, and to her he had always been Uncle Jack.

Then Lovingdon was standing in front of her, a devilish twinkle in his eyes that caused her heart to skip a beat. How long had it been since he appeared less burdened? "Are they serving rum this evening?"

She gave him an impish smile, doing all in her power not to let her cheeks turn red. "Not to the ladies."

He gave her a secretive grin. "More's the pity."

To get his mind and hers away from things they shouldn't ponder, she nodded toward the typing machine. "Interesting contraption. I've never heard of such a thing."

"They're a relatively recent invention. However, I don't know that they have much of a future. They seem rather clunky and slow-going to me."

"You remembered her dream, though, and that's what matters."

"Strangest thing," Avendale said. "All the ladies are speaking so softly I can barely hear them without leaning in."

During dinner Lovingdon had noticed the odd behavior as well. They were presently in the gentlemen's parlor, drinking port and smoking cigars, while the ladies were off sipping tea. He could well imagine Grace fuming over that little ritual. He knew she'd much rather be in here.

He, Avendale, and Langdon had separated themselves from the other gents. He was ridiculously glad that the bachelors on hand were few in number. The men who were here had not given an unusual amount of attention to Grace. He didn't know if it was because of the occasion or that they had given up hope of securing her hand. He hoped for the latter, then wondered at the reasoning behind his hope.

If she were narrowing down her selections, then soon she would make a decision and no longer need his advice. He could avoid exhibits, balls, and other social niceties. So why wasn't he overjoyed at the prospect of his life returning to what it had been before she knocked on his bedchamber door?

"Well, I could do with some cards," Avendale said. "Think I'll head to Dodger's after this. At least there I can hear what's being said." He rubbed the back of his neck. "All that leaning in has given me a cramp in my neck."

They began talking about stopping by Cremorne on the way to Dodger's. But for some reason it didn't appeal to Lovingdon that night, and he wondered why it ever had. "If you gentlemen will excuse me, I'm going out for a bit of fresh air."

He used the side door that led onto the terrace. Gaslights lit the garden path. He had grown up in this house and was familiar with every aspect of it. He could walk the paths in the dark without tripping over anything. He heard the chirping of the insects and the rustling of the foliage brushing over the brick wall. He knew all the normal night sounds. They did not include whisperings.

As quietly as possible he walked off the terrace

and around to the side, where he peered around a hedgerow and spotted three ladies. Were they? No, they couldn't be. Yes, they were—passing a cheroot among them.

"...a failure," Lady Ophelia said. "Every gentleman leaned in. They can't all fancy us."

"We simply need another sampling," Minerva said. "The gathering was too small and it was comprised of people who love us, so naturally they're going to try to hear what we have to say."

"I suppose, but could it be, Grace, that your gentleman had it wrong?"

Lovingdon was dumbstruck. She was telling *them* what he was telling her? Had she gone mad? He thought he had her trust, that what he revealed would go no further.

"He's extremely knowledgeable about such matters," Grace said, "so I doubt it."

"Ask your gentleman what it means if a man spends dinner sneaking glances at a lady near whom he is not sitting," Minerva ordered. "As I noticed one gentleman in particular seemed quite taken with you."

Was Minnie talking about him? He had been sneaking glances at Grace, but every man would have. She'd been radiant, her smiles in abundance, her laughter becoming.

"Who was sneaking glances?" he heard Grace ask.

Before his half sister could reply, he stepped around the hedge. "Ladies."

Jumping back, they released tiny squeaks, rather like dormice caught by the cat, and at that moment he felt feral in a way he suspected most felines didn't. He wasn't tamed, but was ready to pounce.

"Lovingdon!" Minnie chided. "You shouldn't sneak up on us like that."

"And you shouldn't be sneaking off with your father's cigars."

"Only one. And they're for guests. He prefers a pipe so he never notices how many are about."

He held out his hand to Grace, as she was the one holding the pilfered cheroot. She tilted up her chin and took a long inhalation before passing it off to Lady Ophelia, who at least had the wherewithal to hesitate a moment before inhaling deeply. Minnie then took a turn. As none of them were coughing—

"How long have you ladies been engaging in this vile habit?" he asked.

"Oh, I'd say about five minutes now," Grace mused with a righteousness in her voice that implied she'd not be intimidated. Not that he'd ever had any success in that regard where she was concerned.

"I meant: how old were you when you first started smoking?"

"Last year," Minnie responded as she took another drag, before handing it to him. "It's not fair that men get port and cigars while ladies get needlepoint and tea. And my needlepoint is more atrocious than my handwriting."

"Fair or not, ladies are not to engage in such behavior."

"Why is it vile if we do it and not if you do it?" Grace had the audacity to ask.

While it was a rather good point, he had no intention of addressing it. "You know what you're doing is wrong, or you wouldn't be out here sneaking about," he said, using his big brother voice.

"The wrong of it," Grace said, "is what makes it so enjoyable."

He couldn't argue with her there, but it also made him wonder how many other wrong things she might have done. "The gentlemen are finishing up. You should probably go inside."

"Are you going to tell Papa?" Minnie asked.

"It's your birthday, so no." Although Lovingdon suspected Jack would applaud her actions. He'd never been much of a rule follower, and while Jack had encouraged him to stray from time to time, he'd always walked the straight path until he became a widower. Then he'd seen some merit in Jack's advice. "Just promise that you won't do it again."

"I promise not to pilfer Father's cigars."

That promise came too fast, and he was quite certain the words allowed her to do as she pleased without breaking her word, but he wasn't in the mood to examine her statement too closely. She was a young lady now, and he had something else he wished to examine. "Inside with you."

"You're a wonderful older brother," Minerva said,

before she began leading her merry crew toward the back terrace doors.

"Lady Grace," he murmured, "might I have a word?"

All the ladies stopped, and he almost told them to recall their names and the fact that he wasn't talking to them, but Grace shooed them on before coming over to join him.

"Yes, Your Grace?" she asked, her voice more challenge than inquiry.

"You've been sharing my observations with them?"

"They have as much right as anyone to marry a man who loves them."

The thought of Minnie, dear Minnie, marrying a man who didn't love her sent chills through him. He hadn't even attended her coming out. While her father had a reputation that would scare any lord into behaving, it didn't mean the man would love her. He needed to be paying more attention to what was going on in the world, among Society. His world had narrowed down, and for the first time in two years it was beginning to feel too tight.

He dropped the smoldering cheroot onto the ground and smashed it with his boot. He would smash anyone who made Minnie unhappy.

"They don't know who's been giving me the advice," Grace said softly.

And now he knew why all the women were speaking so quietly tonight. God, but he wanted to laugh. But he wanted something else more.

He advanced on her. She backed up until she hit the brick wall.

"Don't be angry," she said.

"I'm not angry, but I just realized that I've never kissed a woman who tastes of tobacco."

"Oh."

Hers was a short, breathless sound that pierced his gut and lower. Dangerous, so dangerous. Yet he seemed unable to walk away. Cradling her face, he layered his mouth over hers. The smoky taste he'd imagined was elusive, but there was Grace, the sweet temptation of Grace.

He must have kissed her a thousand times in his mind since the night she'd come to his library to thank him for the glass stemware. He'd forgone evenings' entertainments to stare at the blasted vase and to think of heat and red and copper. He'd sipped on rum, striving to bring back the flavor of her.

For the past two years women had floated in and out of his life. He couldn't remember the flavor of a single one.

*He'll remember your flavor.*

*He'll remember your scent.*

But he refused to put himself into the category of a man who might fall in love with her. He didn't want to love again, but he had learned that a man didn't always get what he wanted.

Just as at this precise moment he wanted more

from her, a kiss that went on until dawn, an unbuttoned bodice that revealed her breasts, a hiking of her
skirts that exposed the sweet center of her. But the
other ladies would be waiting for her, and he knew
Minnie's impatience well enough to expect her to
intrude at any moment, so he fought down his desires until he thought he would choke on them and
pulled back.

"I prefer the rum," he said.

A corner of her mouth hitched up mischievously
and her eyes twinkled. "I prefer the whiskey to the
port."

"I shall have to see about accommodating you
next time."

Turning on his heel, he started to walk away, wondering why he thought there would be a next time,
knowing all the while that if he had any say in the
matter, there would be.

"Lovingdon?"

He stopped, glanced back.

"What does it mean if a man sneaks glances at a
lady during dinner?"

"I suspect it means she's the most beautiful
woman there."

Grace *had* been the most beautiful woman there.
Lovingdon meant no insult to the others in attendance, especially the ones to whom he was related
by blood, but Grace embodied her name with her
poise and elegance. While her features were pleasing,

her beauty went beyond the physical, to include an inner loveliness that radiated through to the surface.

Now, playing cards in the private room at Dodger's, Lovingdon glanced up when he heard the door open. Waited, waited, not breathing…anticipating—

Cursing inwardly when Avendale parted the heavy draperies and stepped into the room. "Sorry I'm late, gents. Hope Lovingdon hasn't relieved you of all your coins yet."

Good-natured laughter and ribbing followed that pronouncement. He didn't know why he'd wanted to see Grace barging in. She would only serve to upset the others, distract them, change the tenor of the game.

He downed his whiskey and waited impatiently while his glass was refilled by one of the footmen. He'd always enjoyed these games, but tonight he was antsy, and no matter how many times he turned the coin he could not find the calm within the storm.

"Any of you planning to go to Greystone's for the Midsummer's Eve ball?" Avendale asked as he drew up a chair.

"I shall be there," Langdon said. "I'm looking forward to leaving the city for a bit. Seems ghastly hot for some reason."

Lovingdon had noticed the heat, but only when Grace was around. She had a way of raising his temperature, if not his temper. He'd thought the two reactions were related. Perhaps it was the weather. Easier to attribute it to the climate than to her nearness.

"The duchess will be disappointed if I don't make an appearance," Drake murmured as he shuffled the cards. "So I shall be there for the ball although I doubt that I'll stay beyond that. What of you, Lovingdon?"

The annual event at Greystone's estate tended to extend into several days, with balls, plays, concerts, hunting, riding. It was a nice break from the London Season. Lovingdon had always anticipated it, never missed going until Juliette died. "I haven't decided."

"Anyone who is anyone will be there," Drake told him. "It'll be deuced boring here. You might as well join us."

Joining them meant joining Grace. He wondered if she were sneaking into his library at that very moment. He supposed he should have left word with his butler to alert him if he had any visitors, although there was only one for whom he would put aside whatever activity he was engaged in and rush to his residence. Any activity, he suddenly realized. Even if it involved a woman.

It had been a mere three hours since he'd seen her. Why the devil was he thinking about her? Why did he want to know what she'd been doing since his sister's party ended? Any proper woman would have done little more than gone to bed.

And that thought, blast it, had him wondering if she slept on her back, her stomach, her side. She'd watched him sleep. It was hardly fair that he didn't have a clue regarding her sleeping habits.

"…in or out."

He knew how to pick a lock, thanks to Drake's tutelage. Perhaps he would head on over to Mabry House—

"Lovingdon, where the deuce are you?" Drake asked.

He snapped to attention and realized that cards had been dealt, wagers were being made. If he didn't focus, he was in danger of losing badly tonight. The problem was, he didn't care about proving his prowess with cards. He didn't care if he lost a fortune, didn't care if he won. Not the best attitude when the stakes were as high as they were at this table.

"I'm out." He stood. "As a matter of fact, I've decided I'm not in the mood for cards. I'm off to find some other sport."

Lovingdon stood in the doorway of an exclusive drawing room that catered to the needs of the elite. The girls were clean and the clientele wealthy. Business was handled most discretely. Wine flowed into goblets as smoothly as women floated around the dimly lit room. Candles provided a soft glow, the flickering flames causing light to dance with the shadows, swirling them around bodies. Intriguing. Revealing, hiding.

A Titan of a woman approached him. Plenty of her to hold on to. She wasn't his usual fare. She wasn't dark-haired or dark-eyed. Her hair was a fiery red that he suspected was not the result of Nature. But he didn't care.

When she neared, he grabbed her hand. "You'll do nicely." And in the back of his mind he wondered when he had become content with someone who would "do."

Unlike Grace, who wanted sweet words and love, this woman required nothing more than knowing she was the one chosen for the moment. He would make it well worth her time, not only with the pleasure but also with the coins that would follow. Theirs would be a brief but honest relationship.

He escorted her out of the room and up the stairs that led to the bedchambers. At the landing, he continued on down the hallways to the room she indicated.

After opening the door, he stepped back to allow the woman to precede him. Her silky covering outlined her broad hips and floated around her legs as she swayed provocatively with her movements. Everything about her was designed to entice. She knew what she was and was comfortable with it.

Shutting the door, he needed only two strides to have her in his arms, his lips nibbling her throat. She smelled of vanilla, tasted of oranges.

"I know about you, Your Grace," she said in a raspy voice, arching her head back so he had easier access to the long length of her throat. "You don't bother with kissing."

"No."

"I could make you change your mind."

"I doubt it."

Beneath his hands, her skin was soft and warm, but it didn't tremble or quake. She didn't sigh with longing. She skimmed her hands over him, but they didn't dig into him as though if she could she would press him into her until they could no longer tell where one of them began and the other ended.

He inhaled her fragrance again, and it struck him that it was wrong. It wasn't rose and lavender. He could trail his mouth over her but she would not taste of rum, she wouldn't taste of desire.

She would taste of boredom.

Briskly, he moved away from her, marched to the window and gazed out on the night, on a street that would lead to his residence, that would eventually lead to Grace's.

"Did I do something wrong?" she asked.

"No." But neither had she done anything right. She wasn't what he wanted. Not tonight. And what he wanted he could not have.

Grace deserved love, and he didn't love her. He wasn't sure exactly why she plagued him or what he was feeling, but he knew what it was to love. The torment he was experiencing now was nothing more than lust and frustration.

"Shall I send up a different girl?" she asked.

He was struck by how easily interchangeable they all were. Perhaps it was time he took on a mistress, a woman who would know and meet his expectations. He looked back at the woman standing uncertainly near him, knowing he would be sending her an extremely expensive bauble on the morrow to make amends for his disinterest tonight.

He slowly shook his head. "No, I don't want another girl."

"But you don't appear to want me either."

"It's not a question of want. I just shouldn't have come here."

A slow knowing smile crept over her face. "Another is always a poor substitute for the one we truly want."

He was not at all pleased that somehow he had failed at keeping his thoughts to himself. Crossing his arms over his chest, he leaned back against the wall. "And who do you want?"

"Who every woman wants. A man who will appreciate me."

Curled on her side on her bed, Grace stroked Lancelot, but thought of Lovingdon. She felt beautiful with him. She forgot about her scars and imperfections. She became lost in the sensations he elicited with such ease. The moment his lips touched hers, the rest of the world ceased to exist. It was only the two of them, him giving so much, her receiving. She hoped in the receiving that she was giving as well.

She considered slipping out of the residence, going to his, and doing what she might to bring him pleasure, without receiving it herself. But she knew danger rested on that path. She might give her heart to him completely, but he could no longer give his heart at all.

She thought of all his pronouncements.

*He'll know your favorite flower.*

*He'll gaze into your eyes.*

*He'll care about what you're saying.*

Lovingdon did those things, but then he also did the blackguard things—kissing her at every opportunity, bringing her pleasure…

Why would only blackguards do those things? It seemed like a man in love would as well.

Was it possible that he cared for her more than she realized, more than he realized?

# Chapter 12

As Grace sat on the blanket, sketching the swans on the lake, she decided that she very much enjoyed Vexley's company. He seemed not to have a care in the world. He wasn't brooding or irascible. He didn't seek to teach her lessons, no matter that she had implied she wanted those lessons from Lovingdon.

Vexley had invited her to picnic with him. Sitting beneath a nearby tree, Felicity was serving as chaperone. Not that one was really needed here at the park. A good many people were about. Vexley could not take advantage—

And neither could she.

She pretended to be fascinated by the swans, because she found herself spending far too much time studying his mouth, striving to envision it moving over hers. It was no hardship whatsoever whenever she thought of Lovingdon, but with Vexley she couldn't quite see it. He had thin lips. The upper tended to disappear when he smiled, which he did quite often. Would it disappear when he kissed or would it become plumper?

Her own swelled considerably when Lovingdon gave attention to her mouth. It was just that he was so thorough. Whether he was kissing her slowly and provocatively or with a ravishing hunger, he was never brief. He lingered, he sipped, he came back for more. He had done her a great disservice by demonstrating how a man who loved her would kiss her. How could any man measure up to that?

How could she survive a kiss that was not a demonstration but was instigated by love? It would contain an emotional richness, delve deeper—

"You have the most lovely blush."

Familiar with the sight of her blushes, she suspected it wasn't lovely, but it no doubt encompassed most of her body, reflecting the path her thoughts had wandered onto. She also suspected with his comment that the rosy hue was darkening. She forced herself to smile at him and not let on that she was embarrassed to be caught musing about things she ought not. "I've grown a little warm."

Understatement.

"You're a very good artist," he said. He was resting up on an elbow, peering over at the sketchpad on her lap.

"I inherited my father's talent for putting images on paper. Although he prefers oils, I like pencils."

"Most ladies do needlework."

"Is that what you expect your wife to do?"

"I expect her to do anything she likes."

She wondered if he intended to stand by those words or if they were just meant to lure her in. Why could she not take them at face value?

"She will be a most fortunate woman," she said. "Some husbands have keen expectations."

Sybil's had, although Grace had seen her the day before and all continued to remain calm within her household. Lovingdon's influence had made a difference. Would Vexley step up to assist her friends if they were in need of help?

"I want the sort of marriage my father had," Vexley said. "Very amiable, no discord."

Amiable might be pleasant but it could also be quite boring. She thought of how she could speak honestly and openly with Lovingdon. She couldn't imagine posing the same sort of questions to Vexley, nor could she imagine Vexley responding with Lovingdon's candidness. That was what she desired: someone with whom she could be completely herself.

Out of the corner of her eye she caught sight of Lady Cornelia walking with Lord Ambrose. Arms linked, they were both smiling. Grace took satisfaction in her role as matchmaker for them.

"That's an odd couple," Vexley said, and she

glanced over to see that he was looking in the same direction that she'd been.

"They seem to get along famously." As though to prove her point, at that moment Lady Cornelia's laughter floated toward her.

"Her dowry won't allow them to live with any sort of largesse."

During all of his courtship, Vexley had never once mentioned the assets he would gain with marriage to her. She had begun to lure herself into believing that it wasn't important to him—or at least not more important than her.

"And will mine allow you to live more in the manner to which you desire?" she asked.

The change in his features was subtle but she knew he had realized his mistake. "I was only talking about them." Reaching out, he took her hand. While his was warm, his touch was not as powerful as Lovingdon's. As much as she wished she didn't, she felt Lovingdon's touch all through her body, no matter how slight, how unintentional. "Things are very different between you and I. We are well-suited, dowry be damned."

"So would we still be here had I no dowry?"

"Without doubt."

Yet, she doubted. Blast it all.

The mood of their outing changed. He read her poetry, but the poems weren't written by her favorite poet. They wandered among the trees and along the lake, never touching. She wanted the inadvertent placing of a hand on the small of her back. She didn't care how inappropriate it might be. He talked at her, not to her. He never sought her opinion. She would not have cared if he asked her what color she thought the sky was. She was merely seeking some evidence that he cared about what she thought.

When she spoke softly, he didn't lean in. He merely responded with, "Quite right."

Which didn't seem right at all considering her comment had been that she thought she had spotted a whale in the pond. Not that she had, of course. She'd simply been testing his interest, and discovered it lacking.

She'd had such high hopes for the afternoon, but found herself quite relieved when he returned her to the residence with the promise of seeing her at her family's estate later in the week.

When she walked into the foyer, she heard voices coming from the front parlor, one much deeper, one that sent fissures of pleasure spiraling through her. Cursing Lovingdon soundly for affecting her at all, she strolled into the room to find her mother serving tea to the duke.

Very slowly, he shifted his gaze to her, and she felt as though she'd been smashed in the ribs with Drake's cricket bat. In a smooth, feral way, Lovingdon unfolded his body from the chair.

Her mother glanced over. "Oh, you're here. Lovingdon was just telling me about a lecture on the American hummingbird that he's taking his sister to this evening. He thought you might be keen to learn about it."

"I believe you'll find a lecture far more interesting than an exhibit," he drawled laconically, and she couldn't help but believe there was more to his invitation than her mother realized.

"I thought you'd come around regarding the merits of exhibits," Grace said. Had he not purchased the red glass? Had she not found him studying it? Warmth swept through her with the thoughts of how much he had seemed to appreciate it—had appreciated her—that night.

"They have their place, but I prefer the opportunity to listen as knowledge is shared."

She couldn't be sure, but she thought she caught an undercurrent to his words, a warning. Had she somehow managed to upset him? That seemed unlikely as she'd not seen him since Minerva's party. But something was amiss. If she were smart, she would no doubt decline the invitation, but when it came to Lovingdon, she'd never been terribly brilliant. She suspected she might regret the evening, but then she decided it was better to regret doing something than not doing it. She'd once thought there were a great many things that she'd never have the opportunity to do. She wasn't going to shy away from experiences simply because she wasn't certain how they might end.

"I'd be delighted to go. May I have some time to dress properly for the occasion?"

"Take all the time you require."

* * *

The undercurrent became a raging river of fury. Or at least that was the sense Grace had as Lovingdon's coach traveled through the city. Glaring out the window, he sat opposite her, his back straight and stiff. Had she brought her parasol, she might have whacked him on the head with it.

She was acutely aware of the direction in which they traveled—the incorrect one. "Are we not stopping off to retrieve Minerva?" she asked.

"No."

"Are we going to a lecture?"

"I haven't decided."

"So you lied to my mother? For what purpose?"

His gaze landed on her then with the full weight of it taking her by surprise. He was fairly smoldering. "To get you into my carriage alone. Men lie. Often. When they want something."

"And you want something?"

"I want you to stay clear of Vexley. I've already told you that he doesn't love you."

"I like Vexley."

"So you're going to ignore my advice? Why ask me for it if you're going to discount it? My time is valuable—"

"So valuable that you've hardly given me any, in spite of your promise to be more involved. You didn't attend the ball last night. Are you even going to bother with our affair at Mabry Manor?"

He returned his attention to the passing scenery visible through the window. "I haven't decided."

"It seems there is quite a bit you haven't decided." She sighed. "Come to Mabry Manor, stay a few days, make your observations, give me a report. I shan't bother you anymore after that."

"You're not bothering me now."

"I find that difficult to believe considering how disgruntled you sound."

A corner of his mouth quirked up. She longed to hear him laugh. "Come early. We'll go riding," she said.

"How will that help you find a husband?"

Maybe it would help her find her friend. "Blast it all, Lovingdon, don't be so cantankerous. Come to our estate, and I promise you can do it without making observations or presenting me with a report. Just enjoy yourself. When was the last time you truly enjoyed yourself?"

He was enjoying himself at that very moment, dammit all. He'd never had harsh words with Juliette. They'd never argued. She'd never been short with him or looked as though she were on the verge of reaching across the expanse separating them in order to give him a good hard shake.

It was odd that igniting a fire within Grace was such fun. He was riding through the park when he spotted her with that scapegrace Vexley. He almost interrupted them there and then, probably should have, but he feared he would come across as some sort of jealous lover. He wasn't jealous, not at all. He was simply disappointed she didn't have the cunning to see Vexley for what he was—completely undeserving of her.

The problem was that he had yet to meet a man whom he thought *was* deserving of her. He didn't like imagining her laughing with some other fellow, sharing exhibits with him, growing warm beneath his touch, saying his name on a soft moan as passion burned through her.

"Did he kiss you?" he asked, immediately hating that he posed the question.

She appeared surprised. "Vexley? Of course not. He's a perfect gentleman." She released a great huff of air. "The trouble is that I'm not certain I want a perfect gentleman. None of the gents courting me excite me the way that you do."

An inappropriate fissure of pleasure shot through him with her admission.

"I spend far too much time thinking of red vases and what transpired near one," she said. "I think of your kisses and wonder if all men kiss with as much enthusiasm."

"I assure you that if he loves you, he'll kiss you with more enthusiasm."

"And if I love him—"

He stiffened in surprise as she breached the distance separating them and sat beside him. She grazed her hand along his cheek, his jaw. When had she removed her gloves? "I'll want to kiss him, won't I?"

"Naturally."

"I'll want him to be keen on having me kiss him again, so I'll want to ensure that I do it in such a way that he'll be unable to resist begging for more. Mayhap I should practice with someone for whom I haven't a care." She leaned in.

"Grace," he cautioned.

"What's the matter, Lovingdon? Afraid you'll be enticed into wanting more?"

He was already enticed. What he feared was that he might not be able to resist taking more than she was offering. "You play with fire, m'lady."

"I'm not afraid of getting burned. Are you?"

It wasn't the burn she should fear but the aftermath, for it could be painful indeed. But before he could even think of a way in which to explain that to her, she had covered his mouth with hers as though she owned every inch of it, inside and out.

*Practice, indeed.* If he hadn't experienced her enthusiasm the first time he kissed her, he might well believe she had spent considerable time practicing, but passion seemed to be such a natural part of her. What amazed him was how well she managed to hold it in check. When she released it, God help the man she loved. At that moment, however, God help him.

He knew he should show shock at her boldness, but too much honesty resided within their friendship for him to feign surprise or castigate her for doing what he had been contemplating since he first saw her with Vexley. Publicly claiming her mouth, however, would have resulted in her having the one thing she didn't want: a husband incapable of loving her.

He wished he could reach past the shards of his broken heart and find a fragment of love that remained unclaimed that he could offer her, but she deserved so much more than a scrap. She was worthy of the whole of a heart and then some.

She would give to a man all she had to give and she deserved to receive no less in return. A man would be better for having loved her. She would cause him to rise above mediocrity. Of that he had no doubt.

She skimmed her hand along his thigh.

"Grace." It seemed to be the only word he was capable of uttering.

"You've touched me intimately, Lovingdon. Why shouldn't I be able to touch you?"

"Because you're a lady." Thank God, he managed to find more words, not that they were particularly adequate.

She laughed against his mouth, and he breathed in the scent of cinnamon. He wondered if she'd enjoyed a hard sweet while she prepared herself for the lecture.

Then she nipped at the underside of his jaw, and he groaned. Her fingers tugged at his cravat. "This is in the way," she said. "I want to kiss your neck.

Everything is in the way." She reached for the buttons of his waistcoat.

"Grace, we're traveling in a coach through the London streets. Your reputation—"

"Who's to see? When did you become such a prude?"

He'd been born one, had lived as one until two years ago. He'd certainly never taken Juliette in a moving conveyance. He wasn't going to take Grace either, but he could damn well enjoy her, and if she wanted to explore him in the sheltered confines so be it. His neck cloth had disappeared, and she was suckling at his flesh, nipping the tender skin along his collarbone. He might bare evidence of her conquest on the morrow. Wicked, wicked girl.

Bracing a foot on the opposite bench, he drew her across his lap. Her hands were in his hair, traveling over his shoulders, touching, touching, touching. Her mouth slipped inside his unbuttoned shirt collar. "So what can you tell me of hummingbirds?" she asked.

*Hummingbirds?* "Who the bloody hell cares?" he asked, just before reclaiming her mouth. With her, he had no rules about kisses. He kissed her and wanted to kiss her again. He wanted to touch her, be touched by her. Lust, it was only lust, and yet it was a fiery need unlike any he'd ever possessed.

She pushed back slightly, dragging her mouth across his bristled jaw and he wished he'd shaved recently. "My mother will care," she whispered. "She'll ask me what I learned this evening. I can't very well tell her the truth of it."

"They hum," he answered, distracted as she wedged her hand between them and began caressing him through his trousers.

"When they sing?" she asked.

"I suppose. No, that's not right." He couldn't think. "Perhaps it comes from their feet. Is it important?"

"Depends what Mother asks."

"It's a sound they make, when they fly, I think."

"Their wings, then?"

"Yes, all right." He should take her to the lecture but how could he possibly sit contentedly beside her when he knew he could have her sprawled over his lap?

Reaching for the laces on the back of her dress, he began to make short work of the knots and bows. She straightened so quickly that her head nearly sent his jaw out the window, snapping his head back. The suddenness of her movement, with no warning, allowed him only enough time to bite back part of a harsh groan.

"I'm sorry," she said, gently rubbing his chin, massaging his cheeks. "But you can't undo my bodice."

"Grace, I've seen you below the waist."

"Yes, I know. I was there when you did."

Had his passion frightened her? That made no sense as she was the one who instigated what was happening between them now. "You can tear off my clothing, but I can't reciprocate?"

"No. I...I apologize. I think I lost sight of myself there." She scrambled off him, returned to her side of the coach, and gazed out the window. "I'm sorry."

"They have a name for women who lead a man on a merry chase and then leave him in agony. It's not very complimentary."

"Are you in agony?"

He was close to dying. He was angry, but more so at himself for not stopping things before they got to this point. Shifting on the seat, he straightened himself. He would most assuredly be taking a frigid bath when he returned to his residence.

"I'll survive," he said harsher than he intended. "But I suggest you not take such liberties with any gentleman courting you. He might not stop when you ask."

"He will if he loves me."

"It's the ones who don't love you who cause the problems."

"You stopped," she pointed out, and he wondered if she was hoping for some declaration of affection. No, she was too smart for that.

"I stopped because it never should have begun," he told her.

"You care for me."

"Of course, I do, but I don't love you as I loved Juliette. And that's what you're seeking, isn't it? A love such as I had?"

"You judge love by her," she stated. No question, and yet he felt obligated to answer.

"I judge everything by her."

She'd known that of course, which made her wanton actions incredibly embarrassing. His desire for her didn't go below the surface, and while the sensations were incredibly lovely, they left her wanting.

"What aren't you telling me?" he asked.

Her heart hammering with trepidation, she snapped her gaze over to his. "Pardon?"

In spite of the shadows, she could feel his gaze homed in on her like a physical presence.

"Sometimes I have the sense you're not being quite honest with me, that there's something more going on here than a quest for love."

She clutched her hands tightly together until they began to ache. She couldn't tell him everything. She didn't want her truth revealed in a coach, especially with a man who loved another and not her. Love was the key to acceptance. She was sure of it. Yet she knew she must tell him something. "If you must know I don't much like this life you lead. I thought that in your helping me, you might also help yourself to again become the man you were."

"He no longer exists."

"So I'm beginning to realize. You're never going to return to Society completely, are you?"

"No."

His certainty was disheartening. Although she should have expected it.

Reaching up, he rapped on the ceiling. The coach slowed, and she was aware of it turning down another street. She had little doubt he was returning her home.

"I should fasten you back up," he said somberly.

"Yes, all right." While she turned slightly to give him easier access to her back, he crossed over to sit beside her.

With a solitary finger, he caressed her nape. Closing her eyes, she wished she possessed the courage to give him permission to undo all the fastenings.

"I apologize for what I said earlier," he whispered softly. "You're an incredibly beautiful woman, Grace. You entice me, but I am not yet blackguard enough to take complete advantage. I would have stopped short of ruining you."

"But you don't think Vexley will."

"Do you really like him?"

"He seems nice enough. They all seem nice enough. I should be content with that, I suppose."

He began tying her laces. He'd loosened so many so quickly. She fought not to consider where he might have obtained that experience.

"You deserve more than contentment," he said. "You deserve a man who smiles every time he sees you."

"Unlike you, who scowls."

"Precisely. A man who loves you will want an accounting of every moment when you're away from him—not because he's jealous but because he missed you dreadfully and wants to assure himself that your time apart brought you a measure of happiness, because the price he paid was loneliness in your absence. Nearly everything he sees will remind him of you. No matter what he is doing, he will wish you were there to experience it with him. No matter how boring he may find the things that interest you, he'll willingly be there to share them with you.

"Within a pocket, he will carry something that reminds him of you. It can be the silliest or seemingly most inconsequential item: a button from a dress, a handkerchief that carries your perfume, a locket of your hair, a petal from your favorite flower, a missive that you penned. Not a particularly endearing missive, but it's from you and so it matters.

"He'll hoard every smile you give him. He'll want to make you laugh. He'll awaken in the middle of the night simply to watch you sleep."

"How will I know that he's doing all these things?" she asked.

Done with his task, he folded his hands over her shoulders. "You probably won't." He pressed a light kiss to the sensitive spot just below her ear. "Just as he'll never know the myriad ways in which you privately express your devotion to him."

The coach came to a halt, and she couldn't help but believe a good deal remained unsaid, that the task of knowing that a man loved her for herself was an impossible one.

A footman opened the door, and Lovingdon stepped out, then handed her down. He offered her his arm and escorted her up the steps.

At the door, he faced her. "When he leaves you, he'll count the moments until he'll be with you again. He'll find excuses to delay saying good-bye." He touched her cheek. "Good night."

Abruptly, he turned and jaunted down the steps. No delays, no excuses. He might not have intentionally done it, but he'd provided her with another lesson.

"Will you be coming to Mabry Manor?" she called after him.

"I still haven't decided."

"I wish you would."

"Unfortunately we don't always get what we wish for."

No, she thought, as he leaped into the carriage and she watched it disappear onto the street, we don't always get what we wish for.

But it seldom stopped one from wishing.

## Chapter 13

Several days later, as the coach bounced along, Lovingdon couldn't remember the last time he'd gone to the country for merriment. After deciding not to attend the gathering at Mabry Manor, he received a missive from Grace alerting him that his assistance would be required, as she fully intended to narrow the selection down to one.

Which he supposed meant there were some gents she was beginning to love or perhaps was leaning toward loving.

He wanted that for her, to love and be loved.

So why had he nearly thrown his red and coppery vase across his library?

On her wedding day he would send it to her to complete her collection, as he certainly had no plans to attend the ceremony. He needed no reminders of his own wedding, no reminders of what he had held and lost.

Although he was hit with a sudden jolt of guilt, as he had not thought of his loss in…days. He recalled when he counted not thinking of it in minutes. A minute had passed without thinking of them, then two. Sometimes with enough liquor and a woman, he could go hours.

But days?

It was the blasted vase. He would go into his library and see it, and images of Grace would start circling through his mind like a damned carousel. Her smiling, laughing, sipping rum. Then his gaze would drop to the wine stain on his carpet, and he would feel the silk of her flesh against his tongue, hear the cries of her being pleasured.

And here he was thinking of her again. Well, that would end quickly enough when she was married.

He rapped on the ceiling, and the coach slowed to a stop. He leaped out before a footman could open the door. "Prepare my horse. I'm going to ride."

He always brought his horse to Greystone's when he came to visit. While they had a fine stable of horses, nothing was better than having one's own horseflesh beneath him, a horse who knew his moods, his movements, and his hands.

When Beau was ready, he mounted him easily and set off in a hard gallop. The coach driver knew the way, so he didn't have to wait. He needed to feel the horse beneath him, the wind in his face. He needed to concentrate on keeping the beast in line. He needed something to keep his mind off Grace.

Ever since their carriage ride, she had been a constant in his thoughts. If she wasn't so desperate for love, if he didn't care for her as much as he did, if he didn't want to see her happy, he might have considered taking her to wife.

Without a doubt their nights would be fulfilling. She was as carnal a creature as he'd ever met. But she wanted what he dared not give.

And therein rested his dilemma. He didn't love her as he'd loved Juliette.

They were such different women. What he felt for Grace was beyond description.

He would not dance with her while at Mabry Manor. He would barely speak with her. He would seriously observe the men who still held her attention, provide what insights he could, and be done with the entire affair. She would be married by year's end and happy for the remainder of her life. It was what he wished for her, what he would strive—

At the sight of a horse and rider loping over the gently rolling green, he drew Beau up short. He'd forgotten how well Grace rode, how she seemed to be one with the beast. She gave her all to everything she did. She'd do the same with marriage.

It was imperative that he secure her a husband who would give equally.

For half a second, he considered staying on his

current path, but she was so damned alluring. What would it hurt to spend a little time with her before the festivities began?

Kicking his horse into a harder gallop, he raced after her.

Her hair had come undone and was flying out behind her. He'd never seen it unpinned. It appeared that it went past her waist. He had an absurd thought that brushing out the tangles would be a pleasurable task, a task that some other man would have the opportunity to relish.

She must have heard the hard pounding of his horse's hooves as they ate up the ground, because she glanced back. Any other lady would have drawn her horse to a halt, but then he had forever known that Grace was unlike anyone else.

He was near enough that he saw her triumphant grin before she urged her horse into a faster lope. A gentleman would have half-heartedly accepted the challenge and then let her win, but he was far from being a gentleman. He gave Beau the freedom to try to overtake them.

"You won't catch me!" Grace yelled over her shoulder, taunting him.

Impressed with Grace's skill as she maneuvered her horse over the slight hills and around the trees that dotted the land, he considered letting her have the victory. Then decided against it. He was almost upon them.

After glancing back, Grace barreled on. "Three dances if I get to the top of the next rise first!"

Her laughter echoed around them, and the excitement thrummed through him. He wanted this victory. He wanted her. Stretched out on the green grass among the wildflowers. He wanted to run his mouth over her body with the sun beating down on them. Though that was unlikely to last long with the dark clouds gathering in the distance.

They were neck and neck now. She looked over, and he saw the determination in her blue eyes. It ignited his blood. He was tempted to reach out, snag her from the saddle, settle her across his lap, and take her mouth until she begged for mercy.

To escape those thoughts he gave Beau a final kick, and his horse reached the top of the rise a nose ahead of hers.

"Blast you!" Grace yelled, drawing her mare to a halt near his gelding. "I almost had you."

"Almost doesn't count."

"You could have let me win."

"You would have despised me for it."

"True enough." Her hair a wild mess, she breathed almost as heavily as her horse.

Against his better judgment, he took several strands between his fingers. "You have the most gorgeous hair."

"Men seem to prefer blondes or brunettes."

He cocked up a corner of his mouth. "Men are fools."

Smiling brightly, she pressed her teeth to her lower lip. "I didn't think you'd come."

He didn't want to acknowledge the pleasure it brought him to have pleased her so. "One last effort to help you find the right man."

"Someone I've overlooked all Season, you think?"

"Perhaps."

"Such a noncommittal response. Still, I'm glad you're here."

"You won't be so glad when I chastise you for being out here with no escort."

She rolled her eyes. "It's my father's land, Lovingdon. I've ridden out here alone for as long as I can remember. I could walk about blindfolded and not get lost."

"You have gentlemen arriving, and some of those might seek an opportunity to be alone with you."

"Not this afternoon. Drake's keeping them occupied with billiards, cards, and drink until dinner."

"I suppose I should carry on to the residence then."

"I suppose you should." She held his gaze, a question in hers, but more an answer that he recognized.

Slowly he dismounted, removed his gloves, stuffed them in a pocket, and approached her horse. It shied away, but he grabbed the reins and calmed it, before placing his hands on Grace's waist. "You should give your horse a rest after that jaunt."

With a barely perceptible nod of acknowledgment, she curled her hands over his shoulders and he brought her down, deliberately allowing her body to brush against his. He should have released her then, but he was loath to do so. It didn't help his convictions any that she neither moved away nor lowered her hands from his shoulders.

Tucking the hair behind her left ear, he wondered how it could feel so soft when it appeared so untamed, but then it seemed to mirror her: bold, yet with an undercurrent of vulnerability that he would have never suspected had he not witnessed it. "My assisting you in your quest isn't doing either of us any favors. After this affair, I'll be returning to my debauched life."

"Are you saying you left it?"

"I'm saying I haven't been as devoted to it as I once was." The fingers that had curled her hair around the shell of her ear lingered, skimmed over her cheek, and came to rest near the freckle. He touched it with his thumb. "You're not quite so brazen this afternoon as you were in the coach."

Her cheeks flushed. "It's easier in the dark, don't you think?"

"Not always."

Lowering his mouth to hers, he took because he could, because he knew she wouldn't object, and because he was hungry for the taste of her. Kissing her was wrong on so many levels, but he had ceased to care. No one was about to witness their transgressions.

Her fingers scraped his scalp, tugged on his hair,

held him in place while her sweet sighs echoed around them. He wound his arm around her back, and brought her in closer, pressing her breasts to his chest, breasts he wanted to see, touch, taste. Why was she so protective regarding what was beneath her bodice and not what was beneath her skirts? In his experience, the opposite was usually true.

But then again, Grace had never been common, ordinary, or like anyone else.

When she pulled back, her lips were swollen and damp. He wanted to swoop in and claim them again.

"I have the impression that you're not teaching me a lesson," she said.

"No, I'm simply being wicked and taking what I have no right to hold."

"Too much power is given over a kiss."

"I've shown you where they can lead."

"As long as it's mutual, I don't understand why it must be forbidden." She slipped out of his hold and began walking, swaying her hips slightly.

Grabbing the reins of both horses, he fell into step beside her. "Because women are supposed to remain pure."

Peering over at him, she scoffed. "But not gentlemen. So unfair. Perhaps I shall stand in the center of the ballroom and invite every gent to kiss me. Surely if he makes my toes curl, he's the correct one."

*Do I make your toes curl?* hung on the tip of his tongue.

"I mean, I can't possibly wait until my wedding

night to discover if he is a marvelous kisser. What if he slobbers or has rancid breath or doesn't like using his tongue?"

Although he knew he had no right he despised the thought of another man kissing her. Reaching out, he pulled her to him, cupped her face between his hands, and blanketed her mouth with his own. He didn't want to discuss potential suitors for Grace. He didn't want to be here. He didn't want to be elsewhere.

Sometimes he thought he might go mad. But at that particular moment, madness was the farthest thing from his mind. Grace took over his thoughts. The feel of her in his arms, the sweep of her tongue through his mouth. He backed up until he landed against a tree that he could use for support while he nestled her between his thighs.

Sweet Christ. She writhed against him as though she sought the same surcease that he did. But he wouldn't take it, couldn't take it, not with her, not when he couldn't give her a marriage based on love. But that didn't mean that he couldn't make her glad that their paths had crossed.

As smoothly as possible, without breaking from the kiss, he turned them around until she was supported by the tree. Her riding habit was perfect for what he had in mind as it lacked the layers of petticoats that would prove bothersome to his quest. Reaching down, he wrapped his hand around her knee and lifted her long leg, settling it just below his hip. Bless her height and long limbs.

"Lovingdon," she whispered on a breathy sigh, and he gritted his teeth at the thought of her saying another man's name. She opened her eyes, and he saw the heated passion that was burning inside her. Had he ever known a woman who was so quick to ignite? "We shouldn't be doing this."

"No, we shouldn't, but you tend to do things that you shouldn't. Why stop now?"

"Is this a lesson?"

How he wished it was. "No. I just want to feel you shuddering in my arms."

"I want to shudder in your arms."

With a growl, he buried his face in the curve of her neck, inhaling her sweet fragrance along with the earthy scent of her earlier exertions. She dropped her head back, giving him easier access to the silky, sensitive flesh as her fingers dug into his upper arms.

He slipped his hand beneath the hem of her skirt until he could cup the bare skin of her calf. Firm muscle. He skimmed his fingers higher, along the back of her knee.

She gasped, giggled, sighed.

"Ticklish?" he rasped near her ear, wondering when his voice had grown so rough.

"A little, but don't stop."

"I have no intention of stopping." Although if she asked, he would. He hoped only that she wouldn't ask. He wanted to give her this, even as he recognized that in the giving he was also receiving. Her happiness, her joy, mattered to him. It was the reason that he'd made this journey, that he would suffer through this deplorable event when he'd much rather be in London focusing only on his needs. But somewhere along the way, she'd become a need, a need not to disappoint.

He trailed his fingers along the marvelous length of her silken thigh. If they were in a bed, she could wrap her legs around him three times over. He fought back that thought before he became of a mind to search out a mattress. He couldn't put his finger on when she'd become so damned appealing. He'd always liked her, but what he felt now went beyond that. Still, he had no desire to examine it. He wanted only to become lost in her pleasure.

His fingers found her sweet center. She was already so wet and hot. Releasing a tiny moan, she pressed herself against him and clutched his shoulders as though she would soar into the heavens without anchor. Then one of her hands was traveling down his chest, his stomach, lower still—

"No," he growled.

"Not fair," she said on a thready breath. "I want you to feel what I'm feeling."

"I do feel it." He slipped a finger inside, and she throbbed around him. She was so tight. He didn't want to think about how marvelous it would be to be buried inside her. "Let me just enjoy you."

Grabbing the back of his head, she held him near

while her heated mouth worked its way over his neck, stirring him in ways that the most experienced courtesans hadn't. It took so little with her to build a raging fire of need, a need that would go unfulfilled this day. While he stroked and caressed her intimately, he ran his tongue along the shell of her ear, taking satisfaction in her gasps. Latching her mouth onto his, there was a frenzy to her kiss as though she could not have enough of him.

Her hand dug more deeply into his shoulder. Then she flung her head back, her cry echoing around them, as she pulsed against his fingers. Shuddering, going limp, she fell against him. With one arm, he held her upright, absorbing each tiny tremor. Ironically, for a man who wanted no commitments, he knew he would be content to hold her here all day, into the night and morning.

Unfair to tease her with things he was not willing to give her forever. Very slowly, he pulled his hand away, and lowered her leg.

Gently, she pushed away from him, giving her weight back to the tree. Her skin was flushed, her eyes sultry. With a sigh, she looked up at the branches overhead. "You've taught me far too much, Lovingdon. I don't know how I shall ever be content with another."

"If he loves you, it will be even more satisfying."

"If he loves me *and* I love him. That's the secret to achieving both the physical and emotional release, isn't it? Without love, as marvelous as the sensations are, the entire experience is still rather empty."

Empty. An appropriate word. Had he not been feeling the same lately?

"I've upset you," he stated.

"No. I'm simply greedy. I want it all." Reaching down, she shook out her skirt. "I need to bathe before the evening."

An image of wet limbs flashed through his mind. He wanted to see her in the bath, he wanted to see her as he had no right to see her. Turning away, he strode over to where the horses chewed grass and shrubs. Grabbing the reins of her mare, he led the beast over to where Grace waited.

He placed his hands on her waist. Such a narrow waist. If he brought his wrists together his hands would span the width of it. If he were an artist, he would paint a slew of slender women. Her shape was elegant, refined, appealing. Leaning in, he took her mouth gently, lingering, capturing once more the feel and taste of her.

"Why did that seem like good-bye?" she asked, when he drew away.

"Because I can't distract you from your goal while we're here. No clandestine meetings, no wickedness. We're to focus on identifying the man who truly loves you."

He lifted her up onto the horse, watched as she maneuvered herself onto the sidesaddle. "I should probably arrive from another direction," he said.

"After chastising me earlier for riding alone? Besides, I believe we've made it perfectly clear that you are only interested in serving as guardian. No one would ever suspect that you've been naughty."

He supposed she was right. Where was the harm in his accompanying her home?

He'd slipped away from the others because he wanted time alone with Lady Grace Mabry, time to court her with no one to observe his attempts, time to convince her that she should accept his suit. But finding her was a challenge. She didn't seem to be in the residence, so he began searching the grounds.

To his everlasting disappointment, he saw her arriving at the stables with Lovingdon in tow. Lovingdon who always seemed to be sniffing about, who appeared to be her unofficial protector.

He claimed to have no interest in marriage, but if he wasn't careful he was likely to be ensnared by it. It seemed he was forever managing to find time alone with Lady Grace. It was not to be tolerated.

She was the heiress with the largest dowry, a portion of which included land that bordered his own property. He would not be content to marry anyone else, and his own contentment mattered above all else.

He would have to redouble his efforts to convince her that they belonged together.

As she lounged in the copper tub, Grace could not help but reflect that her skin felt particularly sensitive. While she knew that she shouldn't allow

Lovingdon to take such liberties, she couldn't deny that she relished the liberties taken. She yearned for his touch, his nearness, his kiss. She loved him, desperately. It was a pity she desired the same degree of love in return, that she couldn't be content to simply love.

Using her sponge, she rubbed it over her foot, between her toes. As lovely as it was, it didn't elicit the marvelous sensations that Lovingdon did. She imagined herself standing before him completely nude, while he ran his hands and mouth over her. In her fantasy, she had no scars for him to avoid.

She feared tonight's ball might be an exercise in futility. Shouldn't she crave the touch of any man she might be considering taking as a husband? Shouldn't she toss and turn at night with thoughts of his body riding hers? Shouldn't she want him to meet her in the shadows of a garden and have his way with her?

The gentlemen were all pleasant enough. Some of them she dearly liked. Some made her laugh. Some made her look forward to their next dance. But she couldn't imagine a single one of them grazing bare hands along her thigh or cupping her intimately. They would do that, of course. But thinking about it made breathing difficult, and not in the pleasant manner that Lovingdon had of taking her breath away.

This love business was such a complicated thing. She feared she might not figure it out until it was too late.

* * *

Dinner was turning out to be a dreadful affair, Lovingdon mused as he sat between two ladies who were determined to convince him that it was high time he placed himself back on the marriage market. He shouldn't have been surprised by the seating arrangements as Grace's mother was known for not giving a fig about ranking. She treated lord and commoner alike. So it was that Grace was surrounded by the most eligible of bachelors, while he was boxed in by innocent misses for whom he could generate little interest. Not that he could find any fault with them. They were pleasant to gaze upon, possessed sweet melodic voices, but they were too eager to please.

They weren't stubborn, opinionated, or determined to find love. They seemed in search of one thing—a husband and any lord would suffice for the role. Quite suddenly, it struck him that Grace had standards, that she wasn't simply in want of a husband, but something more, something with value, something that placed her above all the other ladies of her station. His admiration for her rose a notch.

She might have an odd way of going about gaining what she wanted, but by God she knew what she wanted.

Grinding his teeth, Lovingdon watched as she smiled at Somerdale, laughed with Vexley, and listened attentively to Bentley. Was she seriously considering one of them?

He tried to imagine each gentleman standing at

the altar beside Grace, but brought himself up short when he envisioned their wedding night. They would do more than touch her as he had. They would know every aspect of her.

They would bring her joy and happiness that he couldn't. He wished that she had never come to him, that he had never realized the young girl he had consoled in the stables had become an enticing woman.

He did care about her, dammit, just not as she wished, not with his entire heart and soul. Those belonged to, would always belong to, Juliette.

He cared for Grace too much to place her second when she deserved to be some man's first.

Grace loved the first night because following dinner they held a ball that continued into the wee hours of the morning. The single ladies had rooms in the east wing, the bachelors in the west. Few of the mamas and papas showed, as the event had always been geared with the younger people in mind. It had begun when she was a child and her parents promised her and her brothers that they could bring their friends to share adventures for a few days during the Season.

Over the years, the adventures had changed. Sometimes she missed the games of her youth, when spending time with the boys was fun. Now it was almost a chore.

Although there was a room set aside for cards and one for billiards, the ballroom was rather crowded.

None of the rooms were for males only. Here the ladies played cards and billiards. Tomorrow some of them would go shooting.

The orchestra was almost finished warming up. She looked around for her first dance partner and spied him talking with Lovingdon. She was glad Drake hadn't sought out an excuse not to come. This had always been a family affair, and he was family, even if he was reluctant to admit it. She knew that he knew he was loved. He had no doubts there but had scars to remind him of his time on the streets, and she doubted he would ever be completely at home in these environs.

As she neared the two men, she thought they were the most handsome in the room. Drake had a roughness to him, a toughness that his evening clothes couldn't hide. In contrast, Lovingdon was elegant, aristocratic. Each man wore self-assurance like a second skin. They were complete opposites, one a lord of leisure, the other hardworking. But friendship bound them.

"Don't you two look handsome tonight?" she said in greeting.

Drake leaned down and kissed her cheek. "You look beautiful. I'm surprised some man hasn't snatched you up yet."

"It wasn't for want of trying, but you know me. I was always hard to catch. Even when we played chase I could outrun the lads."

She turned to Lovingdon to find him studying

her intently. He had always been attractive, but tonight he seemed more so. His dark blond hair was trimmed and styled, his face freshly shaven. He had lines formed by sorrow, but she could make out a few shaped by happiness. Sorrow always dug more deeply. His face contained character that it hadn't in his youth. He had gone through the fires of hell, and while she doubted he would see it as a compliment, to her, he had been forged into a rather remarkable man. He grieved deeply for those he loved; he kept their memories alive. He was keeping his word to help her find love, and she suspected he would assist Minerva as well.

The strains of the first waltz floated on the air.

"Drake, this dance is yours." She winked at Lovingdon. "You're next."

"Not as many suitors here?" Lovingdon asked.

"I have suitors aplenty but I always begin with my favorite gentlemen, so I etched you onto the card days ago."

"Rather confident that we'd be here," Lovingdon said.

"No, but I see no harm in sustaining hope that one's wishes will come true."

Drake offered his arm and led her onto the dance floor. She knew his habits, knew his reservations. Knew he would dance with her and then make his way to the card room or perhaps even the library to read. He thought he knew his place, but he didn't really have a clue.

"You know any of these ladies would be more than happy to dance with you," she told him.

"They're not for me, Grace. They never have been and they never will be," he said, discounting her words. "And you managed to get Lovingdon here, but don't think you've put him back together. That way lies heartache."

It was hardly fair that he wouldn't discuss his love life but seemed to believe it perfectly fine to discuss hers. "I'm well aware. He's adamant that he won't love again."

"But then you've always been a dreamer."

"I dream that someday you'll find love."

He laughed heartily, a deep, rich sound, and she wished the ladies of the Set could see him as she did. She thought of him as a brother too much to ever think of him as anything else, but she knew the goodness in him knew no bounds. Yet she also recognized there was darkness in him that could claim the same.

"Worry about yourself, Grace. My bloodline coming to an end would be no loss, and I'm in no need of heirs."

"But you could use a wife. I've seen the way you live. You need someone to remind you to eat."

"I make out fine."

She wanted more than that for him, but she also knew he could be as stubborn as she. They might not have the same blood, but they had been raised in the same household, and they had some of the same traits.

When the dance ended, he escorted her to where Lovingdon waited. He was the only partner she wanted this evening, but she knew he would give her no more than a single dance. Still, it was better to have one dance than to have no dance at all.

She was aware of his gaze roaming over her as she neared, and when those amber eyes returned to meet her blue ones, they were smoldering with an intensity that heated her core. It couldn't have been more obvious that he desired her if he shouted it from atop the stairs. But in his case, desire was not love. He'd had women aplenty but only ever loved one. She wanted to see evidence that he loved her.

Just a little. That was all she would need.

He offered his arm, and she placed her hand on it, relishing the firmness of his muscles bunched beneath her fingers.

"No lessons tonight," she said. "Don't teach me anything or demonstrate particular behaviors. Just dance with me to dance with me."

She peered over at him to find him watching her steadily. "I can't give you what you want."

"All I want is a dance," she assured him, wondering when their relationship had transformed into one where she could not be totally honest with him.

His eyes never leaving hers, he swept her into the fray of dancers. No words, no conversation to distract. She was aware of every aspect of him. The dark blond locks rebelling to fall over his brow. The smoothness of his jaw, which she wanted to scrape her lips over. The perfectly knotted cravat that she wanted to unknot. His bergamot scent that wafted toward her. The heat of his touch, the nearness of his body.

By all appearances, by all actions at the moment, he loved her. It had been one of his axioms.

*He will look at you as though you are the only one in the room.*

If he were anyone else, she would have thought, *He wants me not my dowry.* But she knew that her dowry was nothing to him.

And he wasn't anyone else. He was Lovingdon, haunted by his first love, by the woman he insisted would be his only love. She could not imagine an emotion so great that it dwarfed all others. Yet even as she thought it, somewhere in the back of her mind she heard, *Oh, but you can.*

She would always love him, but it didn't prevent her from loving another. Why could he not do the same?

She wasn't even aware of the music drifting into silence until he stopped moving. He tucked her arm into the crook of his elbow and they strolled leisurely toward the edge of the dance floor.

*He won't be in a hurry to be rid of you.*

All the signs pointed toward love, and yet—

*I can't give you what you want.*

His lessons had been for naught. He couldn't help

her determine if a man truly loved her, because the signs could be misread, misinterpreted.

*Trust your heart.*

Hers was the heart of a fool.

Never taking his gaze from hers, he lifted her hand to his lips. The heat of his mouth seared the skin through her glove. She swallowed, licked her lips. His eyes darkened.

"Enjoy your next dance," he said, before releasing his hold on her and handing her off to Vexley.

She watched him walk off, then with determination turned to Vexley and smiled. She very much intended to enjoy the entire evening, Lovingdon be damned.

Standing in the gazebo, smoking a cheroot, Lovingdon looked out over the stream where the dappled moonlight danced over the water. The smoke he released momentarily clouded his vision. He wished it would cloud his mind.

He wanted Grace to find love, knew she wouldn't find it with him, but the acknowledgment didn't stop him from wanting her. He had watched her dance with one gentleman after another, and each gazed at her adoringly. He could hardly blame them. Her smile was the sweetest, her laughter warmed the soul. It was when he saw her slip into the garden with Somerdale that he decided he needed to leave, because his first inclination had been to follow them out and plant his fist in the center of the man's face.

He wasn't jealous, but merely being protective. She was wise, smart, able to look out for herself. He had given her enough warnings that she would not find herself forced into marriage by an overzealous suitor.

Hadn't he taken Juliette for walks in the garden at night whether the moon was full or absent, and behaved himself? A kiss on the back of her hand. Twice he leaned over for a kiss on the cheek. Once he had grazed his mouth across hers in much the same manner that Grace had described Somerdale's kiss. Innocent. Respectful. Boring as hell.

Only now did he realize how dull his courtship had been. He had loved Juliette. He held no doubt. He had been a boy on the cusp of manhood, eager to please her, terrified of frightening her with his passions, so he'd held them in check.

Why could he not do the same where Grace was concerned?

He caught the whiff of her rose and lavender fragrance before he heard her slippers crush leaves, before the floor of the gazebo vibrated as she stepped upon it. He felt her warmth as she neared. Out of the corner of his eye he saw her reach for his cheroot. She plucked it from his mouth, turned, leaned back against the railing and took a short puff. He was mesmerized watching the smoke escape through her slightly parted lips.

She extended the cheroot toward him. He took

it, studied it. "Does your father know about your bad habits?"

"There are a good many things about me that my father doesn't know."

He wondered how many of those things were secrets kept from him? A lifetime of exploring her would never be enough. There would always be something new to learn, something new to relish. He couldn't travel that path. "Shouldn't you be inside dancing?"

"I've worn out three pairs of slippers. I've had enough of the ball. I think I've had enough of the Season."

He shifted his position until he was facing her squarely. "What do you mean by that?"

"If one of those gentlemen loves me, it doesn't matter, because I don't love him. I enjoy them. I enjoy them all. But my heart fails to speed up, my skin doesn't grow warm. I don't anticipate their nearness."

"That doesn't mean you won't come to love one of them."

"But it would be a passionless love."

And she so deserved a passionate love, a man who could not live without her. A man who woke up each morning and smiled because she was in his bed, a man for whom she was the sun and the moon.

Without looking at him, she held something toward him. He snatched the bottle from her. "You little minx. No glasses?"

In the light of the full moon he saw her slight smile. "I was attempting to escape from being so civilized."

"Well, you accomplished that." He removed the top from the bottle and offered it to her, not at all surprised when she took it. Too many shadows prevented him from observing the minute movements of her delicate throat as she swallowed, but he could see her faint skin washed by moonlight. His blood thrummed.

He retrieved the bottle from her and enjoyed several gulps, barely savoring the flavor of whiskey. She'd brought his preference, not hers, had known his preference. Juliette had never imbibed with him, nor smoked, nor used profanity. But then he'd kept all his vices on a short leash when she was alive. He hadn't wanted to offend her. He'd loved her, there was no denying that, but in being true to her had he been true to himself?

"You look as though you're deep into heavy thoughts," Grace said.

"Berating myself for failing to discover a man who loves you more than he loves your dowry."

"My father says I'm searching too hard. Perhaps I am."

She grabbed a beam, swung around and stepped through an opening onto the ground.

"Where are you going?" he asked.

"I want to walk along the stream."

"I smell the scent of rain on the air. You should

head back to the manor if you're going anywhere." Taking another swallow of whiskey, he didn't want to admit his disappointment because she was leaving him already.

"You're hardly made of sugar," she called over her shoulder. "You won't melt if you get wet."

No, but he'd get chilled. So would she. Dammit. "Grace, you don't know what creatures are about."

"When did you become a coward, Lovingdon?" she taunted.

Blast her. He leapt off the gazebo and trudged after her, aware of the occasional raindrop pinging off him. "I'm a grown man, not a young boy in search of adventure."

"Are there adventures to be had here, do you think?"

Chuckling, he caught up to her. "Most assuredly. Especially if your father finds us out here. Rifle in tow, he'd no doubt hunt me down."

"He trusts you to behave, at least where I'm concerned."

"Yet you know that I don't always behave where you're concerned."

In spite of the gathering clouds, he could see her smile in the moonlight. The rain began to fall in earnest. He needed to get her back. He didn't want to risk her catching her death. "I think you're out here trying to tempt me into wickedness again."

"It's crossed my mind that wickedness without love is better than no wickedness at all."

"I thought you valued love above all else. If you've been wicked, it'll be harder for him to love you."

At the water's edge she faced him. "Will it? If he truly loves me, shouldn't he love every aspect of me? That's what I want. A man who will love every aspect of me, even the imperfections."

"A woman who admits to imperfections, a rare find indeed."

She abruptly spun about, presenting her back to him, and he had the sense that perhaps she hadn't been teasing and that maybe he shouldn't have either. He moved up until he could see her profile and the tears glistening in her eyes.

"Grace?"

She shook her head. "There's something I haven't told you, something that's not talked about, and yet there are times when I feel this overwhelming need to shout about it."

"You can tell me."

She shook her head.

With one hand, he cradled her cheek. "Sweetheart, whatever it is—"

Lightning flashed, thunder crashed, the air reverberated, and frigid rain poured from the heavens.

Grace hunched her shoulders. Lovingdon tore off his jacket and draped it over her head to shelter her from the rain as much as possible. "Come along, we need to get back to the manor."

"There's an old crofter's cottage just beyond the trees. It's nearer."

He didn't argue as she began trudging away from the river, but worked to keep pace and keep his jacket over her. The wind picked up, slapping rain against them. Blast it! Where had this come from? A flash of lightning guided their steps. Another rumble of thunder cracked above them.

As they passed into a clearing, Lovingdon caught sight of the silhouette of a small building. It looked sturdy enough. As long as it had a sound roof, he'd be happy.

With a bit of fumbling, he found the latch, shoved open the door, and guided Grace inside.

"There's a lamp on the table just inside the doorway," she said, and he felt more than saw her moving away from him.

He found the table, realized he'd clung to the whiskey the entire time. Lightning arced through the sky, provided him with a glimpse of the items spread across the table. He set down the bottle and snatched up the box of matches before all grew dark. He struck a match, lit the lamp, and turned to the room, the only one in the dwelling. Grace was crouched before the empty fireplace. To his right was a bed, neatly made. As a matter of fact, everything appeared tidy. Drawings were pinned on walls around the room.

"It appears to be clean," he said.

"It's where I come to draw."

He glanced back at the bed.

"Sometimes late into the night," she explained, as though she knew he was confused by the out of place furniture. "Father had it redone for me a few years back."

He wanted to examine the drawings, especially the one that appeared to be a bunny with only one ear. He wondered if it was a sketch from her youth, as it seemed an odd choice for a woman. He remembered often seeing her, when she was younger, with sketchpad and pencil.

Crossing the distance separating them, he placed the lamp on the floor and crouched beside Grace. "And you have some firewood and kindling."

"The servants keep it tidy, as I never know when I might want to come here alone."

He worked diligently to get a fire going. "If I didn't know you so well, I would think you'd led us here on purpose."

"Only to escape the rain. I assure you that I'm well aware you'll never love me, and without love how can one *make* love?"

The fire caught and began to crackle. He wished he could make love to her, could give her what she wanted. He turned to find her simply sitting there, rocking back and forth. "You need to get out of those wet clothes. The fire is not going to provide you with enough warmth."

"I'll be fine."

"Humor me. Health is a fragile thing." Standing, he strode over to the bed and pulled off the quilt. "You can use this to cover yourself."

He walked back over and held the quilt up so it

served as a curtain between them. "Come on now, Grace."

"I'm not going to disrobe in front of you."

"You're not in front of me. I can't see you."

"The fire will warm me."

"It'll warm you faster if you're not drenched, and I don't intend to stay in sodden clothes. You'll catch your death and I won't have that on my conscience."

"I'm not your responsibility."

She sneezed, sniffled. Blast her!

He crouched beside her. "Grace, don't be so stubborn. You're safe with me."

She was staring at the fire, refusing to look at him.

"I've seen plenty of women."

"Is that supposed to make me feel better?" she asked, and he could not mistake the pique in her voice or the way it made him want to smile.

"I'm not boasting, but merely pointing out that I'm skilled enough around women's clothing that we can do this without me seeing you at all."

He moved around behind her and began to work on the fastenings. She wiggled her shoulders. "No!"

She started to get up, and he wrapped his hand around her arm, bringing her back down. "You're pale, you have chill bumps that I can see, and your skin is like ice. Perhaps I'm overprotective, but by God, I'll not have you ill on my watch."

She studied him for a moment. He thought she might argue further. Instead, she nodded and presented her back to him. He quickly unfastened her dress and slipped the shoulders down her arms. He should have stopped there. He knew he should stop there. Instead he rubbed his palms briskly up and down her arms.

"How can you be so warm?" she asked.

"I have more meat on me." He moved away, stood, and lifted the blanket until it hid her from view. "Come along now. Discard the clothing."

He could hear her moving about, and fought like the devil not to imagine the bodice skimming down her torso, past her hips, her thighs—

The blanket was snatched from his fingers and she draped it around herself.

"There is little point to removing your wet clothes if you're going to get the blanket equally soaked." He knelt so he could glare at her on eye level, but she once again averted her gaze. He reached for the ribbons of her chemise. She shoved his hand away and it accidentally brushed over her breast.

Something wasn't right. It was too soft, too malleable.

"Grace—"

"Please leave me alone."

He should do as she asked. He'd never forced himself on a woman, but something was going on here. He retrieved the whiskey from the table where he'd left it earlier. "Here, drink this."

She upended the bottle as though her life depended on it. The blanket slid down, pooled at her hips. He could see the beginning of a scar, or perhaps it was the end. It peeked out above the lace of her chemise. To the side something else peeked out.

With his forefinger and thumb, he took hold of the rumpled linen. She grabbed his wrist. Holding her gaze, he saw the discomfort in hers. He was so accustomed to her confidence and boldness. He almost released his hold but realized that he had to know the truth.

She licked her lips, swallowed, gave the barest of nods. Slowly, ever so slowly, he pulled out the long strip of linen. Without it, her chemise appeared painfully empty on the left side.

Calmly, not wanting to startle her, taking the same sort of care that he took with a nervous filly, he tugged on the ribbon of her chemise.

"Lovingdon—"

"Shh." Cautiously, he untied the ribbon, then the next, and the next, the material parting. With great consideration, barely breathing, he moved aside the cloth to partially reveal one side, to reveal the thick rigid scars where once a left breast had been.

"Now you know why it is so important that he love me, for me."

# Chapter 14

Grace had always expected to feel shame at this first moment when a man gazed upon her chest, but she saw no revulsion cross Lovingdon's features.

"What happened?" His voice was rough, scratchy.

"A malignancy."

He leapt to his feet as though she had lit a fire beneath his backside. He tore at his waistcoat, popping off buttons in his frenzy to get it off. His cravat came next. He slung it across the room. He unbuttoned his shirt, stopped and glowered at her. "Are you going to die?"

She heard the devastation, the pain so deep that she wanted to weep. She shook her head. "No, I shouldn't think so. If I weren't so slender, if I were not as flat as a plank of wood, I might not have noticed the growth for years, but I did notice and it was enlarging, so Dr. Graves said the best thing was to remove everything that might have a chance of becoming infected. He examines me every few months to make sure nothing else is amiss. You know how good he is."

Lovingdon glared at her. "Can he guarantee that you're all right, that you won't die?"

"We all die." Thunder sounded, the timing ominous, as though to punctuate her words. "You could walk outside and be struck by lightning. There are no guarantees. But Graves thinks it unlikely that I'll have to deal with it again."

Lovingdon strode around the room. She was surprised that he didn't go out into the rain.

"How could I not know that this happened to you?"

"The timing of it, I suppose." She licked her lips. "It was a little over two years ago. You were in the depths of grief and despair. And it's not as though we took out an advert. Mother and I went to the country, said we were taking a long holiday. I don't think anyone thought anything of it. She and I have always been close. Our going away together wasn't unusual. As I said by the river, it's not something that's shouted about. If people discuss it at all, it's in whispers."

She didn't know why she didn't cover herself up. Only she, Graves, her mother, and Felicity had ever seen her scars. That Lovingdon wasn't casting up his accounts gave her hope that perhaps another man might not be repelled either. He dropped down in front of her.

"I'm so sorry, Grace." He raised a hand, lowered it, lifted his gaze to hers. "I feel as though I should have done something."

"You're doing something now. Assisting me in finding love. I know if a man asks for my hand that I shall have to tell him, but I don't know exactly when I should, or how. I must know that he loves me. I must trust him implicitly. I don't want all of London to know. This is personal, private. And then I think, 'What should it matter?' Lady Sybil told me that Fitzsimmons only ever lifts the hem of her nightdress, that he never unbuttons it, never seems to care much about anything other than what's between her legs. So perhaps my husband would never know. If he's only interested in the lower portions—"

"If he loves you, Grace, he'll want to see all of you."

The problem with his honesty was that he told her things she'd rather not know. "I feared as much."

"You shouldn't fear it, because if he loves you, it won't matter."

"How can it not?"

"It won't." Gently, like a summer breeze wafting over a lake, he parted the material farther. "Is it painful?"

"Not very." She shook her head slightly. "Sometimes it pulls. It looks much worse than it is. Looks ghastly, actually."

"No...no." He lowered his gaze, then slowly began lowering his head. "If he loves you, he'll find every aspect of you beautiful."

But how could he? She didn't utter the words, fearful that he would think she was fishing for compliments. She didn't like being needy or unsure. She had always known her own mind. It was the minds of men that she didn't quite understand. Every time she thought she had them figured out, they surprised her.

Just as Lovingdon surprised the hell out of her now. He laid his lips against the ropy scars. She couldn't feel his touch, but she could see it, the light pressing that didn't smash his mouth. The gentleness of it, the reverence.

His mouth glided up until she felt the heat of it on her collarbone, then her neck. Then his lips were against hers, sipping at the corners. One of his hands came to the back of her head, holding her in place before his mouth smashed hers, his tongue urging her to part her lips, which she did gladly.

With a groan, he delved swiftly and deeply. She forgot about her scars, her imperfections, her fears of disappointing. All she knew was the hunger of his kiss, the urgency of their mating mouths.

He dragged his lips along the sensitive flesh just under her chin, his tongue tasting until he reached the shell of her ear. "Little Rose," he rasped, "never doubt that you're beautiful. I'm going to show you how beautiful."

With hardly any effort at all he lifted her into his arms and carried her to the bed. He laid her down gently. There was more darkness than light here, shadows providing a welcoming cover from his gaze. He walked away, and when he returned brought the glow of the lamp with him and set it on the table beside the bed.

"I'm not going to let you hide from me," he said.

"Lady Sybil says it's done in the dark."

"Lady Sybil is married to a buffoon."

Sitting on the edge of the bed, he took his fingers on a journey through her hair, discovering and removing the pins that had refused to take flight as she'd run to the cottage. He fanned out the strands. They were relatively dry thanks to the protection of his jacket.

Folding his hands around her neck, he eased them down to her shoulders, then slid them down her arms, taking her chemise with them. She considered protesting, and yet when she saw his concentration, words failed her and she couldn't look away.

She saw anger at what she'd suffered; she saw sorrow, but she also saw wonder. The wonder stole her voice, her breath, her worries. During all the times when she envisioned revealing herself to a man, not once had she ever imagined that he would gaze on her with wonder reflected in his eyes.

When all her undergarments were gone, he retrieved the quilt he'd taken to the fireplace earlier and very gently dried whatever raindrops remained on her skin.

"I won't break, you know," she said.

His eyes met hers. "You are like blown glass, to be appreciated for your beauty, touched with care. Admired. So fair." He shifted his gaze down. "Except where you're red."

"It's not right for you to be able to look at all of me when I can see so little of you."

"You tempt me, Little Rose. If I remove my clothes, you won't leave here a virgin."

"I don't want to." Sitting up, she began unfastening the buttons on his shirt. "You tempt me as well."

When the last button was undone, he reached up and over his shoulders, grabbed the back of his shirt and pulled it over his head to unveil the smattering of hair on his chest and the sculpted muscles that revealed his life of debauchery included some sort of strenuous activities.

He was perfection, and he desired her.

She knew because she could see the bulge straining against his britches. His arousal.

Leaning in, he took her mouth tenderly, sweetly, exploring at his leisure as though he had never explored it before, as though the shape of it, the taste of it, were all new discoveries to be savored. It was only a kiss and yet it quite undid her.

He guided her back down to the pillows, then

stood, and began giving the buttons of his trousers their freedom. One, two—

Her gaze shot up to his eyes, the smoldering depths, watching her as she watched him. By the time she dropped her gaze, his task was done, his clothes on the floor—

"Amazing how your body reacts when there is a woman in a bed—"

"It doesn't react this way for every woman I see in a bed. It's actually quite particular."

Stretching out beside her, he threaded his fingers through her hair. She heard thunder, or perhaps it was her own heart beating. The rain pounded the roof, creating a more intimate cocoon. When she had envisioned her first time with a man, she had not imagined this feeling of being whole and complete. He gazed down on her as though there were no imperfections, no scars. Through his eyes she felt remarkably lovely, not at all self-conscious, not at all wanting to cover up and hide.

As his mouth once again blanketed hers, he made her want to be bold, allowed her to be her true self, someone who had never retreated from adventure. What an adventure he was taking her on.

His mouth and hands explored while hers did the same. His skin was hot and slick to the touch, salty to the taste. His muscles coiled and undulated beneath her palms. He guided and encouraged her to touch him intimately, and the heat of him increased her fervor. They were like two flames, a conflagration dancing and writhing and generating more heat, building a bolder fire that ignited passion. She thought she might come away from this as little more than a cinder—

And then she realized that she would come away from this as beautiful hand-blown glass, shaped and molded with care, with precision, with love. For surely only someone who loved her would devote so much attention to every aspect of her. He left no part of her unkissed, no part uncaressed.

He suckled her solitary breast and she nearly bucked off the bed with the pleasure of it. She threaded her fingers through his hair, held him there while his tongue lathed over the tiny pearl.

Then he skimmed his mouth over to the other side, bringing the sensations with him. They were phantom sensations, she thought, because he could only run his tongue over scars, but having a sense of what she should have felt, she felt it now.

Even if it was only in her mind, she didn't care, as he was creating other feelings elsewhere, across her hips, between her thighs, stroking, stroking, urging—

Pleasure escalated. He moved between her legs, wedging himself at her apex. She could feel him nudging at her entry. She skimmed her fingers over his damp chest, his breaths coming short and hard, his heart beating out a steady tattoo. Holding her gaze, he began inching himself in.

"Tell me if it hurts," he commanded.

As though she would, as though she would ruin this moment of their joining with complaints or whimpers. She'd endured much worse. He was slow, but determined, stretching her.

"You're so damned hot," he growled.

Fire, she thought, we're fire, shaping something beautiful and wonderful here.

He sighed with deep satisfaction. Her body curled and tightened around him. Yes, this was love, this melding that made it impossible to tell where she ended and he began.

He slid out, slipped back in. Short thrusts, hard thrusts, teasing ones, determined ones. All the while he caressed and kissed and whispered that she was beautiful, perfect, enticing.

Enticing. She liked it the best, because it meant he wanted her, wanted to be part of her. His tempo gained momentum, the deep thrusts dominated. Liquid sensations began swirling through her. Heating, cooling, taking shape into something that could not be denied.

She dug her fingers into his shoulders, scraped them down his back, curled them into his firm buttocks. They moved in unison as one.

Her sighs turned to cries as the pleasure intensified. Fire consumed her as the sensations exploded, ripping through her and then bringing her back, gasping, stunned, and utterly replete.

Above her, Lovingdon grunted, withdrew, and spilled his hot seed on her thigh. Breathing heavily, he bowed his head. She combed her fingers into his damp hair.

She never wanted to stop touching him, she never wanted them to leave this bed.

After cleaning her and himself up, Lovingdon lay on his side and trailed a finger along a scar, then circled it around her breast. He thought he'd always been there for her, but when she had needed him most, he was secluded in mourning, devastated, thinking that no one else had pain as great as his.

For the past two years he had convinced himself that he alone suffered. He had wrapped himself in a shroud of anguish. Breaking out of the tight cocoon was not turning him into something beautiful now, but perhaps it was making him stronger. Not that he would have ever willingly traded Juliette and Margaret for strength. He would have never let them go, but sometimes life didn't come with choices.

If Grace never found a man who loved her, who would appreciate her, he had wanted her to experience lovemaking at its finest. Two years of debauchery had taught him a great deal, and he'd wanted to share the lessons with her. At least that's what he told himself. In truth, thought and reasoning played no part in what had just transpired.

"I think Fitzsimmons is doing it wrong," she said quietly.

He peered into her eyes. "When you're in a man's bed, it's bad form to mention another man."

She smiled, the mischievous smile that always enthralled him. "I don't intend to make a habit of visiting different men's beds. Only my husband's. It's only that I think Sybil would have told me if she had experienced anything close to resembling what just transpired between us."

"Not all men care about the lady in their bed to such an extent."

"You care about me?"

"I do, very much, yes."

She studied him as though he hadn't said quite enough. He hoped his next words offered reassurance. "The storm has passed. It'll be light soon. We should get back to the manor so I can tidy up before asking your father for your hand in marriage."

She blinked, opened her mouth, closed it, furrowed her brow. "I beg your pardon?"

"I've compromised you, Grace. You can't possibly think that I'm going to shirk my responsibility here."

She quickly moved away from him, sat up, grabbed the quilt and covered herself from chin to toe. "Your responsibility?"

"Yes."

"Do you love me?"

"In a manner of speaking."

The fire in her blue eyes would melt glass. "A manner of speaking. Do give details on the manner, here."

"You know very well, as we've discussed it, I have limits regarding what I will allow myself to feel, especially in regard to—" He dropped his gaze to her chest.

"What does that look mean?"

He did not want to travel there. He did not. "You have no guarantee that the malignancy won't return. You can't guarantee that you'll survive another bout of it." He came up off the bed in a blind rage that took him a moment to get under control. The thought of her dying—he cared for her, yes. Losing her would be painful, but he would not allow her to own his heart and soul. If the disease came upon her again, he wouldn't be able to save her, just as he'd been unable to save Juliette. To lose Grace under those circumstances would send him straight to Bedlam.

He faced her. "You will be happy. And this between us"—he moved his hand back and forth between them—"it's good. We can make this work without the necessity of falling in love."

Staring at him, she shook her head. "I can't make it work without falling in love. I won't. I deserve a man who cares if I die."

"I'll care. Of course I'll care. I just won't—"

"As much as you did when Juliette died."

"I can't go through that pain again. I won't."

"Go to the devil, Lovingdon." She came off the bed in a majestic sweep of bedclothes wrapped around her. She stood before him, her shoulders back, her chin level, a queen sorely disappointed in her subject. "Get dressed and get out. I'll see myself to the manor without you in tow when I'm good and ready."

"I'm not allowing you to traipse about unprotected."

"Good God, Lovingdon, I've traipsed about these grounds unprotected most of my life. I don't want you about. And don't you dare ask my father for my hand. I shan't marry you."

"You won't have a choice when I tell him what transpired here."

"You won't tell him." She turned her back on him.

He wanted to go to her, comfort her, but she was right. She deserved a man willing to give her his heart. He wasn't that man. He'd known all along he wasn't that man. It didn't stop him from admiring her, desiring her. But he would not force marriage on her.

In silence, he snatched up his clothes and hastily drew them on, barely bothering with the buttons on his shirt. With his waistcoat balled in his fist, he headed for the door. "I've left my jacket so you can at least have some protection from the early morning chill."

He opened the door.

"It was you," she called out softly. "You I fell in love with once. You who broke my heart at such a tender age. And now you've gone and done it again."

And with those simple words she eviscerated him.

She didn't know how long she sat in the cottage. Without looking back, he'd slammed the door in his wake. She didn't know why she'd confessed what she had.

Well, she certainly wasn't going to sit here all night feeling sorry for herself. She thought about trying to sketch. She had been working on a story told through pictures of a bunny who had lost an ear and feared no other rabbit would ever love him, because he was scarred and different. She thought she would have it published as a children's book, but at the moment she didn't care about the damn bunny.

She hurt too much to care about anything.

Why had she thought he would open his heart to her, that he would think for a single moment that he could have with her what he'd had with Juliette?

But at least for a few moments with him she'd felt beautiful again.

Somewhere a man existed who would love her, appreciate her, and find her beautiful. But her father had it right. She hadn't found love where she'd been searching for it. Perhaps the key was to stop searching.

She thought of the butterflies she'd chased as a girl, and how she never caught a single one. One afternoon she wanted to hold one so desperately that she'd run herself ragged, until she finally collapsed on the cool grass, breathing heavily, too exhausted to move. She'd felt it. The tiniest touch on the back of her hand. When she looked, she'd seen the orange and black wings, opening and closing in delicate rhythm. A butterfly was taking its rest near her thumb. She could have captured it with ease.

Instead she let it go. She had to do the same with Lovingdon. He'd had his love, short-lived but intense. He was content to live out the remainder of his life with the memory of it. Just as she had been with her singular butterfly. Some experiences were not meant to be repeated.

She'd been a fool for thinking otherwise. She would tell him so when next their paths crossed. She valued his friendship. It was enough. She didn't require more.

With a sigh, Grace stepped outside. The moon was hidden behind dark clouds and the rain had begun to fall again. She should delay, she thought, but was anxious to be home. Besides, she knew the path well.

She had taken but two steps when soft linen covered her mouth. Startled, she inhaled deeply, breathed in a familiar sweet fragrance that she associated with fear, with pain, with loss. Dr. Graves had used it as he prepared her for surgery.

She started to fight, tried to fight, but the drug was already taking effect. Her limbs were too heavy to move. Her knees began to buckle. She was aware of someone lifting her.

And then she was aware of nothing at all.

# Chapter 15

Lovingdon stood at a window in the library gazing out on the thrashing rain. No outdoor activities today unless it involved building an ark.

"You wanted a word," Greystone reminded him.

Yes, he did. When Lovingdon entered the breakfast room it was filled to the gills, and for the first time ever he seriously studied every man there. Which one was right for Grace? Which one would truly love her as she deserved to be loved? Which would treat her better than he would?

Then his gaze fell on Grace's father and he'd known he needed to speak with the duke. He was allowing his daughter to run wild. Did he know she smoked a cheroot, drank rum, and slipped out of her room at all hours of the night? Did he know she cheated at cards? There were a thousand things about Grace that he wished to discuss with Greystone.

Now, he turned to face the man, who was casually leaning back in his chair. "I wish to ask for your blessing in marrying your daughter."

He was as surprised by the words as Greystone appeared to be. He didn't love Grace, refused to love her in the way a man loved a woman who encompassed the whole of his life, but he knew he could make her happy. And he'd compromised her, unforgivably.

He would convince her, one way or the other, that marriage to him was in her best interest. He would find a way to mend the heart he had broken.

Greystone tapped his finger on the arm of his chair. "I didn't even realize you were courting her."

"I suspect there are a good many things about your daughter of which you are unaware."

"Not as many as you might think. What do you offer her?"

Lovingdon was taken aback by the question. "You know me, you know my family well. You know what I offer. Impeccable lineage, title, wealth, lands—her dowry is not a consideration."

"What is?"

"I wasn't expecting a bloody inquisition."

Greystone stood. "So I gathered."

"She'll be happy. Of that I can promise you."

"I like you, Lovingdon, always have, but I can't give you my blessing on this matter."

"Why the hell not?"

"I think you know the answer to that."

The words were in his eyes, if not on his tongue. *Because you don't love her, you'll never love her as you did Juliette.*

The last thing Lovingdon had expected was a refusal. He could argue, he could insist, but he saw no point in it. "Then I bid you a good day."

With as much dignity as he could muster, he strode from the room. It shouldn't have mattered that his request had been denied. He preferred it, actually. He didn't have to feel guilty washing his hands of the entire matter. He didn't want a wife, especially one who might depart this earth before him. He couldn't go through that again. He had merely asked out of obligation.

But Lovingdon knew it was a poor reason indeed, and respected Greystone more for knowing it.

He needed to return to London and he wanted to let Grace know before he left. This assisting her in finding love was a colossal failure. In the process it also managed to ruin their friendship.

*Damn it all to hell anyway.*

He'd been a guest here often enough in his youth that he was familiar with the family quarters, and he made his way to her bedchamber with no difficulty, but stood outside her door, trying to frame the words. He didn't want to hurt her any more than he already had, but neither could he pretend that all was right. She was the actress of their little group.

He considered simply walking in. After all, he had seen her in all her naked glory. There were no surprises left. But still there were privacy and boundaries. Just because she'd quivered in his arms didn't mean she'd be quivering with anticipation if he walked in. As a matter of fact, he rather suspected she might throw something at him.

He rapped lightly. And waited.

He looked up the hallway and down it. He didn't want to be caught here. If her father wasn't going to give his blessing, Lovingdon didn't want her reputation ruined. He rapped again. Pressed his ear to the door. No sound. She was sleeping.

He could come back later, but that would mean that he'd have to stay longer, possibly into the afternoon, and he preferred to be away as soon as possible. He released the latch, pushed open the door. It squeaked. He cringed.

Didn't the servants know to keep the hinges oiled?

He stepped into the room. The bed was made. Grace was obviously awake. He should have checked in the breakfast dining room first. He considered waiting here, but who knew how long she would be? Some gent might snag her and proceed to bore her to pieces in the parlor.

Returning to the hallway, he nearly smacked into her lady's maid. He straightened his spine and glared down at her as though it was perfectly fine for him to be exiting her mistress's bedchamber. "I'm in search of Lady Grace. Have you any notion where I might find her?"

"No, Your Grace. She didn't return to her rooms last night, so I assumed she was at her small cottage—although she doesn't usually go when company is about. When I saw the door ajar, I thought she was finally home. I'm thinking that I should probably alert His Grace to her absence."

"No need for that. I know where she is."

She obviously stayed in her cottage to sulk, although she'd never been one to sulk. Perhaps she just needed some guaranteed time alone.

Lovingdon returned to his room for a coat and hat, then struck out in the rain to retrieve her. He didn't know what he was going to say to her. As long as he'd known her, he never had any trouble at all speaking his mind, speaking to her. Even last night, when the sight of her scars, the knowledge of what she'd endured, should have left his tongue unable to move, he'd known what to say. He hadn't hesitated, hadn't thought through the words.

For the first time in two years he'd spoken without any thought, simply said what he'd needed to say, what he wanted her to hear. The stubborn, courageous, lovely girl she'd been had grown into a remarkable woman. She could have gone into seclusion, she could have hovered in corners. She could have stared out windows and wished upon stars for a different life. Instead she attended balls and soirees. She danced and laughed. She lived, God bless her. She lived.

While he was the one who had gone into seclusion. Not noticeably, of course. But he had withdrawn from life—until she brought him back into hers.

Juliette would have been disappointed in him, but no more so than he was in himself.

He strode past the gazebo, where everything had shifted and changed. If only he hadn't followed her—

If only she'd asked him sooner.

The rain pelted him, and he barely noticed as he approached the cottage. He still wasn't exactly certain what he would say to her. But he knew that when he laid eyes on her again, the right words would fall from his lips.

He arrived at the door, considered knocking, but in the end simply opened it and strode in.

Only to find it empty.

Unease skittered along his spine. If she wasn't at the manor, if she wasn't here, then where the deuce was she?

Rushing to the doorway, he glanced quickly around outside. Perhaps she just took a different path to the manor and they'd been as two ships passing in the night. That was probably it. She was no doubt there now, having a bath, or stretching out to sleep, or enjoying breakfast. Closing the door behind him, he started off—

Halted in his tracks.

Something caught his eye, in the mud, being battered by the rain. As he neared, he realized it was a bit of linen. The stuffing from her chemise? No, not nearly large enough.

Bending down, he picked it up and was assaulted by a sweet aroma that made him grow dizzy. Chloroform?

Bloody damned hell!

Grace was drifting out of slumber, languishing in a vague area where dreams were gossamer mists that hadn't yet faded. Rain pounded a roof, leather cooled her cheek, and a rocking motion threatened to ruin her appetite for breakfast. Her head was heavy. Her entire body was heavy, just as it had been after her surgery. Her mouth felt as though it had been stuffed with cotton. She couldn't swallow without discomfort.

"Would you like some water?"

Opening her eyes fully, she realized she was traveling in a coach. A man sat opposite her. "Vexley?" she croaked.

"Here." He extended a silver flask toward her.

She pushed herself into a sitting position. Dizziness assailed her. She took a moment to let it pass, before glaring at him. "What's going on here?"

"We're off to be married."

She stared at him. "I beg your pardon?"

"I have the special license here." He patted the left side of his chest. "We'll be at my estate by nightfall. When we reach the village, we'll make a quick stop by the church. The vicar owes me a favor. We'll exchange our vows, then off to my manor for our wedding night. We'll return to your father's estate on the morrow with the good news that you are now the Countess of Vexley."

She truly felt ill now, terribly, frightfully ill. Glancing out the coach window, all she could see was countryside and rain and dark clouds. "You can't possibly think that I'm going to exchange vows, that I will sign the registry—"

"Doesn't matter if you do or not. As I said, the vicar owes me a favor. He'll make certain all looks in order, even if it's not. With this little escapade and a night in my manor, you'll be ruined and have no choice except to accept me, and all this fluttering about from gentleman to gentleman that you've been doing will come to an end."

He was so damned smug, so haughty, so arrogant.

"I'm already ruined."

He narrowed his eyes at her, and she wondered why she'd never noticed before how terribly beady they looked when fully open. "Who?"

She met his gaze head on. She would not be ashamed of what had happened between her and Lovingdon. "It doesn't matter. It's done. Very recently, in fact. Should I become with child rather quickly, you'll never know whether it's yours or his."

"Lovingdon. Why else was he with you in that cottage? But it's of no consequence to me. I need your dowry. Rather desperately. Besides, the land that comes with you? A portion of it borders mine. I'm very keen to have it."

"You're mad if you think my father is going to hand over my dowry to a man who forced me into marriage and then forced himself upon my person."

He smiled, a horrid little ugly showing of teeth. "He loves you too much to see you do without. I'm certain we'll come to terms."

Oh, she doubted it very much but could see there was little point in arguing. If this marriage did take place, she suspected she would be a widow before the week was out. Her father, Drake, possibly Lovingdon, would see to it. They were all too familiar with the darker side of things to allow this travesty to stand.

The carriage suddenly lurched to a stop, tossing them both around. She regained her balance first, flung open the door and tumbled out into an immense amount of muck. She scrambled to her feet, but the mud clung to her skirt, her legs, her arms, weighing her down. If she was free of it, she had no doubt she could have outrun Vexley and climbed a tree to safety, one from which he wouldn't have been able to get her down. Instead, she slugged along, slow and clumsy, falling, shoving herself back up to stagger forward.

She felt a hand close firmly and possessively around her arm. Spun around, she found herself face-to-face with Vexley. Not only Vexley—

But a pistol.

She froze. The air backed up in her lungs.

"I'm most serious, Lady Grace. Don't force me to hurt you."

Then the realization dawned that if he shot her, he wouldn't have his bride. "If you kill me, you won't gain what you want."

"I have no intention of killing you, but merely slowing you down. I have no qualms marrying a woman who will walk with a limp for the remainder of her life." With his fingers biting into her arm, he dragged her back toward the coach, where the driver and footman were working diligently to rock the vehicle out of the mud.

As the rain soaked her, she fought not to feel despair. Surely someone would notice that she wasn't about, but would they notice in time? And how in God's name would they find her?

Haste. Haste was of the essence.

With urgency, Lovingdon galloped his horse alongside Drake's. From time to time the mud slowed them down, but they were determined to catch up with Vexley.

Lovingdon had returned to the manor, explained to Greystone his suspicions that he thought Grace might have been taken. Then they'd done a very discreet but incredibly quick accounting of the men present. Vexley was nowhere to be found. His carriage and driver were gone.

So Lovingdon and Drake had set out. While they

could have asked others to join them, they thought it best to keep those aware of the situation to a small group in order to limit the damage to Grace's reputation. They were fortunate. Even with the rain, they discovered evidence of a carriage recently leaving. The direction of the ruts made sense. Vexley's ancestral estate. How many hours ahead of them was Vexley? How long had Grace been his captive? What might he have done to her during that time?

The rain was a blessing and a curse. It would slow Vexley, but it also slowed them. Not as much, though, Lovingdon was certain. His horse was sure-footed and could lope across grassy ground when the roads were mired, while the coachman would have no choice except to stay on the path and slug through. The rain had to stop sometime, and when it did, Lovindgon would be able to push forward faster. But would he get there in time?

He didn't need much of an imagination to know what Vexley's plans were: Grace's ruination, a way to force her to become his countess. His countess when she deserved to be a duchess.

Lovingdon's heart pounded with the force of the hooves hitting the ground. It raced faster than the horse, and yet there were moments when it was unsuitably calm. He would not let Vexley have her, not for the long haul. If the man forced himself on Grace, he would castrate him, then kill him. He would probably do both anyway, regardless of the man's actions.

He just had to find him.

They rode, rode, rode. Through the rain and as night began to descend. They only stopped to rest their horses when absolutely necessary, and even then they trudged forward, horses in tow. He had to keep moving forward. Forward. Forward.

Dear God. Two years ago he'd stopped moving at all—

And then Grace with her schemes, her dodges, her cheating at cards, had started him moving again, reluctantly, slowly. He was squeaky and rusty, in need of oiling, and she had limbered him up, loosened him up. She had made him glad to get up in the morning, given him a reason to do so.

They were nearing Vexley Hall. In the distance he could make out some light, no doubt the village that resided within its shadow. On the other side of it—

A horse whinnied, screeched. Hearing Drake curse soundly, he glanced back to see that horse and rider had taken a tumble into the mud. He was torn. He needed to carry on, but he knew Grace would never forgive him if Drake was badly injured and he left him there to languish. He drew Beau up short and circled back.

The horse had regained its footing and was standing. Drake was kneeling beside it, examining a foreleg. He looked up as Lovingdon drew his own horse to a halt. "She's gone lame. Carry on. I'll catch up."

Lovingdon hesitated.

"I can't leave her," Drake said. "I'll walk her to the village, get a fresh horse there."

"Are you certain you're all right?"

"I will be once we have Grace back. Off with you."

Lovingdon urged his horse around and sent it back into a hard gallop. He knew the frantic pace was dangerous with the dark and the rain and the mud. But he was so near. It never occurred to him that he wouldn't find her. He just didn't know if he would do so in time to spare her Vexley's touch.

He reached the village but didn't bother to stop to make inquiries. Instead, he loped down the center of the road. Few people were about. He could hear merry-making in a tavern he passed. God, he could use a drink. After he had Grace back, they would all have a drink.

He was almost to the other side of the village when he spied the carriage. It had no markings but was a damned fine carriage for a villager to be driving about. He'd bet his life it belonged to someone of noble birth. It wasn't moving. No, it was quite still, positioned as it was in front of a path that led into a church.

"Weddings are supposed to take place in the morning, but not this early in the morning," Grace said. She wasn't quite sure of the hour but it had to be long past midnight. It had taken the driver and footman more than an hour to get the carriage out of the mud and on its way again. Then they'd gotten stuck three more times, before the driver slowed the horses' pace. She had been cold, damp, and miserable with the mud caking to her clothes. Vexley hadn't offered her his coat, only bits of cheese to eat and water to drink.

But he no longer recited poetry, as when they were on the picnic. He didn't speak to her of his unclaimed heart. After today's misadventures, she doubted he had one.

She supposed she should have been terrified, but she was more annoyed than anything else.

In long strides, his footsteps echoing off the rafters, Vexley paced in front of the altar. Only moments earlier he'd sent his driver to fetch the vicar.

"Vexley, rethink this mad scheme of yours," she told him.

"It's not a mad scheme. Do you know how many of my ancestors stole their brides? It's tradition in my family."

She thought perhaps he was striving to make light of his actions, but she saw no humor in it. Neither would her father. For a short while last night she had thought Lovingdon would stand as her champion, but he remained true to his word. He'd not love again.

He could recount every act of a man in love, but he had no heart to give. She envied Juliette to have been loved so much, to have the ability to hold onto Lovingdon's heart, even beyond the grave. Theirs was the sort of love she longed for, not this macabre travesty perpetuated by Vexley.

She glanced around surreptitiously. She had to

find a means of escape. She didn't think asking for
sanction would work, not if the vicar owed this man.
The pistol was the problem, for even now Vexley had
it in his coat pocket. He could retrieve it quickly and
easily enough if she tried to run. He'd offered up a
demonstration when they first arrived.

How could she have been so blind as to consider
him a viable suitor? Who would have thought there
was such a thing as a gentleman being too charming?

He wasn't at all like Lovingdon, who was not
overly charming. He argued with her, got put out
with her. He didn't seek to win her over with flowery
words, but he'd managed to do it with honest ones.
He was good and noble. As angry as she'd been at
his reasons for marrying her, she couldn't deny that
she admired his willingness to go into an arrange-
ment that would bring him nothing but misery, to
make amends for the fact that he'd compromised
her. If only she could be content with that: duty instead of love.

If she had not run him off, she might not be here
now.

Although it was equally likely that Vexley might
have done him harm. She had long ago ceased to
look back and wonder what if…

She heard footsteps echoing in the vestry and her
heart began to race. The vicar.

Vexley grabbed her arm and pulled her to her
feet. "Do as you're told and it'll all go very quickly."

"I do not know how to be any clearer, but I have no intention whatsoever of marrying you."

"You will, that I don't beat you. Make a fuss here and you will be black and blue for a week."

She needed to catch him off guard. Lowering her gaze, she tried to look as docile as possible. "Yes, my lord."

"Now where's that blasted vicar?"

The footsteps increased in tempo, moving quickly, growing louder, nearer. Vexley glanced back over his shoulder. Grace shot her fist straight up, aiming for his chin—

But he flung her aside before she could make direct contact. She merely grazed him as she stumbled and landed hard on the floor. She heard an animalistic growl, and a huge beast was flying through the air. It slammed into Vexley and took him down.

Not a beast. Lovingdon.

She watched as the two men struggled and rolled. Fists flew. Grunts echoed. She rushed to the altar and lifted a gold candlestick. The heft of it would do nicely. Turning back around, she saw that Lovingdon had gained the upper hand. He was on top, straddling Vexley.

Thunder boomed.

*The gun. Oh, dear God, the gun.*

Both men went still. Her ears rang. Candlestick poised, she approached cautiously. "Lovingdon?"

He rose slowly and delivered two quick punches to Vexley's nose. He struggled to stand. As he revealed his foe, she saw the blood on Vexley's chest. It was a horrid sight, but she felt no sympathy. Relief swamped her, and the candlestick clattered at her feet. She rushed to Lovingdon and threw her arms around him. He grunted.

"You're all right," she sobbed, tears welling in her eyes. "You're all right. I was so afraid—"

"I wouldn't have…let him…hurt you."

"I wasn't afraid for me, you silly man. I thought he'd hurt you."

He wrapped his arms around her. "You're safe."

"You saved me."

"I'm not a dragon slayer, Little Rose. I'm only a man."

She felt thick and warm liquid easing through her clothing. Vexley's blood. But why was it still so warm? Why was there so much of it on Lovingdon?

Pulling back, she saw the red blossoming over his shirt. "Oh, my dear God."

He gave her a sweet, sad smile as his fingers barely grazed her cheek. She could see the pain in his eyes. He dropped to all fours.

"Lovingdon!"

He slid the rest of the way to the floor. She fell to her knees, placed his head on her lap, and pressed a hand where the blood flowed. And then she screamed at the top of her lungs, "Help! Dear God, someone help!"

## Chapter 16

Grace sat in a chair beside the bed where Lovingdon lay as still as death. They were into the second night since his encounter with Vexley. After collapsing onto the floor, he'd not awoken. From time to time he mumbled incoherently. She wiped his fevered brow, held his clammy hand. It all seemed so futile.

Thank God for Drake. He'd found them at the church, and with the aid of the vicar and Vexley's driver, carried Lovingdon to an inn. He'd roused a constable to place Vexley in gaol until it was decided what to do with him, then secured a rested horse and fairly flew back to Mabry Manor to retrieve Dr. Graves.

Drake hadn't wanted to risk Lovingdon in a bouncing carriage over rutted and mud-slogged roads. He hadn't trusted the local physician, whom he'd thought in all likelihood was another of Vexley's men. He stayed only long enough to see the bleeding stanched and then left Grace in charge. She had thrown her father's name around to give weight to her words, and while many may not have heard of the Duke of Greystone, enough had that she was listened to. Or perhaps it was simply that she wouldn't tolerate not being obeyed.

Lovingdon had lost a good deal of blood before Graves took the scalpel to him to do what he could to repair the damage done. But she could tell by the expression on the physician's face that he didn't hold out much hope for Lovingdon returning to them as strong and bold as he'd been before the bullet struck him down.

Her family and Lovingdon's had taken over the inn. It was as quiet and somber as a church, and while people offered to relieve her, she wouldn't leave him, wouldn't give up these last minutes to be with him.

She wanted to hear his voice, just once more, to see his smile. She wanted to gaze into his eyes and know that he recognized her. She wanted to thank him for showing her that she could be beautiful, even with imperfections.

However had he borne it when Juliette was dying? And precious Margaret?

She understood now—with resounding clarity she wished she didn't possess—why he had broken. Her own heart felt as though it had turned to glass and at any moment would shatter beyond all recognition.

Somewhere a clock struck two. She was alone with this man whom she loved more than life. She wanted to beg, plead, cajole him into fighting—but his pain was so much more than physical. She understood that clearly now.

She pressed her lips to the back of his hand, a hand that had brought her pleasure and comfort and now brought her strength.

"What a silly chit I was. I thought love only mattered if I were loved in return, but I have learned that it is enough to love, and that one must love enough to care more for the other's happiness. I want nothing more than for you to be joyful and unburdened. So let go, my darling, go to Juliette. I know she awaits. Let go."

*Let go. Juliette awaits.*

Lovingdon was vaguely aware of the mantra urging him to let go, to release his hold on this aching body.

Yes, he needed to let go. He understood that now as he floated in oblivion. It was time, time to let go.

With a clarity born of deep memories, he envisioned Juliette as he'd loved her best, with her pale hair floating around her shoulders like gossamer moonbeams, of her blue eyes dancing with devilment. Her smile that welcomed and warmed.

And Margaret. Almost a mirrored reflection.

He loved them so damned much. But for the first time it didn't hurt to think of them. A kaleidoscope of memories washed through him, and each one lightened the weight of their passing. Why had he held the recollections at bay? Why had he thought they had the power to rip him apart, when in truth they were strong enough to lace him back together? So many wonderful moments. He wanted to hold them close, but they slipped through his fingers. They weren't solid. They were mist.

They didn't hold his hand. They didn't press warm lips to his knuckles. They didn't splash salty tears upon his skin.

Slowly, so very slowly, he cracked open his eyes. The room was dimly lit, but enough light escaped the lamp to cast a halo around Grace. She looked awful...and beautiful. With her eyes closed, she held his hand against her cheek. Her hair was a tangled mess. Her dress looked to be that of a servant. His last conscious memory was of her standing in the church. He vaguely remembered voices circling about him—Drake, Graves, his mother.

And Grace. Always Grace speaking to him.

"It's all right," she whispered now. "You can let go."

"I did."

Her eyes flew open and she stared at him as though he had risen from the dead. Perhaps he had. Dear God, he'd certainly felt dead these past two years. Until this marvelous woman had knocked on his bedchamber door. Until she challenged him and irritated him. Until she'd shown him what it was to want, to desire, to dream of something grand that would last a lifetime. Until she'd revealed profound courage and strength that far exceeded anything he'd ever possessed. She thought she needed someone who truly loved her because she believed herself imperfect, when in truth she was perfection. He'd known her when she was a girl but never truly known her as a woman—not until recently. Now she haunted him and occupied his thoughts.

"I let Juliette and Margaret go." His voice was rough, ragged, sounded strange to his ears.

Tears welled in her eyes. Because she hadn't released his hand, he had only to unfurl his fingers to touch her cheek. Her soft, damp cheek. "God help you, Grace, but I love you. I want to marry you. I need to marry you. I will marry you."

She shook her head. "You're delirious. You don't know what you're saying."

"I'm deliriously in love with you, and I do know what I'm saying." Sliding his hand around, he cupped the back of her neck. "I am too weak to sit up, however, so come lay down beside me."

She gave him some water first before nestling against his uninjured side. "I feared he'd killed you," she said softly, her hand curled on his chest.

"I feared it as well, and all I could think was that I hadn't had enough time with you. I want years with you, so many that we'll lose count."

"I don't know if I can promise you that, Lovingdon. We never know how much time we'll have."

He knew she was thinking of the malignancy, that it could return, that this time it could take her. The thought terrified him, but he wasn't going to hide from it, he wasn't going to deny himself time with her just because of what *might* happen. "Whatever time you have, Grace, whatever time either of us have, I want to spend it with you."

He heard a small sob, felt hot tears hit his skin.

"I thought you wanted a man who loves you," he teased.

Nodding, she lifted herself up on her elbow and skimmed her fingers along his jaw. "I love you. We shall be so happy together. But first we must get you well. I should fetch Dr. Graves so he can examine you."

"In a bit." His eyes began to grow heavy and he pulled her back down to him. "For now, just sleep. Sleep with me and never leave me until I am a crotchety old man."

He thought he heard her promise, but it hardly mattered. He would be grateful for whatever time he had with her. Be it a day, a month, a year. A moment.

He didn't know how long he slept, but when he awoke, light spilled in through the window. Grace was sleeping against his side. His arm was numb and would no doubt hurt like bloody hell when she left him, but like all hurts, it would subside, and she would soon be back in his arms. Tenderly, with his other hand, he brushed aside the strands of hair that partially hid her face. He was quite looking forward to all the mornings he would awaken to her in his bed.

Her nose twitched, she smiled, and slowly opened her eyes. So like her to be optimistic and smile before she saw what the day held.

"Good morning," he rasped.

" 'Morning."

"Not exactly how I envisioned our first morning together."

"You can't flirt with me just yet, not until Dr. Graves has seen you." Leaning up, she brushed a quick kiss across his lips, rolled out of bed, and with a tiny squeak came up short. "Father."

Lovingdon saw him now, standing near the foot of the bed, arms crossed. He didn't appear at all pleased to see that Lovingdon had survived. Or perhaps he merely looked as though he had grand plans for a painful death for the man who had taken his daughter into his bed without benefit of marriage. Even if nothing except innocence had transpired the night before.

Lovingdon struggled to sit up, fell back against the pillows. He supposed an inch was better than none. "I know you refused to give us your blessing when I asked for it, but I intend to marry your daughter with or without it."

Grace jerked her head around. "You asked for his blessing?"

He nodded. "The morning after…the night that we argued."

She looked at her father. "And you didn't give it?"

"I didn't give any of them my blessing."

Grace blinked, stared. "Any of them?"

Greystone looked at the ceiling. "Hmm. Yes. I think there were twenty-two, twenty-three, who asked for your hand in marriage."

"You denied them all?" Grace asked.

The duke looked unabashed. "You wanted love, sweetheart. I knew to a man who truly loved you that it wouldn't matter whether I gave my blessing." His gaze came back to bear on Lovingdon. "Seems I was right." His brow puckered. "Although I didn't take a man of Vexley's ilk into consideration."

"He asked for my hand in marriage?" Grace asked.

"He cornered me at the ball. He seemed to take my response civilly enough. I misjudged him."

"I think we all did," Lovingdon said, once again feeling his strength draining.

"I'll fetch Graves," Greystone said. He began to walk out.

Grace rushed after him and wound her arms around his neck. "Thank you, Papa. Thank you for your blessing."

"Be happy, sweetheart. Be very happy."

Grace turned, strode back to the bed, sat on its edge and took Lovingdon's hand.

He threaded his fingers through hers. "You will be happy."

She smiled. "I know."

# Chapter 17

As Grace sat at her vanity while Felicity pinned her hair, she gave her gaze freedom to wander over to the red vase filled with her favorite flowers— red roses. They had arrived first thing that morning with a missive.

*Because they're your favorite, you should have them today.*
*—L*

Her heart had done a little somersault. It had been six weeks since the Midsummer Eve's ball. Lovingdon's wound had healed. When he needed fresh air, he had invited her for an open carriage ride through the park. As he'd grown stronger, they walked.

And talked. They spoke of everything. Their up-coming wedding. The trip they would take to Paris. All the exhibits they would see.

While rumors concerning what exactly had trans-pired following her family's country ball were scarce, everyone was well aware that the Earl of Vexley was persona non grata in the eyes of London's most pow-erful families. He'd lost his membership at Dodger's. No woman with any dowry welcomed his courtship and he courted no woman who had no dowry. He was seen about London sporting two black eyes and a broken nose. As he had taken to mumbling when he spoke, many thought he might have a broken jaw.

They were right.

Grace knew the nose was the result of Lovingdon's punches in the church, and she suspected that Vex-ley's broken jaw was the result of Drake spending a little time with him in gaol. As a lord of the realm, Vexley had neatly sidestepped arrest for abduct-ing her and shooting Lovingdon. He'd claimed self-defense on the latter charge, asserting he was con-vinced Lovingdon meant to kill him. Considering the murderous rage she'd seen on Lovingdon's face when he flung himself at Vexley, she suspected the earl's assumption was correct. But with the other families delivering their own messages to Vexley—and no doubt additional blows—she was convinced he'd suf-fered enough. He was ostracized. She doubted he'd ever regain his place in Society, and was rather em-barrassed to admit she'd ever found him charming.

Her attention wandered again to the red roses and the vase that held them. She would have them delivered to her new home so they were waiting for her when she arrived this evening. The other glass pieces were already there, as were most of her belongings.

Today she was going to become a wife, but more than that, she was going to marry a man who loved her, imperfections and all.

When her hair was done, she stepped into her wedding gown of lace and pearls. Felicity gently padded the left side. Grace knew that Lovingdon wouldn't care if it was flat on one side but she liked the symmetry, and on this day, at least, she was vain enough to care.

Carefully, she placed the pearls at her neck, pearls her mother had given her, pearls given to her mother by the man she believed to be her father. Grace sometimes found it difficult to believe the life her mother had led, the life that had brought her here to capture the heart of a duke.

Now she possessed her own duke's heart.

She had no doubts that Lovingdon loved her. Even if he hadn't known her favorite flower, she had no doubts where his affections lay. It was strange to think that she once doubted her ability to gauge love, but Lovingdon had told her to trust her heart, that it would know. By Jove, but he was right about that.

Flowers, listening, gazing into her eyes, touching her, small but important things he had cited as examples—Lovingdon did them all, without thought or artifice. He didn't need her dowry, but apparently what he did need was her love. He possessed it in abundance.

A rap sounded on her door all of three seconds before her mother opened it. She smiled. "Don't you look beautiful?"

"I feel beautiful. He makes me feel beautiful."

"As well he should. Are you ready to be off to St. George's?"

"I've never been more ready for anything in my life."


Lovingdon stood at the front of the church, Drake and Avendale beside him, while he waited for Grace. He didn't want to think of Juliette, and in fact could only vaguely recall the last time he had stood here. He'd been so much younger, more boy than man, filled with promise and promises.

He was more tempered now, not quite so eager or brash. More cautious about life. More determined to never take Grace for granted. His wound was healed. He was as fit as ever. He'd need that fitness tonight. While he had been with Grace since the night he rescued her from Vexley, he'd had very few moments alone with her—a kiss here, another one there, but nothing beyond that. He ached to touch all of her again, to sink his body into hers, to know her again as he'd known her in the little cottage, but not quite the same. There would be a deepness and richness to their lovemaking this time. He'd once thought that he loved nothing more than being nestled between a woman's thighs. But now he knew he loved nothing more than being nestled between hers.

The organ began to play, and he looked up the aisle to see her maid of honor and bridesmaid leading the way: Lady Ophelia and then Minerva. Minnie winked at him and smiled. He wondered how much longer it would be before she was a bride.

The music rose in crescendo, and he turned his attention toward the back of the church. With her arm tucked around her father's, Grace glided up the aisle, taking his breath. The hair she had once despised was the most colorful part about her. She was a vision in white, a gossamer veil covering her face. Such a silly bit of frippery that would prevent him from gazing on her fully. Then she was near enough that he could inhale her lavender and rose scent. The rose was a little heavier, as she held a bouquet of red roses.

Yes, he'd known her favorite flower. He'd always known, from the moment he'd likened her to a red rose and she gave him a gap-toothed grin. He'd known her all of her life, had so many memories of her growing up. It still astounded him to realize that he had managed to overlook her blossoming into the woman he once promised her she'd become.

What a fortunate man he was that her suitors had not seen beyond the dowry, did not recognize the beauty that he did.

When the Duke of Greystone turned her over to

his keeping, Lovingdon felt a tightness in his chest. The responsibility, the fears, the doubts, they were all there. That he would make promises he could not keep. He'd done that once before.

But then Grace smiled at him, and he saw the determination and the understanding in her eyes. She had been forged by her own fires and was stronger because of them. She'd not require that he watch over her, but watch over her he would.

He listened intently as she recited her vows, then he recited his with a sure voice. When he was told he could kiss the bride, he lifted her veil to find her blue eyes fastened on him.

"You never looked away from me," she said in wonder.

"That's because I'm in love with you." He lowered his mouth to hers, wishing hundreds of people weren't about.

Soon, very soon, he would have her all to himself.

# Chapter 18

Grace waltzed with the first man she had ever loved: her father.

While it was not customary for the bride and groom to attend the evening ball usually held on the day of their wedding, she'd wanted one more dance with her father, and her husband had been inclined to indulge her whim. She suspected he would do quite a bit of indulging over the coming years.

While the orchestra played, she and her father were the only ones on the dance floor. He moved with ease, as he had no worries about stumbling into anyone. He was tall and handsome, and she could easily understand why he had swept her mother off her feet. She hoped he still had enough vision remaining that he could see her joyous smile and the sparkle in her eyes. She had never known such happiness. And she knew it was only the beginning.

"You're beautiful," he said, "so much like your mother on the day I married her."

She could not have received a compliment that would have pleased her more, but she knew the truth of it. "Love does that to a person, I hear."

Grinning, he bowed his head in acknowledgment. "It does indeed."

"You should know that as Lovingdon has no need for my dowry, we're going to use the land to establish a sanctuary where women can heal when faced with surgeries about which people will never speak. They can confide in each other, draw comfort and strength from similar tribulations. We're going to place the money that comes with the dowry into a trust fund to cover the expenses of the upkeep and servants."

"I suspect even if Lovingdon were in need of funds, he would still allow you to do with your dowry as you pleased. He loves you, Grace. For him, the dowry was never a consideration."

"I know." She couldn't seem to stop herself from smiling broadly. "I'm the most fortunate woman on earth."

"I may be a bit biased, but I say he's the fortunate one."

Out of the corner of her eye she watched as Lovingdon led her mother into the dance area and swept her across the floor. She and her mother did favor each other. She hoped that she would still have an opportunity to dance with Lovingdon when her hair had faded and lines created by years of joy creased her face.

Lovingdon caught her gaze, and with smooth yet swift movements managed to change dance partners. The Duke and Duchess of Greystone now waltzed together, while Grace waltzed with the man she loved.

"I do believe this is the longest song I've ever heard," he grumbled.

"I asked them to play it twice, without stopping. Thank you for delaying the start of our wedding trip so that I could dance with my father. It means a great deal to me to have a final waltz with him."

"I love you too much to deny you anything, Little Rose."

Her heart somersaulted, once, twice, thrice. She would never tire of him saying the words, and it seemed he wouldn't tire of saying them. He never missed an opportunity to remind her that to him she was everything.

The music drifted into silence. He brought her gloved hand to his lips and held her gaze. "I would very much like to take my wife home now."

His wife. She was his wife. She could hardly fathom it. She nodded. "I should very much like for my husband to take me home."

As they journeyed in his coach through the dark London streets, Lovingdon kissed Grace sweetly, gently, and she knew that he was holding his passion in check. She also knew she had no reason to be nervous, and yet she was, just a bit. While he'd been healing, they'd shared an occasional kiss but nothing more. Tonight they would finally be alone, but more than that they were allowed to be alone. His restraint made her worry that perhaps the hunger of their previous encounters had been a result of doing things they shouldn't. Now they were legal. Now she was his wife, and she couldn't help but wonder if he viewed her differently.

While she viewed him quite the same. She could hardly wait to be in bed with him. She could look at him to her heart's content. Touch him, snuggle against him.

The coach came to a halt. A footman opened the door. Lovingdon leaped out. When she leaned into the doorway, he slid an arm around her, lifted her out, and quickly placed his other arm beneath her legs. She wound her arms around his neck.

"What are you doing?" she asked.

"Carrying my wife."

"But your injury—"

"Is completely healed."

She nestled her head against his shoulder and protested half-heartedly, "Whatever will the servants think?"

"That the Duke of Lovingdon loves his wife to distraction."

He climbed the steps. Another footman opened the door, and Lovingdon carried her into the foyer.

She'd expected him to put her down there, but he continued up the wide sweeping stairs to the upper floor.

He stopped before the door to his bedchamber, and she thought of the long-ago night when she had knocked on it. She couldn't help but wonder if a secretive part of her had wished then that she would end up here.

"You need to take me to my chamber so I can prepare myself for you," she told him.

He grinned broadly at her, and she couldn't help but believe that she had managed to put joy back into his life. "I'll see to preparing you."

"But I bought a lovely lace nightdress to wear for you."

"Why bother putting it on when I'll only tear it off you?"

With a light laugh, she tightened her arms around him. "I feared as my husband, you might get all proper on me."

"Because I only kissed you in the carriage? I've been anticipating this night too much to ruin it on the journey here. I want you in my bed." His eyes darkened. "Open the door."

Leaning over, she released the latch and he kicked the door open. As he carried her in, she was assailed by a faint familiar scent.

"I smell paint," she told him.

"Yes, I had some work done. I was hoping it would all air out by now."

She glanced around. "But your walls are all papered."

"The ceiling isn't."

Glancing up, she released a bubble of laughter. "The nymphs!"

Gone were the voluptuous maidens who had greeted her before. These vixens were slender and long-limbed, every one of them. Their red hair—the exact shade as hers—cascaded wildly around them.

"Oh, Lovingdon." She planted her mouth on his, kissing him deeply and passionately. She was vaguely aware of him walking, then carrying her down to the bed. Without breaking from the kiss, he stretched out beside her, cradled her face with one hand, and began to ravish her mouth with all the enthusiasm she'd hoped for. She didn't know if he could have done anything that would have pleased her more.

But then his hot mouth trailed along her throat, and she realized that everything he gave her was going to please her.

"You like them?" he murmured against her skin.

"Very much so."

Raising himself on an elbow, he began plucking the pins from her hair. "It was rather fascinating to watch as Leo transformed what was there into what I desired."

"In spite of being up in years, he's a remarkable artist." She was familiar with him as he'd done several portraits of her family.

"He is indeed. I would lie here at night in torment because my favorite nymph wasn't in my bed. Now you're here, and I intend to make you very glad that you are."

He rolled out of bed, brought her to her feet, and turned her so she was facing away from him. He went to work on her lacings, his mouth following the path as skin was revealed. His hands made short work of the tasks, and in no time at all, her clothes were piled on the floor. Cupping his palms over her shoulders, he slowly turned her.

It wasn't fair that he remained clothed, but she couldn't quite bring herself to reach for him, not when he was studying her as he was. He lowered his gaze, and she fought not to hide herself from him. Lovingdon loved her. He'd seen her scars. They weren't a surprise.

Finally, he slid his hands down until one cradled her breast and the other flattened against her scars.

"These terrify me, you know," he said quietly, "because of what they could portend."

"Don't think about that."

He lifted his gaze to hers, and she was taken aback to see the thin veil of tears. "I also find them remarkably beautiful because they are part of you, your strength, your courage. I don't know that I'm worthy of you, Grace, because I have neither your strength nor your courage. But I swear that you will never find a man who loves you more than I do."

Leaning in, he pressed his lips to the corner of her

mouth before sliding his mouth over to cover hers. The kiss was deep, hungry. It reached into her soul, caused everything inside her to curl inward like a rose closing up for the night, and then sensations blossomed like petals unfurling.

Tearing his mouth from hers, he trailed it along her throat, her collarbone, nibbling, licking, teasing.

"I want your clothes off," she breathed on a heady rush.

Stepping back, he held out his arms and grinned. "I'm all yours to do with as you please."

Her fingers were not as nimble as his as she worked to remove his clothing, but she took great pleasure in revealing him inch by inch until his clothes were resting on the floor beside hers. She flattened her palm on the puckered scar at his side.

"I always thought scars were hideous things, but I was wrong. You have these because you saved me. You have them because you lived. To me, they are quite beautiful."

Cradling her face between his hands, he tilted up her chin until she held his gaze. "Nothing, no one is as beautiful as you."

His mouth blanketed hers as he carried her down to the bed. She loved the feel of his silken skin against hers.

Once again, he began to take his lips on a sojourn along her throat. "I love the length of your neck," he rasped. "Truth be told, I love the entire length of you." He closed his hand over her breast. "I love the way you fit within my palm." Kneading her flesh gently, he leaned over and kissed her scars.

She loved that he didn't avoid any inch of her, that he relished every part of her. She had so hoped to find a man who would appreciate each aspect of her, and Lovingdon did. Just as she appreciated all of him. She ran her hands over his shoulders, through his dark golden locks. She skimmed her fingers over his jaw.

He moved lower, leaving a hot trail of kisses along her stomach. Lower still. Then he adjusted himself so he was at her feet and she couldn't reach him at all. But when she protested, he simply said, "Patience."

After massaging her feet, he ran his hands up her legs. "I love your long legs. I want them wrapped around me."

She crooked a finger at him. "Then come back up here."

"Not yet."

He kissed his way along her calves, one then the other. He lingered at her knees, before giving attention to the inside of her thighs, again one side then the other. He kissed all of her, every inch, front and back, over and under. She felt very much like the coin he so often rolled over his fingers. Constantly being touched, constantly moving.

But she couldn't simply receive. She had to give as well.

She began following his lead: caressing, tasting, exploring the peaks and the valleys, the flat plains.

He was firm muscle, hot skin. He was perfection, scars and all.

Sensations became all-encompassing. Their breathing grew harsher, their bodies slick. There was no rush and yet there was a hunger that couldn't be denied. Suddenly it wasn't enough to be a tangle of limbs. She needed more and based on the tightness of his jaw, she knew he did as well.

Opening herself to him, she welcomed him, relishing his fullness as he sank into her. She would never have to resist again, never have to curb her passion, her desires.

Nuzzling her neck, he said, "You feel so good. So good."

Bringing her legs up, she wrapped them around him and squeezed. He groaned, before proceeding to ravish her mouth. Every sensation was more intense, every aspect of their coming together was richer.

Because he loves me, she thought. Because I love him.

He possessed her heart, her body, her soul.

He began rocking against her, slowly at first, increasing his tempo as she urged him on with her cries. Scraping her fingers over his back, she wondered how it was possible that so many different sensations could be spiraling through her at the same time. They consumed her, just as he did.

The feel of his mouth on her skin, the caress of his hands, his growls, his arms tightening around her—all served to increase her pleasure as it rose to a fevered pitch.

They moved in unison, touching, kissing. He whispered sweet endearments, and she responded in kind. She wanted to give as much as he gave her, wanted him to take all she had to offer.

Undulating waves of pleasure began coursing through her, taking her ever higher. Beneath her fingers, his sinewy muscles bunched and bulged.

"Come with me, Grace," he urged.

And she did. She followed him into a realm where there was nothing except sensations, where her body sang, her heart soared, and her soul rejoiced.

Breathing heavily, he buried his face in the curve of her neck. They lay there replete and exhausted. She thought she might never move again.

It was long moments before he rose up on his elbows and gazed down on her. With his fingers, he moved aside the damp strands of her hair.

"I hope you didn't find that an empty experience."

She laughed with abandon. "I most certainly did not."

"Good. I didn't either. Now, I have something wicked in mind that involves brandy. Are you up for it?"

She was the one who made use of the brandy, dripping droplets on his chest, then lapping them up like a greedy little cat, purring as she did so, a vibration in her throat that sent pleasure coursing through him.

He wondered why he ever thought he had the strength to deny his love for her. Why he had denied it, why he hadn't embraced it sooner. She made life fun again, laughing and teasing him in bed. She was open to whatever manner he might devise to bring her pleasure. She was willing to learn all she could about bringing pleasure to him.

Not that he needed much. Kissing her, touching her, being buried inside her was enough. Sometimes he thought the heat generated between them would scald them both—but all it did was leave them breathless and anxious to rekindle the fire.

He nudged his wife over until she was straddling his hips. Then he plowed his hands into her hair and brought her mouth down to his. She tasted of brandy mingled with him, yet underneath it all was her own flavoring, so sweet. A man could never have enough of it, could never fill up on it. Her luscious kiss could bring him to his knees if he wasn't already prone.

She wasn't timid, she didn't hold back. Her tongue parried with his on equal terms. He would not compare her to what he'd had before except to acknowledge that she was unlike anything he'd ever known. He hadn't been able to keep up with her when she was younger. He hoped to God he could keep up with her now.

Tearing his mouth from hers, he dragged it along her silken throat. "I love you."

She smiled, dropping her head back to give him easier access. "I adore you."

"Then come to me."

He lifted her up, settled her down, feeling her heat envelop him as she sheathed him. She felt marvelous. So tight, so molten. God, she was like a furnace.

She rocked against him, rode him. Unbashful, unrepentant, unapologetic. She was wildly beautiful when passion caught hold of her. Her blue eyes dazzled, her skin flushed, her hair danced around her like living flames. Red and copper.

His rose. A bud who had unfurled into something rare and precious.

She was his, as he was hers. For whatever time they had. He would relish every moment. He didn't fear losing her. He feared wasting moments that they could have shared. She would no doubt grow tired of his constant attentions.

He cupped her breast. It barely filled his palm, but it was enough. Gently, he kneaded, his thumb circling the pearl of her nipple. She looked down on him. With his free hand, he cradled the back of her neck and brought her down.

"I love you," he rasped again before taking her mouth. He should not be this hungry for her again, and yet he was. She stirred something deep inside him that had never been touched. Odd for a man who had loved as deeply as he had to discover that there were depths yet to be explored.

Breaking off the kiss, she pushed herself up,

pressing her palms to his chest, leveraging herself, riding him with wild abandon. The pleasure built. Her cries echoed around him, her spine arched, and she threw her head back.

"Gorgeous," he rasped, just before his orgasm shook him to the core.

She sprawled across him. He draped his arms over her, holding her near, while his heart settled into a normal rhythm, a rhythm that beat for her.

Grace awoke to an empty bed, something she'd not expected. It was still night. The clock on the mantel indicated that it was a bit past two. Reaching out, she touched the rumpled sheets where Lovingdon had lain. They were cool.

Slipping off the mattress, she donned her nightdress, but didn't bother with the wrap at the foot of the bed. She wanted her husband.

She found him in the library, standing in front of the life-size portrait of his wife. It was no longer above the fireplace but perched in front of it. She didn't resent it, knowing that Juliette and Margaret had shaped him, would always be part of him. But something inside her twisted. She'd hoped that at least on their wedding night it would be only the two of them in this house, in his bed. It seemed they could not escape the memories or the ghost of his previous life.

Lovingdon glanced over his shoulder. He hadn't

bothered to straighten his hair, mussed from her fingers. She wanted to muss it some more. "Grace?"

"I'm sorry. I didn't mean to disturb you."

"Come here, sweetheart."

She hesitated, knowing she was being silly to feel as though she were intruding. This was her home now, their home. She forced herself to move forward. When she was close enough, he took her hand and drew her in against his warm solid body.

"I didn't expect to find you gone from our bed," she said quietly.

"I was just saying good-bye to Juliette."

She looked up at him. His gaze wasn't on the portrait, but on her.

"When I was unconscious, fevered, in pain, I kept hearing this strong, determined voice urging me to let go, of life I think."

She nodded. "I wanted you to be happy."

"But if I let go of life, it meant releasing you, and I could not find the strength to do that. So I let go of Juliette. I am not the man who fell in love with her. Nor am I the man with whom she fell in love." Turning, he cradled her face. "I am the man who fell in love with you. God knows I didn't want to love you. I think losing you would kill me—but the thought of not having some days and nights with you because of my own cowardice…I could not live with myself if I missed out on a single moment with you." He kissed her then, gently, sweetly.

She understood what he was telling her. She was

right for him, perfect for him. He had changed, and she loved the man he was now. She loved everything about him.

When they broke apart, she could have sworn that the smile on the portrait seemed softer, warmer.

"I'm going to put a portrait of her and Margaret in my study, so I don't forget them. The rest are going into storage. You are my life now."

As much as she relished his words, she couldn't be so selfish. "I don't want you to forget them."

"I shan't forget them; I couldn't if I tried, but it is time for me to begin anew." He lifted her into his arms and began carrying her from the room.

"I love you, Lovingdon," she said against his neck.

"When I'm done with you, in an hour or so, you're going to love me just a little bit more."

She laughed. "What have you in mind, my wicked duke?"

He smiled at her, and she realized that she already loved him just a little bit more.

# *Epilogue*

*In my lifetime I loved two women. I cannot say which I loved more because I was a very different man when I loved each of them. And I loved each of them differently.*

*I began adulthood with Juliette.*

*When my life comes to a close, it shall be with Grace at my side.*

*She blessed me with an heir, a spare, and a daughter. While I know that a father should not have favorites, I must admit my ginger-haired little girl wrapped herself around my heart the first time she wound her small hand around my finger. Watching Lavinia grow into* womanhood was one of the most joyous, yet bittersweet aspects of my life. She resembled Margaret not at all, but there were times when I watched her that I could not help but mourn my first daughter.

Being as strong-willed as her mother, Lavinia did not serve as a substitute for Margaret.

Just as Grace did not serve as a replacement for Juliette.

When she was forty, Grace exhibited signs of another malignancy, and Graves did what needed to be done to ensure that she not yet leave me. She had once asked of me, "Is it not better to hold someone for a short span of time rather than not to have held them at all?"

During the agonizing hours while I waited for him to assure me that she would be well, I came to accept with startling clarity the truth of her words. All the moments we'd shared—I would not have given up a single one of them in order to spare myself the sorrow of losing her.

Holding her for a short time was indeed preferable to never having had the pleasure of holding her at all.

But this time the Fates were kind, and they allowed me to hold awhile longer that which I treasured above all else.

We are up into our years now. I see no signs that we shall be parting anytime soon.

*My darling Grace wished only to marry a man who loved her. She met with astonishing success in that regard. For I loved her yesterday, I love her today, and I shall love her for all eternity.*

*Whether or not the Fates are kind.*

* * * * *

## *Author Note*

The beauty in writing fiction is the license I have to change facts so they match what is needed for the story.

Public awareness of breast cancer is a recent phenomenon, which is why only Grace's parents knew of her condition. Unfortunately, the mores of Victorian times made it something of which to be ashamed, but in quiet corners I'm certain Grace encouraged women to pay attention to their bodies.

By this time in history a good many physicians had begun removing lymph nodes when they performed mastectomies. As anyone who has read the Scoundrels of St. James series knows, Dr. William Graves was ahead of his time when it came to caring for his patients. While I didn't go into the details of his treatment for Grace, rest assured he took all measures known at the time to ensure she lived a long life.

The beauty in writing romance fiction is the license I have to ensure my couples always have their happy ending. Lovingdon and Grace are no exception. They lived long, joy-filled lives.

I enjoyed sharing their story with you and look forward to sharing Drake's next.

Warmly,
*Lorraine*

# THE WORLD IS BETTER WITH

# *Romance*

Harlequin has everything from contemporary, passionate and heartwarming to suspenseful and inspirational stories.

Whatever your mood, we have a romance just for you!

Connect with us to find your next great read, special offers and more.

**f** /HarlequinBooks

🐦 @HarlequinBooks

www.HarlequinBlog.com

www.Harlequin.com/Newsletters

**⊕ HARLEQUIN®**

A *Romance* FOR EVERY MOOD™

www.Harlequin.com

SERIESHALOAD2015

# Love the Harlequin book you just read?

Your opinion matters.

Review this book on your favorite book site, review site, blog or your own social media properties and share your opinion with other readers!

**Be sure to connect with us at:**
Harlequin.com/Newsletters
Facebook.com/HarlequinBooks
Twitter.com/HarlequinBooks

HREVIEWS

**HARLEQUIN**®

A *Romance* FOR EVERY MOOD™

# JUST CAN'T GET ENOUGH?

Join our social communities
and talk to us online.

You will have access to the latest
news on upcoming titles and special
promotions, but most importantly,
you can talk to other fans about your
favorite Harlequin reads.

Harlequin.com/Community

Facebook.com/HarlequinBooks

Twitter.com/HarlequinBooks

Pinterest.com/HarlequinBooks

™ HSOCIAL

**HARLEQUIN**®

A *Romance* FOR EVERY MOOD™

Stay up-to-date on all your
romance-reading news with the
*Harlequin Shopping Guide,*
featuring bestselling authors, exciting new
miniseries, books to watch and more!

The newest issue will be delivered right to you
with our compliments! There are 4 each year.

Signing up is easy.

## EMAIL

ShoppingGuide@Harlequin.ca

## WRITE TO US

HARLEQUIN BOOKS
Attention: Customer Service Department
P.O. Box 9057, Buffalo, NY 14269-9057

## OR PHONE

1-800-873-8635 in the United States
1-888-343-9777 in Canada

Please allow 4-6 weeks for delivery of the first issue by mail.